THE BUTCHER OF BELARUS

BRIAN SHEA

TY HUTCHINSON

Severn River
PUBLISHING

THE BUTCHER OF BELARUS

Copyright © 2022 by Brian Shea and Ty Hutchinson.

Severn River Publishing
www.SevernRiverBooks.com

ISBN: 978-1-64875-256-8 (Paperback)
ISBN: 978-1-64875-257-5 (Hardback)

ALSO BY THE AUTHORS

The Sterling Gray FBI Profiler Series

Hunting the Mirror Man

The King Snake

The Butcher of Belarus

The Green Samurai

BY BRIAN SHEA

The Boston Crime Thriller Series

Murder Board

Bleeding Blue

The Penitent One

Sign of the Maker

Cold Hard Truth

The Nick Lawrence Series

Kill List

Pursuit of Justice

Burning Truth

Targeted Violence

Murder 8

To find out more, visit

severnriverbooks.com/series/sterling-gray-fbi-profiler

1

The little girl walked slowly through the woods, her focused gaze scanning the damp ground. The rain had stopped earlier that morning, making it a perfect time for picking mushrooms. She was bundled up in a puffy jacket and wore gloves. A beanie her mother had knitted sat snugly on her head with her brown hair flowing out from under it.

She kept her eyes peeled for two types of mushrooms: chanterelle and honey. The honey mushrooms tended to cluster around dead trees, while the chanterelle, her favorite, was often found around the base of the silver birch trees that populated the forest.

"Salma, don't stray too far from me," her mother had called as she bent down to pick a cluster of honey mushrooms.

"I won't," she called out without so much as a glance in her mother's direction.

Salma was determined to find the chanterelle. Her mother had plans to make mushroom soup later, and the chanterelle tasted the best. Not much later, her nose caught a whiff of something familiar, the fruity scent of apricots. That meant one thing: a large patch of chanterelles was nearby. Salma spotted the orange-yellow caps and hurried over to them. It was a large cluster, certainly enough for soup. Salma carefully plucked the mushrooms from the soil and put them into a plastic bag.

This will make a delicious dinner later tonight.

That first patch had given Salma hope that she would have a good hunt and even pick enough mushrooms to last a couple of days. A few steps farther, she spotted more chanterelles and even a large cluster of honey mushrooms that had sprung up by a fallen tree. Salma couldn't believe her luck. She almost had her entire bag filled. But when she looked up to share her good fortune with her mother, she wasn't anywhere in sight.

"Mama?" she called out as she spun in a circle.

That particular part of the forest was dense. The trees grew only an arm's length apart, and after twenty yards or so, the silver trunks of the birch trees blended.

Worried about being lost in the woods, Salma began to backtrack as best as she could remember. Still, the forest looked the same no matter what direction she walked.

"Mama?" she called out once more.

Salma's ears picked up rustling nearby, and she hurried in that direction.

"Mama, are you there?"

A raccoon appeared and scurried away, but Salma's eye caught sight of something: a shoe.

Seeing that it looked about her size and that she might be able to use it if it were part of a matching pair, she went to retrieve it.

But what Salma found instead caused her to scream.

The body of an olive-skinned girl that looked a lot like Salma lay motionless on the ground. Her throat had been cut, and the front of her jacket stained red.

Salma turned and took off running.

"Mama!" she screamed.

She darted around the trees, using her hands to help move around them. All she wanted was to find her mother. But as she pushed off a tree to avoid running straight into it, she stepped on uneven ground and rolled her ankle.

"Oww," Salma called out as she fell.

She grabbed hold of her ankle as she winced in pain. That's when she noticed someone standing next to her. And those boots did not belong to her mother.

Salma slowly raised her head to find a man carrying a rifle standing next to her. His penetrating stare sent chills through her body, causing the back of her neck to tickle. The man bent down and grabbed Salma by her coat, yanking her to her feet. He smiled, revealing a mouthful of crooked teeth.

"Ow, ow," she cried out. "My ankle hurts."

"Let go of her!"

Salma's mother appeared and forced herself between the man and her daughter, breaking his grip on her.

"What are you doing here?" He spoke English with a Belarusian accent.

Just then, more men like him appeared. They were Belarusian soldiers on patrol.

"You know the rules. Get back to the camp!" He pushed Salma's mother. "Next time, I won't be so nice."

"We were only looking for mushrooms." Salma's mother held up a bag. "We're hungry."

"Are there more of you?" he asked.

"It's just us."

"No, there's someone else," Salma said through gritted teeth as she sucked up the pain. "I think she needs help." She pointed behind her.

"Who is there?" Salma's mother asked.

"I don't know her."

The soldier looked at one of his comrades and ordered him to find out what the girl was talking about.

"Can you walk?" Salma's mother held her to take the weight off her foot.

"I can."

"Go!" the soldier ordered them.

The soldier tasked to check out Salma's story reappeared.

"Did you find someone?" the soldier who gave the order asked.

He nodded. "It's a dead girl. Just like the others."

The man dressed in torn blue jeans and a black turtleneck, with bed hair and a heavy five-o'clock shadow, was Chi Gaston. He was a DI with the Metropolitan Police in London.

"Let me tell you something, mate. Nobody in their right mind calls them sneakers. What are you doing? Sneaking around? Everyone knows those shoes are called trainers because it fits the purpose." He took a hearty swig from his pint glass before placing it back on the table.

The clean-shaven man with a buzz cut sitting opposite Gaston was Special Agent Sterling Gray, a profiler for the FBI.

"They were originally called sneakers because the guy who invented the shoe put a rubber sole on the bottom, so it was quiet when you walked, like you were sneaking," Gray said. "That's how it got the nickname. It's not meant to be literal. It's just what Americans call workout shoes."

"You see, even the name 'workout shoes' is better." Gaston looked around the pub. More people had filled up the place since he and Gray had first arrived. He slipped off his stool. "I'm going for another pint. You ready?"

"Yeah, sure."

Gray had met Gaston months ago when Interpol brought him to consult on a murder investigation in London. Gaston was the lead inspector on the case, and they had gotten along since day one of working with each other. Gray's consultancy should have been a one-off, but Interpol was impressed by his profiling abilities; they worked out a deal with the Bureau. Gray was officially on loan to Interpol to help with investigations that might need his particular skill set.

Gaston returned with three full pint glasses and set them down on the table. "Look who I found at the bar."

Accompanying Gaston was a woman with short blond hair dressed in a black pantsuit. She was Lillie Pratt, an analyst with Interpol. She was responsible for tapping Gray for Gaston's investigation. Now she and Gray worked together.

"Lillie, so glad you could join us," Gray said as he scooted his stool over so Pratt could slide another one up to the table.

"That meeting I had didn't take as long as I thought, but I can only stick around for one, maybe two pints. What are we gossiping about tonight?"

Gray lifted up a leg to show off his shoes. "What do you call these?"

"They're trainers."

"And why do you call them trainers?" Gaston asked.

"Well, because they're used to train or exercise."

A smug look appeared on Gaston's face. "You see, mate. I told you."

"Someone want to fill me in?" Pratt asked before taking a sip of her beer.

"We're discussing the correct name for these shoes," Gray said. "I call them sneakers."

Pratt crinkled her forehead. "Why would you call them sneakers? Do you intend to sneak around?" Pratt used two fingers to imply someone tiptoeing.

"Like I told Chi, the name isn't literal. It's just a stupid nickname."

"I'll say it is," Gaston said.

"I'll back you on that one." Pratt tipped her glass and clinked it against Gaston's.

"That meeting you had, what was it about?" Gray asked.

"Budgets. Apparently, people are spending a wee too much when out of the office."

"Bloody hell," Gaston said. "Do they expect you to eat chips for every meal?"

"They expect us to be prudent."

"That's code for work more." Gaston chugged his beer.

"Lillie, any word on new assignments coming up on the horizon?" Gray asked.

"Not at the moment. I know you're eager to get your hands on your own investigation."

"I don't mind looking over other profiles and weighing in on other investigations, but, you know, it would be nice to have one of my own."

"Be careful of what you're asking," Gaston said. "You'll soon find yourself neck-deep in it."

"Patience, Sterling," Pratt said. "Interpol has been pushing your profiling skills, and there is a lot of interest but nothing of merit to really pull you in. No need to waste your time on an investigation that doesn't require your level of expertise."

"Listen to Lillie. She's got the right idea. Look at all the time we've had to spend in the pub together."

"You're right," Gray said with a smile. "What was I thinking? Cheers!"

3

Salma hopped alongside her mother as the two slowly made their way back to the camp. Night had fallen, and it was cold and dark away from the campfires that appeared up ahead. There were hundreds of them dotting the landscape, and each one had a small tent erected behind it.

They had arrived at the makeshift migrant camp a month ago from their home country of Syria. They and thousands of others from Syria, Iraq, and Afghanistan had come to Belarus with the hope of easy passage into the European Union through Poland. The Belarusian government had relaxed its visa process and posted a promise of entry into the EU for asylum seekers all over social media.

Thousands and thousands took flight from their countries to Minsk, the capital. Salma's mother, Farida, had even heard from others that the Belarusian government had paid for their flight. All of the arrivals were given food and a place to stay for the night. The very next day, soldiers transported them to an area along the border of Poland.

Before Farida and her daughter arrived, migrants crossed easily into Poland via the border checkpoints until the

Polish government stopped accepting them. At that point, the Belarusian soldiers had resorted to showing the migrants parts of the border that weren't guarded or heavily fenced and told them to cross there. They even supplied tools to cut through the fence. The Polish government quickly erected better fencing and increased guards along their border. Without passage, a camp formed and started to grow.

Nearly five thousand migrants were now living in the forests on the Belarusian side of the border. Once there, the soldiers didn't allow them to leave. Their only way out was through Poland, and that route had all but been sealed. To make matters worse, the Belarusian soldiers stole whatever money or supplies the migrants had, leaving them helpless as the Belarusian and Poland governments bickered over who should accept the migrants. Aid relief organizations were finally allowed into the camp to provide food, water, shelter, medicine, and other basic human needs.

Farida managed to secure a tent and pillows and blankets for her and Salma. Her husband had suffered a heart attack a few weeks before their journey to Belarus, so they only had each other.

Like everyone else, they wanted to cross into Poland and travel to Germany. Farida had relatives waiting for their arrival. But now, they were stuck on the border with no money and relying entirely on aid from relief organizations to survive.

"Lay down and rest," she said to Salma.

Farida removed Salma's shoes and then placed a pillow under her ankle to keep it elevated.

Salma still had her plastic bag of mushrooms in her grip. "I didn't lose the mushrooms."

"No, you didn't." Her mother chuckled as she took the bag from her. "Tonight, we will have warm soup."

During their walk back to the camp, Farida had not mentioned what had happened in the woods.

"Mama...that girl... She was dead, right?"

"Don't talk about that," Farida said quickly.

"But she must have a mama and a baba."

"Bad things happened in the woods. That's why I always tell you to never go there alone. You must listen to me."

"I will, but what do you think will happen to her?"

"What do you mean?"

"Will the soldiers find her family and tell them? Will they bury her?"

"I don't know, Salma. All I can do is worry about our safety. That's it. I don't want you talking to anyone about what you saw."

"Why?"

"Because I don't want trouble. Life is hard enough inside this camp. I don't want people to think we had something to do with what happened."

"But we didn't."

"I know, but people will think what they want. That's enough talk. Rest, Salma."

Farida tended to the campfire she kept outside of the tent. She wanted to boil water for tea.

Another family from Syria occupied the tent next to them: a woman, her husband, and two teenage daughters.

"Farida, did you have luck with the mushrooms?" a woman asked as she peeked her head outside her tent.

"Yes, I did. Salma did well today. She even gathered more than I did."

The woman stepped outside and pulled the hood of her oversized jacket over her head for warmth.

"Wait here. I will prepare a bag for you."

Farida disappeared into her tent and returned a few moments later with a small bag filled with mushrooms.

"For you and your family. These are called chanterelle mushrooms. They're delicious when cooked."

"Thank you so much," the woman said. "You must take me with you the next time. I want to learn how to find these mushrooms."

"Of course, of course. We must all help each other during these hard times."

"Did you hear?"

"Hear what?"

The woman looked around, making sure no one was within earshot. "They found another girl, young, just like the others."

"I know. It's terrible," Farida said as she shook her head. "Do you know the family?"

"I do not, but I pray for them."

"As do I." Farida looked away as she wiped her eye.

"What is it, Farida?" the woman asked.

Farida sniffed. "Life is already hard here. But to have to worry about someone killing the young girls in the camp, it's too much."

"I know what you mean."

Farida opened her mouth to speak but stopped.

"What?"

"Salma," Farida said in a lowered voice. "She found the girl."

The woman's eyes widened. "Are you serious?"

"Yes, while we were looking for mushrooms, we got separated. She saw the girl lying on the ground. We bumped into some soldiers right after and told them."

"What did they do?"

"I don't know. They made us leave right away."

The woman tsked as she shook her head.

"You must watch over Salma carefully. She is the same age as the others. All have been eight or nine."

"God willing."

"Be careful of who you tell this story to," the woman said. "There are many bad people in the camp, and desperate ones as well. You don't know how they will react. Everyone is scared. I don't want any trouble for you and Salma."

"Thank you."

The woman nodded before heading back inside her tent.

As Farida checked on her campfire, she couldn't help but wonder if Salma would be the next victim. It was more important than ever that she find a way into Poland.

4

Deputy Prime Minister Aleksy Salamon took hurried steps through the halls of the Chancellery, an imposing neoclassical building located on Ujazdów Avenue in the city center of Warsaw. This building housed the executive office of the Prime Minister of Poland and his office.

Salamon was always visiting the prime minister's office, more so as of late, thanks to the humanitarian crises that had quickly developed along Poland's border with Belarus. He muttered under his breath as he approached the PM's office. It seemed every recent conversation was about the problems at the border. It would be no different today.

There were always two guards stationed directly outside of the doors to the PM's administrative office. His staff worked there and served as a buffer to his office. Salamon nodded to the guards, and they let him pass. Inside the office, the PM's personal administrative assistant met him.

"Deputy Prime Minister," she said. "I didn't have you on the schedule today."

"Sorry, I've just come into urgent news. I can't wait. Is he available?"

"Give me a moment." She made a quick call. "The prime minister will see you. You may go inside."

Salamon pushed through another door. The office was rectangular, with a sitting area off to one side, where the PM preferred to conduct his meetings. His desk sat in the center of the room facing the rear, where large windows lined the wall, allowing generous amounts of natural light into the room. It also provided a beautiful view of the gardens.

"Salamon, what's so important?" the man sitting behind the desk asked.

Brajan Paszek had only been in office eight months as the country's prime minister when the problem with the migrants erupted along the border. In the beginning, Poland accepted thousands of migrants seeking asylum. As an EU member state, they had a legal obligation to offer asylum to any non-EU national seeking to escape violence in their own country. That is, until it became clear to them that this wasn't a one-time group of migrants.

They had learned through their own observations and by interviewing the migrants that the Belarus government had helped thousands travel to Belarus for the sole reason of crossing the border into Poland. They were arriving by plane daily. Most had heard of the simplified visa process via family, friends, and social media posts from the Belarusian government. Upon their arrival in Minsk, the government then transported them to the border and instructed them to cross.

This was not an established migratory route. Obviously, the Belarusian government was funneling migrants into Poland by the thousands, knowing legally they had no choice but to accept them. The EU quickly recognized this was in response to the economic sanctions imposed on Belarus due to their systemic human rights violations.

"Tell me we're making progress with the Belarusians." Paszek sat up and straightened the coat of his navy blue suit.

Salamon took a seat in one of the guest chairs in front of the PM's desk.

"It's getting worse. The camp has grown to over five thousand people, and there doesn't seem to be any shortage of new arrivals every day."

"Those bastards. They manufactured this crisis on purpose, and now it's out of control."

"We all know that, but they're sticking to their story that they have nothing to do with the migrants traveling through their country."

"If they think they can do what Turkey did last year, force sanctions to be lifted or allow hundreds of thousands of migrants to cross through their country and into Greece, they're crazy. I won't allow Poland to fall for this ruse. The Belarusians fabricated this humanitarian crisis. It's nothing more than hybrid warfare."

Salamon crossed one leg over the other. "There have been more deaths."

"Aren't the relief organizations in the country providing food, water, shelter, medicine?"

"They're there, and it's helping tremendously, but the deaths aren't coming from that."

Deep lines formed on Paszek's forehead. "Stop talking in riddles and give it to me straight."

"Little girls have been found dead, murdered, three that we know of so far. We have an intelligence officer embedded in the camp as an aid worker. He's one hundred percent positive the girls were murdered. The third was found a few days ago. All three girls were eight or nine, had their throats slit, and were then dumped in the forest."

"What are you implying?"

"Someone is murdering those girls—a serial killer is loose in the camp. The Belarusian government isn't checking the backgrounds of the migrants; many are criminals escaping persecution in their own countries. It wouldn't surprise me if the governments of Syria, Iraq, or Afghanistan purposely sent their criminals to Belarus to rid themselves of those problems. It's completely plausible that a person of this nature could end up in the camp."

Paszek rested his forehead in his palm. "This is the last thing we need. Why aren't the Belarusians doing anything about this?"

"I'm not exactly sure. They might think it's nothing more than migrant-on-migrant violence."

"Is there anything we can do diplomatically? Something that will force Belarus to act."

"There might be a better approach than that, but it's unusual, and the window to act is small."

Paszek rested his forearms on his desk. "What are you proposing?"

"We find the killer ourselves."

"And why would we want to do that?"

"It will stop the senseless murders, and it will prevent this crisis from escalating. If the media finds out, it'll only add to our problems."

Paszek let out a defeated breath as he nodded. "Do what is necessary to catch the killer."

Gray sat on the chair, hunched as he held his phone against his ear. His sister, Fleur, had called to check on him.

"Everything is fine with me," Gray said.

"Where are you, Sterling?" she asked in a calm voice. "I hear a lot of noise in the background."

"I'm at Heathrow, waiting to board a flight." Gray stood up and walked away from the crowd surrounding him to hear his sister better. She always spoke quietly.

"Are you coming back to the US?"

"No. I've been put on an investigation at the very last minute. I just found out this morning that I'm needed in Warsaw."

"Warsaw? I thought you would only be in London for a few months."

"The situation has changed. It seems I'm officially on loan to Interpol."

"What does that mean?"

"It means until the powers that be at the Bureau decide otherwise, I'm here to help."

"The kids miss their uncle. They ask about you all the time."

"I miss them too."

"Sterling, you need to come and visit. It's been way too long. You know you can always stay here at the house with us."

"I know. As soon as I free up some time, I'll fly to New York."

"You always say that. How long will you be in Warsaw?"

"I'm not sure, maybe a week at the most. I'm assisting local law enforcement. They need a profile."

"Another serial killer?"

"Yes."

"Don't you ever get tired of chasing those lunatics around?"

"Someone has to go after them. We can't leave people like that unchecked."

"Sterling, you've spent your entire life helping other people. I hope one day you can turn some of that energy back onto yourself. Do you have a girlfriend?"

"I'm working on it."

"You always say that as well."

"Fleur, my flight's boarding. I'll talk to you again soon."

"Take care, Sterling. We all love you."

Gray disconnected the call and boarded the plane with his one carry-on bag. Interpol had booked him into business class, which afforded him more privacy. It's not that Gray didn't like sitting next to other people. It's just that they always ended up asking what he did for a living or peeking at the paperwork he was looking over. That always led to conversations Gray would rather avoid.

The flight to Warsaw was a two-and-a-half-hour flight, enough time to prep himself. Gray took out his laptop. Pratt had emailed him a briefing of the assignment while he waited for his flight. He had just begun to look it over when his sister had called.

A quick review didn't tell him as much as he had hoped. There were three victims, all girls between the ages of eight and nine. No names or descriptions or any personal information. Gray assumed they were of Polish descent. The victims were all killed the same way. No mention exactly how they were killed. No autopsy reports on any of the victims. No interview notes. No suspects. No names of suspects being investigated. In fact, the dossier was nothing more than a rehash of the information Pratt had told him the night before. There should have been more information since there were three victims. There wasn't even a timeline. Was it over a couple of weeks or a couple of months? All Gray had were questions and absolutely no answers.

This report makes no sense. All I've learned is that the victims are little girls. That's it.

Gray checked the email Pratt had sent him. Nothing in her correspondence suggested additional information was forthcoming. She didn't even comment on the lack of information. Gray closed his laptop and gave it no more thought.

Gray's flight touched down at Warsaw Chopin International Airport in the early evening. He had been told a contact from Interpol would meet him at the airport. After passing through baggage claim, he made his way toward the exit, where he saw people holding signs with names written on them.

"Special Agent Gray, welcome to Warsaw." A tall woman with long blond hair was suddenly walking beside him. "Is that all the luggage you have?"

"Uh, um. Yes, it's just the one carry-on. You snuck up on me there."

"Sorry. My name is Julianna Pakulski." She smiled as she offered her hand.

"Sterling Gray. You can drop the special agent. It's not necessary. Are you with Interpol?"

"I am not. I'm an aide for Deputy Prime Minister Aleksy Salamon."

"I was under the impression someone from Interpol would be meeting me."

"There's been a slight change in plans. Come, I have a car waiting for us outside."

Gray spun around, searching. "I need to get a SIM card for my phone."

"We'll provide you with one. Come on. We don't want to keep the deputy prime minister waiting."

Inside the car, Gray studied the woman a bit more. She was dressed in a form-fitting skirt suit, black stockings, and matching heels. She didn't carry a purse or bag.

"I apologize for hurrying, but the deputy prime minister is eager to meet with you. After your briefing, I'll drop you off at your hotel."

"Will the investigators on the case also be in the briefing?"

"No, they will not."

Gray raised his eyebrows. "Oh, okay. What can you tell me about the investigation? I received a report, but it was a little light on details."

"Mr. Gray—"

"Sterling's fine."

"Sterling, I understand that you have many questions. All of them will be answered in your briefing."

Gray decided to go with the flow and drop the questions. There wasn't much to look at outside the window until they arrived at the DPM's office. Gray stepped out of the vehicle in front of a large building with neoclassical architecture. The outdoor lighting on the building's exterior gave it a grand appearance, especially the lights highlighting the tall pillars near the entrance.

"Welcome to the Chancellery," Pakulski said.

"Very impressive," Gray gazed around as he followed her, dragging his carry-on behind him.

Pakulski led Gray down a spacious hallway with marble flooring. Wooden console tables and armchairs lined the hall. Gray assumed the paintings hanging on the wall were previous prime ministers. He didn't recognize anyone. Most of the staff had left the Chancellery since it was after hours. The *click-clack* of their shoes against the polished floors echoed in the silence.

Pakulski stopped in front of two wooden doors and pushed them open, leading the way in. There was a large office area with four desks. She continued past them to another pair of double doors. She knocked twice before pushing one open and entering the room.

The office inside was equal in size, except there was only one desk. The floor was carpeted, and more paintings hung on the walls. A tall, thin man dressed in a gray suit came around to the front of the desk with his hand extended.

"Special Agent Gray, this is Aleksy Salamon, the deputy prime minister of Poland."

"Special Agent Gray," he said. "It is a pleasure to meet you."

"I'm honored to meet you," Gray replied as they shook hands.

"Julianna, could you please summon the others?"

Pakulski nodded before leaving.

"Please, Agent Gray. Have a seat." Salamon motioned to a sitting area. "Thank you for coming on such short notice. I wish we were meeting for more positive matters, but the issue at hand is of great importance."

"I received a report, but as I mentioned to Julianna, it didn't have a lot of details."

"Ah, yes, that's because I wanted to brief you in person. I must tell you right now that what we're about to discuss is a sensitive matter for our government. It goes without saying that what is discussed in my office stays here."

"Understood."

"I read your file earlier. You have a very impressive background, Agent Gray. Before joining the FBI, you spent time as a Pararescue man with the United States Air Force. And from what I understand, you've become their best profiler. I don't know why you're working with Interpol instead of with your own department, but I'm glad you are. It allows countries like mine to utilize your special skills."

"I'm happy to help."

"I'm a man of few words, so I want to get directly to the point. Agent Gray, how determined are you in the pursuit of justice?"

"Uh, well. If you're asking if I believe in good and bad, right and wrong, then yes. And bringing people to justice is of great importance to me."

"I'm glad to hear that. I believe this investigation will not only test your abilities but your determination to get the job done no matter what challenges you face."

"I approach every investigation in the same manner. I want to win."

Just then, the door to the DPM's office opened, and two men entered. One in a suit, the other in military dress. Salamon stood, and Gray followed suit.

"Agent Gray, let me introduce Gabriel Filipek. He is in charge of Poland's Foreign Intelligence Agency. The other gentleman is Jurek Janda. He is the commander of Poland's Border Guard."

"I see the confusion on your face," Filipek said after shaking Gray's hand and taking a seat.

"I was under the impression that I would assist on a murder investigation," Gray said, managing a smile. "Normally, I meet with the lead detective or inspector on the case. It's not often I find myself in such impressive company."

"We are normal men just like you, waking up every morning ready to solve the day's problems," Filipek said.

Janda flipped through a pack of paper-clipped files. "You caught the Jack the Ripper serial killer in London."

"Not the original, but a copycat," Gray said.

"You had a failed mission in Ethiopia when you were a Pararescue man with the Air Force," Janda continued. "Can you tell me what happened?"

"Our mission was to meet up with a platoon that had injured men and help them to the extraction point. We received bad intel and were dropped off course, and the time it took to make up that ground did not work in our favor. The platoon came under fire from a local militia."

Janda looked up from the papers. "Did you lose everyone?"

"No, but their platoon did suffer casualties, as did my team."

"How many men did you lose under your command while serving in the Air Force?

"Three."

"And now you work for the FBI. Have any of your cases gone cold?" Janda continued his line of stern questioning.

"No, but I have solved a few cold cases."

Gray held up a hand, stopping Janda. "If I may say something. You have received a very detailed file on me. That doesn't bother me one bit. Everything in my file is correct and up to date. But I'm a little confused about where all this questioning is heading. I've sat through more briefings than I can recall. None of them focused on my background instead of the investigation."

"I apologize if you feel like you're out of the loop," Salamon said. He looked over at the two men. They both nodded and then left the office without so much as uttering another word.

"I'm sorry," Gray said. "Did I offend them?"

"They wanted to meet the man joining the team. That's all."

"Okay, so where is the rest of the team?"

"You'll meet them soon. Agent Gray, are you aware of what's happening on the border of Poland and Belarus?"

"I did catch a brief report on the news a few weeks ago, something about a group of migrants wanting to cross over into Poland."

"That group of migrants is five thousand strong and growing by the day. Have you heard of the term 'hybrid warfare'?"

"I have."

"Good. These migrants are from countries like Syria, Iraq, and Afghanistan. They all want into the EU, which is not the issue here. The issue is that flying into Minsk and traveling west to our border to make their way into the EU states is not a typical migratory route. It's been fabricated."

"You're saying the Belarusian government brought them to the border?"

"I am. They deny it, but intel tells us they're behind it. Their end goal is to force the EU to lift economic sanctions or face an influx of migrants into our Poland. We've already accepted thousands but have since closed our borders."

"The border closure has resulted in the camp growing."

"That's correct."

"What does this have to do with the serial killer here?"

"The serial killer is not here. That person is in the camp. Those little girls are Arabic. The Belarusians are refusing to investigate. The situation is already fragile. Until we can resolve this migrant problem with Belarus, we need to ensure the camp doesn't explode into a humanitarian crisis. Murdered children won't help."

"So are the Polish border guards investigating?"

"Yes and no. It's a little hard to do from our side. Right now, the Belarusians are convinced it's nothing more than migrant-on-migrant violence. And they might be right, but we don't want to take that chance. A profile from you would help narrow down the person we're looking for. I know this is an unusual approach, but the situation itself is anything but ordinary."

"Yes, I can see that, but how will you force the Belarusians to act?"

"We can't, so we've decided to take this investigation one step further. We believe *we* need to apprehend the killer for anything to be resolved."

"But the camp is in their territory, where you have no juris-diction."

"You're right about that. We intend on sending a team of aid workers into the country. Along with another investigator, you will be embedded in a team of doctors there to help the migrants. While in the camp, it will be your job to work up a profile so that our investigator can zero in on the killer."

"And then what?"

"We'll take it from there. We just need your expertise in locating this person. If we cannot determine who the killer is, we'll pull the team out. No harm, no foul."

"This explains the lack of detail in the investigation report. How do you know there even is a killer in the camp?"

"We had an intelligence officer living among the migrants. The intel is good. We wouldn't be having this conversation if it wasn't."

"I see."

"Agent Gray, do you understand what I'm proposing here?"

"I believe I do."

"Great. I'll need an answer right now if you're on board. If it's no, we have a car waiting to take you directly back to the airport. If it's a yes, then we'll get started."

7

Pakulski met up with Gray outside of Salamon's office. "I'm happy to hear everything worked out."

"Yeah, it looks like I'll be staying," Gray said as he followed Pakulski back through the same spacious hall with his roller behind him. "Do you know anything about my contact at Interpol? I should probably check in."

"They know you're here. Because of the nature of the assignment, you will only have contact with people directly involved. You can understand that, right?"

"Sure. So when do I meet the rest of the team?"

"You'll meet your handler a little later tonight."

"My handler?"

"I'm sorry, I meant to say your partner. He'll also be embedded."

"Is he with the Polish National Police?"

"Gray, we all have tremendous faith in you. There can't be anyone better suited for this assignment than you. Do you realize how hard it is to find a profiler who is also a doctor?" Pakulski smiled.

"Let me guess. It's just me?"

"Yes."

It wasn't lost on Gray that Pakulski had just deflected. *I guess I'm also on a need-to-know basis.*

"I have you staying at the Hotel Warszawa. It's an elegant five-star. I think you'll be very comfortable there. I've already had suitable clothing to wear inside the camp placed in your room. A new SIM card is also in the room. If there are issues with sizing, or you feel you need something else, please let me know."

She handed him a business card.

The hotel wasn't too far from the Chancellery, about a twenty-minute ride. Gray bade goodbye to Pakulski after she helped him check-in. Once inside his room, Gray looked over the clothing: a heavy jacket, durable cargo pants, long-sleeved shirts, a multi-pocket vest, and a beanie. The shirts, vest, and beanie had the Doctors Without Borders logo stitched onto them. There was also an array of personal medical equipment in a backpack: a stethoscope, an ophthalmoscope, an otoscope, a reflex hammer, and a stopwatch.

Gray switched out the new SIM card for his old one before heading into the bathroom for a shower. No sooner had he stepped out of the bathroom than the hotel phone rang. Gray wrapped a towel around his waist and hurried to answer it.

"Mr. Gray, this is reception. I'm calling to let you know Mr. Gorecki is waiting for you in the lobby."

"Thank you."

Gray quickly got dressed and headed down to the lobby. He walked up to a man in a suit sitting alone.

"Excuse me, are you Mr. Gorecki?" Gray asked.

"I'm sorry, I'm not," the man said.

"Sorry to disturb you."

Gray spun around and saw another man tapping on his phone. He had brown curly hair, an olive skin tone, and five-o'clock shadow, and he was dressed casually in jeans and a windbreaker.

"Excuse me, are you Mr. Gorecki?"

"Mr. Gray." He stood, and the two shook hands. "How was your flight?"

"Quick."

"Are you hungry?"

"I'm starved."

"Perfect. I know a great place not far from here that serves Polish comfort food."

The restaurant was a fifteen-minute walk from Gray's hotel. The décor outside resembled a cottage.

"This is one of my favorite places to eat," Gorecki said. "Whenever I'm in the area, I have to stop by."

"Smells good," Gray said as they took a seat at a table.

The inside of the restaurant had a rustic farmhouse feel to it. Most of the other diners were couples.

"Are you familiar with Polish food?" Gorecki asked as they looked over the menu.

"No, I'm not. What do you recommend?"

"I recommend you let me order."

Gray closed his menu. "Done."

Gorecki quickly put in an order, and a few moments later, large bottles of Tyskie were placed on the table.

"Na zdrowie," Gorecki said as he and Gray clinked their bottles.

"I'm sure you have a lot of questions," Gorecki said. "Probably the first thing you noticed is that I don't look like your typical Pole. I'm half Arab. My father immigrated here as a very young man and ended up marrying a young Polish woman."

Gorecki reached into a small backpack he'd been carrying and removed a large envelope. "Your new alias. You'll find all the details of your identity right there: name, age, background, work history, and more. Memorize it in case you're questioned at the border."

While Gray looked over the information, the server returned and placed the dishes on the table.

"We'll eat family-style if you don't mind. This is golabki, or stuffed cabbages. It's wonderful if you top it with a little sour cream. This is sausage with a sauerkraut hash. These kielbasas come from Krakow. Wonderful stuff. We also have placki ziemniaczane, or fried potato pancakes, and lastly, stuffed zucchini."

Both men dug into their food while they continued to talk about Gray's new identity.

"There's no covering the fact that you're a Yankee. You definitely look like someone who would be called Dr. Clark Sanders. But don't worry. Doctors Without Borders are always a mix of ethnicities. You and I will fit in just fine."

"What's your code name?" Gray asked.

"I'm Dr. Rasheed Ajam."

"Do you have medical training?"

"I took a crash course. I'm about as knowledgeable as a mother who diagnoses her kid's sicknesses. Anything out of the realm of headaches, colds, and fevers, I'll refer to you."

"Are we the only ones embedded?"

"Yes, none of the other members of the team will know who we really are. There will be about twenty of us in total. You and I will keep to ourselves. As for timing, we have five days."

"Five days? You mean to develop a profile?"

"No, five days total to find the killer. If we're not successful, we'll be pulled out. You'll need to work very fast so that I have time to hunt this person down."

"I'm not so sure you understand how this works. Do you really think it's that easy to catch a killer?"

"He's contained in a camp. It's our job to root him out." Gorecki popped a bite into his mouth. "Come on, Dr. Sanders. I bet you've taken craps that were harder than this."

8

Farida dreaded the nights in the camp. Almost everyone remained in their tents out of fear. The ones who chose to walk around weren't people she wanted to meet. Many men in the camp preyed on others, primarily women and children. It didn't help that she and Salma fit that profile.

Usually, Farida kept to herself, not wanting to draw any attention to their tent. But word about the third girl and the knowledge that Salma had stumbled across the body had spread quickly. Other women, who were friendly with Farida, had stopped by.

The women gathered around the campfire in front of Farida's tent to listen to her recount their experience. Farida had Salma stay inside the tent. She didn't want her involved any more than she already had been.

"Did you see the body?" one of the women asked.

"I didn't. Salma and I had gotten separated briefly. She found the body during this time and then ran back to me. I'm sorry that she had to see that. I wish she hadn't."

"What did the soldiers do? Did they..."

"Suspect us? No, but they weren't nice about it."

"They never care about anything."

"They accused us of doing something wrong in the woods. They wanted to know why we were there. I had to show them the mushrooms, and even then, they were suspicious. When we told them about the body, they didn't believe us at first. But once they saw it, they quickly told us to get back to the camp. I don't think they care."

"Of course they don't care," the woman said. "If they did, they would be trying to find the killer. But I don't see that."

Just then, a couple cautiously approached the group.

"Excuse me," the man said. "We were told one of you found the girl in the woods."

"And who are you?" Farida asked.

"My name is Waleed, and this is my wife, Oma. The girl… she was our daughter. Her name was Sabah."

"I'm so sorry. Please join us."

Farida then told the couple how she and her daughter had found Sabah. After she finished, the couple sat there quietly gazing at the campfire. Oma had tears running down her face.

"Thank you for telling us this," Waleed said. "It helps."

"Did you bury your daughter?" one of the women asked.

The man nodded. "The soldiers never took her body from the woods. They only pointed in a direction. We had to search for her."

There was a collective groan from the group.

"We thought this was our chance for a better life," Waleed said. "We sold everything we owned, gave up our home, and came here. Everything was open arms and smiles when we arrived. And now we just buried our only child."

"The government lied to us all," one of the women said. "There was no deal with Poland or the EU to accept us. The food, the water, the shelter they provided when we all arrived in Minsk was part of a show. Even if we wanted to go back to our country, they wouldn't let us return to Minsk."

"It is done to trap us here," another woman added. "I am so sorry about your daughter. You have it worse than all of us. Did the soldiers say anything about finding out who did this?"

Waleed let out a long breath. "We asked many times, but they said it's not their problem. They don't care."

"They really don't," Farida said. "I could see it in their eyes when we told them about your daughter. The soldier smiled. I don't understand who could act that way. A child was killed."

Oma's tears increased upon hearing Farida's words, and Waleed wrapped an arm around her for comfort.

"Thank you very much for talking to us," Waleed said. He then helped his wife to her feet, and the couple walked away.

"Such a terrible thing to happen," one of the women said after the couple left. "I wish them to have justice. Farida, you must watch Salma carefully. Don't let her out of your sight. Everyone here will help."

The rest of the women nodded in agreement.

"Thank you," Farida said. "It's comforting to feel like I'm not alone here. Salma and I are also like Waleed and Oma. We have nothing in Syria to return to, even if we wanted. Our only hope is that the Polish government will change their mind and open the border."

It was late, and the women needed to head back to the safety of their tents. They bade each other goodbye and left. Farida remained outside her tent for a few minutes longer as she looked around the camp. *How much longer can we survive here?*

Salma stuck her head out of the tent. "Mama, please come inside."

"Why are you still up?"

"I can't sleep."

Farida entered the tent and tied the flaps shut.

"Were you listening?"

She nodded. "I'm sorry. I feel bad for that man and woman. Will the same thing happen to me? I'm the same age as those other girls."

Farida lay down next to Salma and drew her into her arms, hugging her gently. "Nothing will happen to you. I will keep you safe. I promise."

9

The following morning, Gray met up with Gorecki in the hotel lobby.

"Did you sleep well?" Gorecki asked.

"I slept like a baby."

"Good, because in the camp, all you'll have is a narrow cot. And it'll be cold. No snow yet though."

Gorecki led Gray to an SUV waiting outside. Gray threw his gear into the vehicle's rear and then joined Gorecki in the back seat.

"We're heading to Kuźnica. It's a village close to the border. That's where we'll meet up with the rest of the aid team. It's about a three-hour drive. Did you have a chance to study and memorize your alias?" Gorecki asked.

"I did. "

"Mind if I test you?"

"Not at all."

Gorecki proceeded to spit out questions in rapid-fire. "What's your name? Where are you from?"

"Dr. Clark Sanders. I grew up in Connecticut but currently live in Washington, DC."

"How long have you been with DWB?"

"On and off for six years."

"Where did you last provide relief efforts?"

"Nepal, after the massive earthquake."

"You're a quick study. I like that. I'll say this now just so that it's been said. You need to treat our time in Belarus as if we're behind enemy lines. There is an autocratic regime in power. There will be no forgiveness from them if they discover our true intentions. Do you understand what I'm saying?"

"It's clear."

"Aside from whatever diplomatic support Doctors Without Borders has, we will have no weapons or support from the Polish government. If things go sideways, we'll pull out immediately. Not just us, the entire team. How's your Russian?"

"I studied language as a Pararescue. I'm capable in Russian and Arabic, more so if we're discussing medical services."

"Belarusian soldiers patrol the camp. They speak Belarusian, a mix of Russian, Ukraine, and Polish. You should get by, but don't let the soldiers know you understand them. Be cautious of your surroundings when you communicate with the migrants."

"I'm assuming I'll actually be treating people," Gray said.

"Yes, they'll be lined up all day with problems ranging from colds to broken arms. We'll have access to an array of medical supplies and equipment, as well as medicines to prescribe. Outside of performing major surgery, we should be able to handle most of the patients' problems. You'll use the time treating patients to gain information. We'll have breaks where we can walk around the camp, but keep in mind we're there to treat patients. That's our cover. You should carry a medical satchel and help people whenever you leave our area. Any questions?"

"None that I can think of at the moment."

Gray spent the remainder of the drive looking at the passing scenery. It was a mix of farmland and woods with the occasional village they drove through. When they arrived in Kuźnica, Gray was surprised by the size of the DWB contingent. The convoy consisted of seven SUVs and two trucks filled to the brim with supplies. Gray also noticed the mix of ethnicities was just as Gorecki had stated.

"That's a lot of stuff," Gray noted.

"We're strictly medical. You should see the relief teams that provide food, water, and shelter. It takes a while to get through the border checkpoint. I think the camp's total population now is about five thousand people. Just a month ago, it was three thousand. It's growing fast."

"How stretched out is the camp?" Gray asked.

"The Belarusians have tried to keep the camp contained, but with the rate that people are arriving, it's expanding rapidly. Right now, it stretches north and south about two kilometers. It's long and skinny."

"That's a lot of border to secure. Isn't it easy for the migrants to cross over?"

"At first, the fence was easy to cut through. It's since been reinforced. The farther north you go, the easier it is to cross. There isn't any fencing, just border markers. But that area is also comprised of dense forest. It's hard to survive out there, especially when all the food and water are back inside the main part of the camp. I want to stress: be careful about being too friendly with migrants. We're not there to help with their situation. We're there to find a killer. Many will want your assistance in crossing the border or claiming asylum. You must resist."

10

Belarusian Border Guards were thorough when searching Gray's body and belongings. They were cold in their approach, not that Gray expected a warm welcome. They were also outfitted in full combat gear. They had their faces covered in tactical balaclavas, which would be intimidating for most people to be around. Each one carried an HK MP5.

The soldiers assigned to the camp were dressed casually in fatigues, a jacket, and an ushanka on their heads. They carried the standard AK-47 assault rifle.

On the way to their designated area, Gray and the team were given explicit instructions not to move their camp. Gray noticed right away that life in the camp appeared awful. People were living in slum-like conditions. There were no visible lavatories. He could only assume these people hadn't had a bath since their arrival. It didn't help that skies were overcast, the weather cold, and the ground was hard. He couldn't imagine sleeping on the cold ground when they first arrived. Since then, most of the migrants had been given tents and cots. There were hundreds of them scattered about.

Almost all of them had little campfires burning just outside their tents for warmth and cooking.

As soon as they dropped their gear onto the ground, migrants began to flock to them for treatment. The soldiers quickly established order by knocking the individuals back with the butts of their rifles. There seemed to be no concern on the soldier's part regarding the assault and that the aid team could see what they were doing.

Gray and Gorecki spent the next hour or so setting up their tent. A queue had already formed.

As soon as he had his area set up, Gray began seeing people and treating them. He hadn't noticed that Gorecki slipped away without saying anything. Gray was too busy to be concerned.

In the beginning, Gray focused solely on treating people. Their needs ran from something as simple as a common cold to something more severe like pneumonia. Some migrants arrived with injuries such as cuts and bruises, even broken fingers. It was obvious they had been beaten. A few pregnant women really needed prenatal care, but Gray looked them over the best he could. It all seemed routine until the women and girls who had been raped showed up, some as young as thirteen. That got under Gray's skin, and anger boiled. He tried talking to a few of them, but none were willing to say what had happened. They were frightened.

Next in line was a mother with her daughter, who had injured her ankle. The girl had a smile on her face when she took a seat, and her big brown eyes were filled with intrigue.

"Hello, I'm Dr. Sanders. What's your name?" Gray asked in Arabic.

"Salma," she replied.

"Do you want to tell me how you hurt your ankle?"

"I tripped and fell when I was running."

"That will do it."

Gray carefully examined her ankle. "Can you move it?"

The little girl wiggled her foot.

"I don't think it's fractured. It's just a bad sprain. I'll need to wrap your ankle with an elastic bandage to help keep the swelling down."

After wrapping her ankle, Gray gave her mother some pain medication.

"This is ibuprofen. It'll help with the pain and also reduce the swelling. Keep her ankle elevated and give it as much rest as possible."

Gray also provided Salma with a pair of crutches he adjusted for her height and made sure she knew how to use them.

"Thank you," Salma said. "I feel much better."

The line of people outside Gray's tent never seemed to dwindle. Before he knew it, four hours had passed, and it was late in the afternoon. Gorecki finally appeared.

"How is everything?" he asked.

"It's fine. Where did you go?"

"I took a walk to familiarize myself with the camp and locate the military headquarters."

"And?"

"There are a lot of soldiers housed there, probably a thousand or so. They've constructed barracks toward the east side of the camp, about a fifteen-minute walk north of where we are. I watched how they patrol. I get the impression that the camp is broken up into sections, with soldiers appointed to watch each section. How's the profile coming along?"

"Profile? I've barely had a chance to come up for breath. Did you see the line outside?"

"I did, but you need to find a way to do both, and if you

need to choose one over the other, choose the profile. I'll take over. It'll give you a chance to rest and think."

Gray didn't argue but immediately stood up, grabbed a medical satchel, and slipped it over his shoulder. "I'll see you in a few."

11

Gray decided to walk south, avoiding the barracks in the other direction. He figured there would be a larger contingent of soldiers in that area. He wanted to be around the migrants, to get a feel for life in the camp. It also felt good to stretch his legs.

Along the way, Gray stopped to check on people. It was unavoidable, since his jacket and beanie had logo patches on them. Gray didn't mind, though, as it was an opportunity to talk to them and earn their trust. The few he did try to engage with earlier were too frightened to speak in any real detail about life in the camp.

During his walk, Gray spotted a woman he had seen earlier who had been raped. She sat outside of her tent, tending to a campfire. He thought maybe she'd be more inclined to talk without anyone around.

"Hello," Gray said.

The woman smiled.

"Remember me? I'm Dr. Sanders."

"Yes, of course, I remember."

"How are you feeling? Everything okay?"

"Yes." She glanced around to see if others were watching them talk.

"May I sit?" Gray pointed to the ground.

Gray took a seat. He removed a blood pressure monitor from his satchel and began to take her blood pressure.

"Do you know who attacked you?"

She remained quiet, eyes glued on the campfire.

"It's okay. I'm only here to help."

Still, the woman seemed nervous. Gray thought taking her blood pressure would ease her concerns about why they were talking. It wasn't working. He finished taking her blood pressure and mentioned that she could always come and speak to him, night or day. She nodded, and Gray got up and walked away.

Gray knew abuses took place in camps like this. It was unavoidable. There would always be the strong preying on the weak. He continued his walk, stopping every so often. He decided to make his way toward the edge of the camp. This area had more silver and skinny birch trees, and the woodsy scent was much more robust. Gray drew a deep breath.

Rustling and muffled noises caught his attention, and he walked in that direction. A beat later, he spotted a woman being held down by two men. One had his hand covering her mouth while he fondled her breasts. Another was busy removing her pants.

"Hey!" Gray shouted as he ran over to them. One of the men let go of the woman and stood up to Gray. Stupid move. Gray planted his fist right into his face, and the guy dropped like a sack of potatoes. The other two men stopped what they were doing and ran off, their friend trailing not far behind.

"Are you okay?" Gray asked as he helped the woman put her clothes back on.

"Yes, thank you for helping me."

"Are you hurt?" he asked as he looked her over.

"I don't think so. You are a doctor? American?"

"Yes. I'm Dr. Sanders."

"My name is Kamaria," she said as she switched to English with an accent.

"Did you know those men?" He helped her stand.

"No, but it's very dangerous here. The men mostly are the ones to worry about. Those men who attacked me are Arabic. People only care about themselves in the camp. Everyone is trying to survive. It doesn't help that the soldiers also take advantage of us."

"What do they do?"

"They harass and beat us for no reason. They steal our money, our supplies, whatever is of value. They even sold a piece of bread to a young teen boy for forty dollars. He had no choice but to pay because he had just taken some insulin and needed something in his stomach. I've had everything taken from me. Even if I wanted to go back to my home country, I have no money to travel. I'm stuck in this camp just like everyone else."

"It's terrible. I heard of other crimes taking place here, really horrible ones involving little girls."

The woman looked around to see if they were being watched.

"What is it?"

"I must be careful," she said in a lowered voice. "If people see us talking, they will start to think and spread rumors."

Gray removed his stethoscope from his bag and hung it around his neck. Then he slipped a blood pressure cuff around the woman's arm and squeezed the bulb, pumping air into the cuff.

"Better?" Gray asked.

She nodded. "You're talking about the girls that were murdered, right?"

"I am."

"It's true. Three of them so far."

"Do people have their suspicions?"

"Of course. It's the gossip in the camp. Everyone suspects someone."

"Who do you suspect? What about those men who attacked you?"

"No, they're too stupid to kill someone and get away with it. They only care about sex."

"Rape can lead to murder, especially if the attacker feels they could be caught. Do you know if the girls were sexually abused?"

"I don't, but whoever is doing this is smart because they haven't been seen by anyone."

"What about the soldiers? Have they said anything? Are they investigating?"

"They don't care."

Kamaria raised an eyebrow. "Why are you asking? You're a doctor."

"I'm concerned. I've come here to help, and to hear that something like this has happened. It's very disturbing for me. Did you know any of the girls?"

Kamaria shook her head. "No, but I know who the mother of one is."

"Could you take me to her? I would love to pay my respects."

Kamaria led Gray to the area where the victim's mother stayed and pointed in the distance.

"That's her tent. I'm sorry I can't introduce you."

"It's fine. I can manage from here. Take care of yourself, Kamaria."

Gray removed the stethoscope from his satchel and hung it around his neck. The campfire was burning outside the tent, so he assumed someone was inside.

"Hello? I'm a doctor. Can I help you?"

A few moments passed before a woman stuck her head out of the tent. She looked to be in her late thirties and was bundled up in a thick jacket with the hood covering her head.

Gray held up his medical satchel. "May I come inside?"

The woman nodded and pulled back the tent flap, so Gray entered the tent. Inside the tent was a teen girl. She looked about fifteen or sixteen. She sat toward the rear with her legs pulled up against her chest. A small battery-powered lamp lit the tent. It was just the two women and their meager belongings.

"My name is Dr. Sanders. I'm with Doctors Without Borders. I'm here to make sure you're well."

"I'm Sada, and my daughter's name is Gamila."

Gray started with the mother. He listened to her heartbeat and breathing before taking her temperature and blood pressure. He asked if she had any pain anywhere in her body, to which she replied no. He looked at her eyes with a flashlight and checked inside her ears. She had a slight cough, so he gave her cough drops. He then repeated the procedure with her daughter. He noticed bruising along her arms.

"Does it hurt?" he asked.

"A little," she said.

"Can you tell me how this happened?"

"Men attacked her," her mother answered quickly. "They wanted to rape my daughter."

"These are men in the camp?"

"Yes. There's a gang of them that go around and rape women and girls."

"Have you reported this to the soldiers?"

"They don't care. They laugh at us. It's getting worse every day. Before, we used to only fear the nights. Now we fear the day. In this area around us, it's all women. We've come together to protect each other. No men are allowed in this area."

The woman had become agitated, and Gray didn't blame her at all.

"I'm very sorry to hear that. I know rape is a problem in the camp. I also know there are other crimes being committed."

"You know, then?"

"I've heard about the little girls, but very few people are willing to talk."

"I'll talk to you. My daughter Haya was the first one. She

was only eight. Boys were playing in the woods and found her. Her neck was cut, and she bled to death."

The woman's eyes welled, and she wiped them with her coat sleeve.

"I'm very sorry for your loss. I truly am."

"Coming here was supposed to be the start of a new future for my children and me. Now one is dead, and every day I fear my other daughter will be raped."

"Can you tell me what happened?"

"Yes. I woke in the morning, and she was gone. I thought she went into the woods to use the bathroom, but after twenty minutes, she didn't return, so we went to look for her."

"And you didn't find her?"

"No."

"Do you know when she might have gone into the woods?"

"We think she went at night while her sister and I were sleeping. I told her never to go at night without her sister or me. If she went in the early morning, people would have seen her, but no one did."

"When did the boys find her?"

"The next day."

"So a full day passed before she was discovered?"

"Yes."

"Is it possible to show me the area where your daughter was found?"

"Yes, I will take you there."

Gray followed Sada and Gamila to an area in the woods away from the central part of the camp. It would be easy for someone to get turned around and not find their way back, especially at night.

Sada pointed to the ground. "She was found near that tree."

"When did this happen?"

"A month ago."

Gray knew there'd be little chance of any physical evidence, but he walked the area carefully, scanning the ground. He bent down next to the tree and imagined the girl lying there. He looked around and noted she could have been killed here and not been heard or seen for days. It was extremely dense, and visibility disappeared after thirty feet. All he could see beyond that were silver vertical lines. If those boys hadn't played in this area, her body might never been found.

"Do you know the boys who found your daughter?" Gray asked as he stood.

"I know one. I can show you who he is in the camp. But I'll warn you now, his father is a dangerous man."

"Why is that?"

"He's a rapist."

13

Sada took Gray close enough to the boy's tent to point it out and not a foot closer. Gray thanked the woman for her help. Once she was out of sight, Gray decided to wait and watch. He wanted a chance to observe the man Sada called a rapist.

He took the opportunity to check the health of a few migrants while keeping watch on the tent. After twenty minutes or so, a man emerged from the tent. He was on the shorter side but bulky. He had a shaved head, a heavy brow, and bushy eyebrows—it was an intimidating look.

The man bent down and added more wood to his campfire. He seemed a bit jittery, constantly looking around as if wanting to prevent someone from sneaking up on him. Gray finished his examination and then made his way over to the man. He spotted Gray approaching and kept his gaze locked on him. The man took a defensive stance.

"What do you want?"

"My name is Dr. Sanders. Do you or does anybody inside your tent have any health problems?"

Just then, a girl strolled close by the tent. Seconds later, her mother grabbed the girl by her arm and yanked her away. Gray could see the fear in the woman's eyes.

The man looked Gray up and down a few times before relaxing his stance. "My son. He has a rash on his leg." He pointed to the tent.

Inside, a teen boy lay on a cot.

"Hi, I'm Dr. Sanders. Your father told me you have a rash on your leg?"

The boy nodded and pointed to his right leg. Gray asked him to remove his pants so he could take a look. Gray recognized the problem right away: contact dermatitis.

"It's nothing serious," Gray said. "Probably an allergic reaction from some plant or bush in the area." Gray slipped on a pair of latex gloves. "This is anti-itch cream. It'll provide relief." He rubbed some of the ointment on the boy's leg. "Apply twice a day, and the rash should clear up in a few days."

Gray looked over at the father. "Take off your shirt. I want to check your breathing. You sound a little breathy."

The man did as he was told, and Gray placed the stethoscope on the man's back. He noticed several scratches. Gray asked the man to turn around, and he listened to his breathing from the front. There were more scratches on the man's chest. His forearms also had scratching and bruising.

"What happened here?" Gray said, pointing to the man's forearm.

"It's nothing," the man said.

"Where are you and your son from?"

"We're from Iraq. Are you American?"

"I am. I came here to help."

"Why? Are there not people in your country who need your help?"

"There are, but I think the people here need it more. Is it just you and your son?"

The man nodded. "His mother died years ago."

"I'm sorry to hear that. I've heard from many people in the camp that the soldiers are very abusive. Have you had any problems with them?"

"They don't scare me. They leave me alone. I scare them." He pointed at his chest and laughed a little.

"You can put your clothes on now. Do you mind if I ask your names?"

"I'm Arif Fadel. My son is Tahir."

"I'll need a photo of each of you for patient records." Gray used his cell phone to snap a photo of the man and son individually. "If you have any more health issues, my organization's tent is north of here. You can't miss it."

Gray exited the tent and made his way back to his campground. The line outside of his tent had gone down considerably. There was just an old man waiting to be seen. Gray looked the man over while Gorecki finished with a woman.

"What did your explorations lead to, Gray?" Gorecki asked after the last two patients cleared out of the tent.

"I met the mother of the first victim."

Gray quickly brought Gorecki up to speed on what he'd learned and his meeting with Fadel and his son.

"Rapes are widespread in migrant camps," Gorecki said.

"Do you know if the girls were sexually abused? Were autopsies conducted?"

"My government never had possession of the bodies, so your guess is as good as mine."

"Where are the bodies?"

"Probably buried in the woods or carted off by the soldiers. The intelligence officer in the camp wasn't able to determine that, as he was pulled out shortly after discovering the murders."

"Finding those bodies could answer a lot of questions," Gray said.

"You're right, but this man, Fadel, the accused rapist, he seems like a person of interest."

"If we could determine if the girls were sexually abused, I could see him being one."

Gray sent the photos of Fadel and his son to Gorecki.

"He had bruising and scratches on his body. He's not afraid of the soldiers. He might have some sort of impunity from them. Maybe he's worked out a deal with them."

"What? Like he points out people the soldiers can steal from and they let him rape freely?"

"Yes, exactly like that."

14

Later that evening, Gray took time to work on the profile. He lay on his cot, tapping away on his phone while Gorecki went out into the camp. It was too dangerous to work on a laptop out in the open. A soldier could enter his tent at any time without notice. Gray was better off hiding the document on his phone.

Gray was in full concentration mode when a giggle broke the silence in the tent. Gray sat up and found the girl with the sprained ankle peeking into his tent.

"Hello, Salma. This is a nice surprise. Is there something I can help you with? Is your ankle bothering you?"

"No. I came to say hello to you."

"Come inside and have a seat." Gray pointed to a chair. "Is your mother with you?"

"No. She doesn't know I'm here." Salma crutched it over to the chair and sat.

"You learned to use the crutches very well."

"I've been practicing."

"Salma, the camp is dangerous at night. You really shouldn't be wandering outside by yourself."

Gray got up, reached under his coat, and removed a box of chocolate chip cookies. He handed it over to Salma. She dug her hand into the box and took a cookie.

"Mmmm, this is very good."

Gray laughed. "I'm glad you're enjoying it, but I'm sure your mother is worried about you. Come on, I'll walk you back to your tent."

Gray held the flap to his tent open so that Salma could get out.

"How did you find my tent, Salma?"

"Everyone knows where your tent is. You're a doctor."

"That's right."

"How long will you stay here?"

"I'm not sure. It's not really up to me."

"I hope you stay a long time."

"Why do you hope for that?"

"Because you make me feel safe."

When they neared Salma's tent, her mother spotted them and came hurrying over.

"Salma, where have you been? Why did you leave?"

"I'm afraid she came to visit me," Gray said. "I brought her back right away.

"Salma, you can't just leave like that, especially at night."

"But I wanted to see Dr. Sanders."

"Salma, you must listen to your mother. She's right. It's very dangerous in the camp." Gray bent down to one knee. "I want you to promise me you'll never run off alone again. Okay?"

"Okay, I promise."

"Farida, how is everything? Anything I can help with while I'm here?"

"We're fine. Thank you for bringing her back."

Gray said goodbye and hurried back to his tent. Gorecki was inside sitting on his cot when he got there.

"Where did you go?" he asked Gray.

"One of my patients, a little girl, paid me a visit. So I walked her back to her tent."

"How's the profile coming along?"

Gray removed his phone from his pants pocket. "Here's what I have. Our guy is twenty-five to forty years of age and single. He's a predator and likes to be in control. He isn't afraid to display his authority in front of others. In fact, he thrives on it. Anger issues related to the camp could have triggered the killings. Due to the sheer number of rapes, our guy may be a sexual deviant. It's also possible the migrants in the camp know or at least highly suspect who it is."

"How good do you feel about this profile?"

Gray shrugged. "Fifty-fifty. I need more information to be more certain. Talking to the mother of the first victim helped a lot. If I could interview the other victims' parents, that would help as well. Any idea how we can figure that out fast?"

"Keep asking around," Gorecki said.

"I don't know if you picked up on this, but there's a high level of fear in the camp. It's difficult getting people to talk."

"You've got to earn their trust. And do it quickly. It's the only way."

"It's the timing that's not working in our favor," Gray said.

"It's not, but that's the situation we're in. It's dangerous for us to be in here. Every day we're here is an opportunity for them to realize our true identities. Anything else come to mind for you?"

"One thing bothers me. The camp is dense. These tents are pretty close to each other. Once you get outside the camp, the woods are thick and very dark at night. I'm struggling with how a killer is abducting and killing these girls without being seen." Gray took a seat on his cot.

"It's like you said earlier, he might have been seen, but people are too afraid to say anything."

"It still feels a little off. You would think after the first two murders, people would keep a tight leash on their children, especially those who have little girls. But as I said earlier, one of them visited me without her mother knowing. And she was on crutches. Talk about putting oneself out there as bait. It leads me to believe the killer might be stalking and targeting his victims. What are your plans if we do pinpoint a suspect? Do you plan on interrogating him? How would you even get him out of the camp, or is the plan to turn him over to the Belarusians?"

"Let me worry about that. You just concentrate on profiling."

Gray straightened up. "That's ridiculous. We need to work together."

Gorecki leaned forward. "I know you're familiar with the chain of command. So I'll remind you who I am...your commanding officer."

15

The shrill scream pierced Gray's ear and pulled him right out of his sleep.

"What the hell was that?" he asked.

Gorecki had also heard it as he was sitting up in his cot.

The high-pitched scream echoed across the camp again. Definitely a woman. Gray and Gorecki quickly put on clothes and hurried out of the tent. Again, the woman's cry rang out. It was coming from the woods. Migrants began poking their heads out of their tents as Gray ran around them toward the woods.

There was more screaming, and this time Gray was positive it was coming from someone young, a little girl. He hustled as fast as he could, using his hands to dodge around the trunks of the trees. It was dark and hard for Gray to move quickly.

Then he spotted her curled up against a tree.

Gray scooped the shivering girl into his arms. Gorecki arrived right behind him.

"Take her!" he said as he shoved the girl into Gorecki's arms. "I saw someone running away."

Gray didn't wait for an answer, and as soon as Gorecki had the girl in his grip, Gray turned and ran. The woods got dark and dense real fast. Gray slowed, not wanting to run smack into a tree. He couldn't exactly see the person he was chasing, but he could hear his footsteps and heavy breathing. Gray continued, even though it was extremely dangerous. He had only his fists to defend himself with, and Gorecki wasn't around to back him up. Whoever he was chasing could be armed with a weapon.

Gray was breathing pretty hard and could no longer hear the person ahead of him. He had gotten away.

Gray drew deep breaths. Streams of perspiration ran down the sides of his face, and his neck felt slick. He bent over, resting his hands on his knees.

A beat later, something hard and moving fast slammed into Gray. The force of the blow caved Gray's lungs and sent him flying through the air until he bounced off a tree and landed on the ground. Gray groaned in pain as he tried to comprehend what had just happened. A heavy weight fell onto his chest. Something hard struck him in the face, and again, and again, until Gray had the presence of mind to lift his arms and protect himself.

Gray managed to grab the sleeve of his attacker and hold on to one of his arms while striking back with his free hand. He knew he had connected with the side of the face of his attacker at least twice. But then a crushing blow slipped through Gray's defenses and knocked him out cold.

~

Gray's eyes fluttered open briefly, enough for him to realize someone was standing in front of him. Then a sharp sting erupted on the side of his face from a hard slap. Gray quickly regained consciousness. The person who slapped him was a Belarusian soldier. Off to the side were two more. Gray was sitting in a chair in a small room with no windows and just a light bulb in the ceiling.

"Answer me!" the soldier said with a heavy Belarusian accent. "What is your name?"

"My name is Dr. Sanders," Gray said. "I work with Doctors Without Borders."

"You lie!" The soldier slapped Gray again. "Why are you here? Who do you work for? What is your mission?"

"I told you. I'm Dr. Sanders. I work—"

This time the soldier punched Gray in the jaw. "Stop lying!"

"I'm not lying. I'm here on a humanitarian mission."

The soldier bent down so he could look Gray directly in his eyes.

"I don't think he's lying," one of the other soldiers in the back said in Belarusian.

Gray understood but didn't let on.

The soldiers began discussing what to do in their own language. Still, Gray picked up enough of it to understand that they realized they had been beating up a doctor.

A knock on the door grabbed their attention. One of the soldiers unlocked the door and opened it. In walked another soldier, followed by Gorecki.

"There you are. I'm so glad you guys found him. We were so worried about him being lost in the woods. He's our best doctor. To lose him would hurt our objective here. Thank you so much for rescuing him. Thank you." Gorecki looked at the soldiers with pleading eyes. They looked at each other with a bit of surprise.

The soldier who had been beating Gray spoke. "Your doctor friend, why was he in the woods?"

"He sometimes has nightmares and walks in his sleep. Normally, I keep the tent locked so if he does wake up, he can't leave. I must not have secured it tight enough. This is my fault. But I'm thankful that you guys found him."

"Your friend is lucky to be alive. The woods are not safe," the soldier said.

"Yes, I can see that. It looks like he fell down." Gorecki pointed to the swelling on Gray's face.

"We found him like that. He must have run into a tree."

"Yes, probably so. Can I take him? I think rest is what he needs."

The soldier nodded, and Gorecki helped Gray to his feet and escorted him out of the room.

Once Gorecki and Gray were in the privacy of their own tent, only then did Gorecki drop the act.

"What the hell were you thinking back there? Running off like that? Of all the stupid things you could have done. Do you know how much pleading I had to do to get to you? You could have easily ended up in a shallow grave. This is not America, where there are rights and everyone follows the rules. Really, a shallow grave would be a gift if they found out you were a spy. Have you ever been tortured? I mean really tortured, brought within inches of your life? I have. And you know what? I'm not looking to put myself back in that situation for something as stupid as what you did back there. You not only jeopardized your safety but mine as well."

Gray took a seat on his cot. "I know. I screwed up. It was a knee-jerk reaction. But what was I supposed to do? Let the guy get away? I almost had him."

"Yes, you were supposed to let him get away, because this time, it's not your job to catch a criminal. From now on, I don't want you chasing after anyone or even trying to detain someone. You leave all of that to me. Your only job here is to give me a profile. Is that clear?"

Gray nodded. "Understood."

Gorecki removed a bottle of vodka from a bag under his coat.

"What are you doing?"

"I need to make sure everything is fine and there are no second thoughts about either of us. Do not leave this tent."

16

Gray let out a soft groan as he rolled over onto his back. Every inch of his body seemed to ache, and the cot wasn't to blame. Gray looked over at Gorecki's side of the tent. His cot was empty.

He sat up and groaned once more as he rubbed the left side of his rib cage. Gray lifted his shirt and saw bruising. He took a moment to assess the other areas that hurt on his body. Gray ruled out fractures. He'd just gotten the crap beaten out of him, that's all. He glanced at his watch. It was seven in the morning.

The flaps at the entrance to the tent opened, and in walked Gorecki with two cups of hot coffee. He handed one to Gray.

"Drink up. It'll breathe life back into you."

"Thanks," Gray said before taking a sip.

"How are you feeling?"

"Sore, but I'll manage."

"Why don't you fill me in on what happened last night when you gave chase?"

Gray did that.

"One of his punches must have knocked me out, because I

woke up to a soldier slapping my face. They thought I was there for other reasons other than providing medical help. They wanted to know who I worked for, what was my mission. Stuff like that. I just kept repeating that I was Dr. Sanders, I worked for Doctors Without Borders, and I was here on a humanitarian mission."

Gorecki nodded.

"How did your nightcap last night go?"

"I convinced them that you were only trying to help. You thought someone was attacking the girl and wanted to catch the person and turn him over to the soldiers. I told them your face is a good indication that you're not a threat." Gorecki smiled.

"Are they watching us now?"

"They'll be watching, but I think we'll be fine so long as we don't do anything to grab any more of their attention. It's important to blend and become invisible for our remaining time in the camp."

"You're serious about us being pulled out after five days, aren't you?"

"I am. I agree with you, we need more time, but it's not my call."

"What happened to the girl?"

"She's fine. She wasn't hurt, just scared. I convinced the family to bring her over to the tent so I could examine her and make sure she had no injuries."

"Did she give up any information?"

"She'd wandered off while the family had been sleeping. Probably to use the bathroom."

"What is it with these little girls walking into the woods by themselves?" Gray asked. "Don't they know better?"

"I can't answer that. But I can tell you the rapist you pointed out, he was at the scene last night. Right after you took off after the culprit, migrants from the camp caught up with us. The family was one of the first. Then I spotted Fadel watching. He hung in the background. When our eyes met, he immediately turned and hurried off. It's possible he went after you or had a partner. Do you think it was Fadel who attacked you?"

"Hard to say. It was dark, and I was being punched repeatedly in the face." Gray took a moment to think. "I can't be sure."

"Do you know where Fadel's tent is? I want to give him extra attention. There's a line outside. Are you ready to get to work?"

"Yeah, I'm good to go." Gray downed the last of his coffee. "Let me get dressed, and I'll start seeing patients."

Gorecki walked out of the tent without saying another word.

Gray was getting used to his abruptness. He changed and freshened up the best he could before greeting the patients outside.

One by one, Gray took care of the people while doing his best to pick their brains about what happened the night before. Most were not interested in talking. A few had questions of their own about Gray's face. One, a woman with her small son, gently touched his cheek.

"You must be careful," she said. "It's very dangerous in the camp. Even you are not safe here."

"Thank you," Gray said. "Do you know who the dangerous men are?"

A look of confusion appeared on her face. "They're all dangerous."

"I'm interested in the ones who are hurting the little girls."

"Hurting or killing? Because many hurt; only one is killing."

"Do you know who that one is?" Gray asked in a lower voice.

"I don't, but he won't stop. I can feel it."

The woman and her son left, and another person took their place. As the day wore on, the overall mood he sensed from the people had worsened. Whether they said it or not, they all believed that the girl who was attacked the previous night was fortunate. She should have been the fourth victim.

The pressure to deliver the correct profile was real. Gray had already been in the camp for three days. There wasn't much time left. If nothing materialized soon, Gray and Gorecki would be pulled out. The killings wouldn't stop.

Gray was essentially working the investigation alone. Gorecki was off doing other things, but Gorecki wasn't a crime investigator. He was an intelligence officer. Gray wished they'd sent someone with an appropriate skill set, someone with a history of investigating crimes. But Gray figured it made sense to pair him with an intelligence officer given the situation.

Gorecki wasn't the best when it came to a sounding board. He tended to take in information and digest it. He wouldn't spit anything back out until he was ready to act. Gray thought of putting a call in to Interpol and seeing what help they could offer, but really, what could they do? Gray was operating in Belarus, not Poland. Gray had to figure out a way to make it work, on his own, in that particular situation. Any "buts" would just be an excuse for not getting the job done. For the DPM of Poland to personally request Gray told him they were counting on him to do what they felt no one else in Poland could do.

A man clearing his throat pulled Gray out of his thoughts. To his surprise, Fadel stood in front of him. He kept his gaze down and off to the side.

"Hi, how can I help you?" Gray asked, trying to catch Fadel's eyes.

"I want to tell you the medicine you gave to my son is working."

"I'm glad to hear that."

Fadel still refused to look Gray in the eyes, keeping his head turned to one side. Gray stood up and walked around to the other side of the table. Only then did Fadel look up as he took a step back. The other side of his face had bruising, as if he'd been punched.

"What happened to your face?"

Gray reached out to further examine it, but Fadel stepped back again.

"It's nothing. I'm okay. I just wanted to thank you for helping my son."

Before Gray could manage another question, Fadel left and disappeared in the crowd of people outside Gray's tent.

17

The number of migrants keeping Gray busy that day seemed never-ending. As much as he wanted to run off after Fadel, he had disappeared quickly. Gray couldn't exactly leave his tent unattended with all those people outside. It took about an hour to find another doctor to cover for him. As soon as he did that, he made his way to Fadel's tent. No one was there, not even his son.

Gray looked around at the other tents in the area. Nobody seemed to be concerned with him standing there. They were simply going on about their day. Gray realized then he hadn't heard or seen Gorecki since he left that morning.

How are we supposed to catch a killer if we're working independently of each other? That's an excuse, Gray. Deal with it and figure out a solution. Maybe Gorecki is doing other things to try to find the killer.

Rather than wonder what Gorecki was up to, what Gray really needed to do was his job: finalize the profile. Gray thought back to his conversations with Sada, the mother of the first victim, Haya. He never did inquire what happened to her daughter's body. It might be worth it to know.

Gray set out for their tent. It took about twenty minutes to reach it. He saw Sada sitting outside, tending to a pot on the campfire.

"Hello, Sada. Do you remember me? I'm Dr. Sanders."

"Yes, I remember you. It's a nice surprise to see you again."

"I was in the area, so I thought I would stop by."

Gamila, her teenage daughter, stuck her head out of the tent just then. "Dr. Sanders. I thought I recognized your voice. What brings you here?"

"I had to check on some patients not far from here, and I thought I'd stop by."

"Dr. Sanders, if you have time, please join us for a meal," Sada said. "I've made mushroom soup, and it's ready now."

Gray was about to decline Sada's offer, as he didn't feel comfortable taking food away from her and her daughter.

"Please, there is plenty."

"Are you sure?"

"Yes, it will be an honor to do something nice for you after all your help for everyone here."

"It's my job to help."

"I know, but you don't have to be here. Please, sit."

Gray knew enough that it could be offensive if he continued to politely decline.

"Thank you. It's very kind of you."

Gray sat down, and Gamila took a seat next to him. Sada filled three containers with a brown soup.

"Gamila and I picked the mushrooms in the woods, not far from here."

Gray scooped up a spoonful and blew on it gently. "Wow, this is really good. What type of mushrooms did you use?"

"Those are chanterelle mushrooms. I also added chopped onion, and rice."

"It's a wonderful soup. I never thought this would be

possible here."

"The onion and rice were given to us by the World Food Program. They've been very helpful."

"I know them. Their camp isn't too far from mine."

After they finished eating, Gray thought it was time to broach the subject of Haya's body. "Sada, I'd like to ask you something, and you can decline to answer. It'll be okay."

"What is it, Dr. Sanders?"

"I want to know what happened to Haya's body."

"Her body?"

"Yes, did the soldiers take it?"

"No, we buried her in the woods."

"Is it possible for you to take me to Haya's grave? I'd like to see it."

"Yes, of course. We should go now, before it gets late."

"Is it far from here?"

"No, not at all."

Sada and Gamila led Gray into the woods to the gravesite. When they reached it, Gray noticed a tiny headstone that had been carved out of wood.

"A few men in the camp helped us bury her. One of them carved the headstone."

Gray stood back and gave Sada and Gamila privacy as they knelt down and prayed. During that time, Gray made notes in his phone on the grave's location and any worthwhile observations.

"What are you thinking, Dr. Sanders?" Sada asked when she finished.

"It's a beautiful area."

"Thank you. Now it is time for me to ask you something.

"Of course, Sada."

"What is the real reason you're interested in seeing Haya's grave?"

"I have a few contacts back in Poland who work in law enforcement. I want to talk to them and see if there is anything they might do to bring Haya's murderer to justice."

"Do you really think that's possible?"

"I do. With the right evidence, it is possible to find the person."

"What evidence do you need?"

"What are your thoughts on exhumation?"

Sada covered her mouth as she gasped. "You want to dig her body up?"

"Yes, but only with your permission. If we can arrange an autopsy, we might be able to learn more about what happened."

"I see." Sada looked away for a moment. "Under Islamic law, the exhumation of a body is only allowed for a good reason. An autopsy would qualify. But how would you arrange it? How would you transport her body? I don't think the soldiers will allow you to take her. I had to fight to bury my daughter. They wanted to take her body somewhere."

"I don't have the answers. I only wanted to see if it was something you would be open to. Now that you are, I will find out exactly what I need to do. Sada, do you know the parents of the other victims?"

"I don't. The soldiers told us not to speak to them or find them. They threatened punishment."

"Why would they do that?"

"I don't know, but we listened because we are afraid. Will you make the same request from the others?"

"Yes, the more evidence we can collect, the easier it might be to find the person responsible."

"I will ask around and see what I can find out. Promise me you will find the killer."

"I promise to do my best."

18

It was nightfall when Gray made his way back to his tent, walking around the numerous campfires dotting the grounds. Gorecki was inside the tent, eating.

"There you are," he said.

"I met with Sada, the mother of the first victim. Her daughter is buried in the woods."

"Yeah, and?"

"She agreed to allow the body to be exhumed for an autopsy."

"That's a big ask. We'd need to retrieve the body and get it back across the border for an autopsy."

"It could lead to evidence that might identify the killer."

"Might. We don't have the time for that right now. But I have been thinking more about your profile and our identified rapist, Fadel. There's a good chance he could be the murderer. I've been observing him. He's always out at night, roaming. I've interviewed women in the camp. A large number of them all say the same thing about him—he's always creeping around and making sexual comments. Two have admitted to being attacked by him but were able to escape. They both said his intent was to rape."

"Did these women notify the soldiers or the NGOs?"

"Telling the soldiers resulted in laughter and sexual abuse from them. Most of these soldiers were conscripted into the military. They're young and immature and don't want to be here. It's hard to expect anything from them. As for the NGOs in the camp, they aren't in a position to do much either."

"Anything else?" Gray asked.

"A young teen reported to her father that Fadel had groped her."

Gray drew a deep breath. "He's a son of a bitch, but it's not enough to pin the murders on him."

"Your profile suggests he is a sexual deviant."

"It does, and I wouldn't argue Fadel isn't one, but I need more information."

"We have testimony from other women that he's attacked and tried to rape them. I'm sure there are women I haven't spoken to or who are simply too afraid to admit Fadel raped them."

"I do not doubt you there. But these are women. The murder victims were little girls."

"Finding a little girl who was abused by Fadel will be hard."

Gorecki rested his hands on his hips. "You know, he could have decided to murder the little girls he was successful in raping to keep them quiet. A child rapist is the worst."

"I'm not saying rape can't be a trigger. But if he murdered to cover up his crimes, he put a lot of thought into everything from the initial abduction all the way to dumping the body. An autopsy could really shed some light on this."

Gorecki went back to eating, and Gray lay down on his cot.

"He's not a loner."

"What's that?" Gray lifted his head and looked at Gorecki.

"I said he's not a loner."

"Can you expand on that?"

"He has a small group of men he interacts with. I've seen them. They tend to do whatever he says, and they follow him around. I haven't heard from anyone that they have actually raped. I think for now they're entertained by watching, but they could step up and start abusing, considering nothing is being done to stop Fadel."

"That's interesting. It could signal that this dynamic fuels his need for control and power. He could be using them to further his abuse."

"Like helping him single out victims and contain them."

"Yes. But like I said earlier, there's too much of a jump from a rapist to a killer. But if we can prove those little girls were sexually abused, then we have something."

"Or we could interrogate him and find out the truth that way."

"Yeah, that's one way to go as well. But we have no jurisdiction here. In fact, we're simply doctors. If word were to get out to the Belarusians that we were questioning migrants in that manner, it would blow our cover."

"It would. That's why it's important they don't find out."

"What are you planning?"

"We're running out of time. We need to make moves. My supervisor is dead serious about pulling us out. Do you think your profile would change drastically if you were to learn more information?"

"It's hard to say. It could depend on the information I receive. This profile was developed on what information I've acquired so far. Normally, I have access to a lot more information. Sometimes a small detail can shift the profile."

"I get the science, but part of your ability is your gut. There are many profilers for hire. Why is it *you* stand out? It's your gut instinct. That's unique to you. What is your gut instinct telling you right now?"

"Fadel isn't our guy."

19

Gray woke to Gorecki shaking his arm. He had a finger pressed against his lips.

"Get dressed," he said.

"What time is it?" Gray whispered.

There were two other men in the tent who weren't part of the DWB team.

"Who are they?" Gray asked as he put on his boots.

"They're here to help."

Gray understood right then that they were probably intelligence officers embedded into the camp as migrants. He was under the impression there were none. It was just more of this need-to-know crap.

"Where are we going?" Gray asked. "Can you at least tell me that?"

"It's time to make our move."

"What move?"

"We're taking Fadel in for questioning. You wanted more involvement. You're being involved."

"Where are we questioning him? Did you secure a location?"

"Hurry, we don't have much time."

Gorecki and the two other men left the tent with Gray bringing up the rear.

Gray checked his watch. It was two thirty in the morning. Most of the campfires had died out by then, and soldier patrols were minimal, if any.

Gorecki stopped about thirty yards away from Fadel's tent.

"Gray, stay here and keep watch."

Gorecki and the others left before Gray could respond. As he watched them make their way toward Fadel's tent, he moved closer. All three IOs disappeared inside. There was some visible shaking of the tent, followed by muffled noises. A few moments later, they emerged with Fadel. He had a gag in his mouth, and his hands were zip-tied behind his back. The two other officers gripped each of Fadel's arms and were moving him toward the woods. Gorecki approached Gray.

"You good?"

"Yeah, I'm fine. What about the son?"

"What about him? Let's go. We don't have time to chat."

The men moved out of the camp and into the woods. Fadel started to trip and fall, having to be jerked back up to his feet over and over. Every once in a while, Fadel would slam into a tree purposely.

"Do you have a location, or are we questioning him in the woods?" Gray asked.

"We can't question Fadel in Belarus. We're crossing the border."

"Are you serious?"

"Yes, it's right there."

Gray looked ahead, and about forty feet out, the trees gave way to a large clearing. It was dark, but from where they were in the forest, in the clearing, he could make out the fence separating the two countries.

Just then, Gorecki pressed a hand onto Gray's shoulder, forcing him down.

"Border guards," he whispered.

In the distance, Gray spotted a few shadowy figures. The patrol was walking right along the edge of the woods and the clearing. They all moved behind a tree trunk as they watched the patrol slowly pass by in front of them. There were four of them, spread out while walking in a line.

Fadel was moving and making noise. One of the officers put him in a chokehold and quickly rendered him unconscious. But it wasn't quick enough. The last guard to walk by stopped and looked in their direction. Just when it seemed like he would continue, he took a step toward them.

Gray and the others froze as the guard moved closer. He was about fifteen feet away when he stopped. Gorecki suddenly produced a handgun with a suppressor attached.

The guard took a few more steps.

Gorecki raised his gun and took aim.

At ten feet away, the guard raised his rifle.

Gray felt the trickles of sweat running down the sides of his neck. He couldn't believe the situation they were in. That he was in. He was unarmed, and ten feet away was a Belarusian border guard armed with the same rifle as the guards at the checkpoint. An HK MP5. He could easily cut them all down, not to mention there were three other guards not far away and equally armed.

At eight feet away, the guard appeared to be looking directly at Gray's position.

He took another cautious step forward. A twig snapped under his boot.

Gray swallowed and realized his throat was dry. It almost triggered him to cough, but he suppressed the urge.

The guard slowly allowed his gaze to pass over all four

men. Deep down, Gray knew he couldn't see them, but that didn't make him feel any better. If Fadel regained consciousness at that moment, they were screwed.

The guard took another step. Gray was convinced the guard could hear him breathing, so he held his breath.

Just then, another guard from the patrol called out, "Alexi, what is it? Let's go."

Alexi stared for a beat longer before turning around and rejoining the patrol.

Everyone in the group let out a collective breath of relief. Fadel woke suddenly and drew a sharp breath.

"That was close," Gorecki said in a matter-of-fact tone. "Wait here."

He moved to the edge of the woods and turned a small flashlight on and off. On the other side of the border, another light flashed on and off.

"They're ready for us," he said when he returned. Gorecki dug into the small backpack he carried and took out two miniature bolt cutters. He handed one to Gray. "We need to cut through the fence."

All four men moved forward and came to a halt at the tree line. Once convinced the coast was clear, they made their move. Gorecki and Gray moved quickly to the fence and began snipping and cutting out a hole big enough for them to pass through. Minutes later, they were through the hole and moving toward the forested area in Polish territory.

Waiting for them was a sole man. The two officers handling Fadel were not coming back to the camp.

"Give me your cutters," Gorecki said to Gray.

Gray handed over the cutters.

"Let's go. We need to get back to our tent. That patrol will notice the hole in the fence on their next pass."

～

The following morning, word had spread quickly of Fadel's disappearance. Most wouldn't have blinked an eye, as Fadel wasn't a well-liked man. Nobody had a problem with the son, and many took pity on the boy and helped him search for his father.

Gray and Gorecki remained at the tent that morning, attending to people lined up outside. They'd heard that the border guards had found the hole in the fence, and a few migrants had already been taken away for questioning.

Gorecki had ordered the rest of the team for DWB to begin packing up and moving back across the border. Their time in the camp had come to an end early. Gorecki and Gray would be the last to leave.

The guards spent extra time searching through Gray's and Gorecki's belongings at the border checkpoint.

"Why are you leaving so soon? Most organizations stay longer," one of the guards asked.

"We need a break and time to resupply," Gorecki answered.

"You did not plan to stay longer? It's only been four days."

"We hope to return soon."

"When?"

"I'm not sure. It's not up to me."

The guard looked at Gray. "Your passport."

Gray handed his passport over.

"You are American."

"I am."

"Why did you come here, Dr. Sanders?" he asked as he flipped through Gray's passport. The Polish government had provided Gray with a fake US passport, complete with all the visas for the places he'd traveled with DWB.

"I'm here to help."

"Where were you before here?"

"Nepal."

"And before that?"

"Puerto Rico."

The guards checked the passport to see if those answers were correct.

"How long have you been working for Doctors Without Borders?"

"Six years, but I had a few breaks during that time."

The guard eyed Gray for a few moments before handing him back his passport. Once safely on Polish territory, Gray asked Gorecki if he thought the guards had suspicions.

"Of course they did, but they have nothing concrete to pin on us. Had we stayed longer, they would have manufactured something. Leaving now took away that opportunity."

20

During the drive back to Warsaw, Gray tried to pick Gorecki's brain and find out the next steps with Fadel. Was he already being questioned? Were they waiting for him and Gorecki to return? Would Gray even have a chance to interview Fadel? He certainly wanted the opportunity, since he didn't think there was enough evidence to implicate Fadel. Heck, he had no idea abduction was even on the table. Apparently, it was. But it made sense. How would they interrogate Fadel in the camp? But Gorecki deflected and eventually shut down. Perhaps he was in the dark as well.

Gorecki kept to himself, focused on the scenery outside his window for the rest of the drive. Gray did the same.

It was early afternoon when Gray was dropped off at the hotel. He had made one more attempt at the next steps, but Gorecki gave him the same answer. "You'll be briefed soon." Gorecki told Gray to stay put in his room until he heard from him or Pakulski.

Gray headed up to his room, where all his belongings had been held for him while he was in the camp. The first thing

Gray did was order a pot of coffee from room service. He was craving a decent cup. He also figured, since he was on house arrest, he'd work on a status report.

While he waited for the coffee to arrive, Gray took a quick shower. It felt good to clean off the grit, dirt, sweat, and whatever else he'd picked up in the camp. There had been no showers, and the best he'd had were wet wipes.

After a warm shower, Gray found the coffee had already been delivered. He poured himself a cup and then tried calling Pratt. He wanted to update her and relay what was happening, as he'd yet to meet anyone from the local Interpol office. But every attempt resulted in a busy signal. Gray gave up and started work on the status report.

∾

In another room in the same hotel but one floor below, two men were busy monitoring video footage on their laptops. It was a live feed of Gray's hotel room: the cameras covered every angle of it, including the bathroom. There were also live mics, and they could hear everything, even Gray slurping his coffee. In addition, the team used an IMSI-catcher to reroute every call Gray made on his cell phone to a dummy cell tower and on to a third party monitored by them. Calls made outside the country were never connected, and a fake busy signal was given. In fact, all electronic communication, whether on his phone or via his laptop, was monitored and filtered. None of it would reach its intended recipient.

∾

It was coming up on five o'clock, and cabin fever started to set in. Gray hadn't heard a peep from Gorecki or Pakulski. He'd left a couple of messages for his contact at the Interpol office but hadn't heard back from them either. He figured he would just step out for a walk and get some fresh air. No sooner had that thought entered his mind than there was a knock on the door. A hotel employee was delivering a tuxedo.

"I'm sorry, are you sure you have the right room?" Gray asked.

"You are Mr. Sterling Gray, are you not?"

"That's me."

"Then this is for you."

The man handed Gray a garment bag along with a pair of black shoes and dress socks. He smiled and left. The hotel phone rang, and Gray laid the tuxedo over the back of a chair and answered the phone.

"Hello, Sterling. It's Julianna. Did you receive the tuxedo I sent?"

"I got it just now."

"Great. I'll be stopping by in an hour. I have plans to entertain you tonight."

"In a tuxedo?"

"It's a nice place. See you soon."

Gray hung up the phone, thinking at least someone got back to him that day. Gray took another shower and shaved before changing into the suit. It fit him perfectly. Julianna had a good eye. He assumed she'd arranged for it like she had all of the other clothing he'd worn at the camp.

At an hour on the dot, there was a knock on the door. It was Julianna. She was dressed in a black cocktail dress that perfectly showed her figure. Her blonde hair had been put up in an elegant braid, with tendrils framing her face. The heels she wore brought her right up to Gray's height.

"You clean up well, Sterling," she said as she gave him a once-over.

"As do you."

"Come on, I have a car waiting for us downstairs."

In the elevator, Pakulski turned to Gray and said, "I hope you're thirsty. I'm in the mood for champagne."

21

After a short drive, Gray and Pakulski arrived at a striking six-story building with an art nouveau design. It sat on the corner of an intersection along what was dubbed the Royal Route: a north-south boulevard featuring several historic buildings.

"Welcome to Hotel Bristol," Pakulski said as the car came to a stop out front.

"I'm impressed," Gray said.

They climbed out of the car and headed inside.

"Most visiting dignitaries choose to stay here because that's where they've always stayed. It has been a political hot spot since it opened its doors in 1901, and the first hotel in Europe to feature this fabulous art nouveau design."

Gray slowed to admire the architectural details in the lobby.

"This way," Pakulski said as she walked toward the elevators.

Gray had assumed they were heading to a bar or restaurant on the ground level.

"It's a beautiful building," he said as they waited for the elevator.

"The Hotel Bristol has survived two world wars, the Great Depression, and the command economy of communism. It's been closed down and reopened and had to endure many restorations to bring it back to its full glory."

"It's certainly worth it."

Pakulski removed a hotel key card from her black clutch and used it to access the top floor.

They exited into a hallway filled with hotel rooms. No restaurant. No bar. No rooftop. Gray tilted his head in confusion. Pakulski smiled at Gray as she hooked her arm around his and led him down the hallway. Gray began to wonder if he'd gotten this outing all wrong. Pakulski stopped outside of room 1902. A lump rose inside Gray's throat. *This can't be what I'm thinking.*

Pakulski pressed the key card against the security pad and the door unlocked. "I hope you like what I have in store for you." She pushed the door open and led the way in.

Gray and Pakulski emerged onto an elegant yet very intimate rooftop bar with sunset views of the city.

"This is the Belle Époque Champagne Bar," she said. "I told you I was in the mood for champagne."

Gray and Pakulski enjoyed Perrier-Jouët as they learned more about each other. Pakulski wanted to know more about Gray's background, finding it fascinating and rich with experiences.

"From Pararescue to FBI profiler. One doesn't hear about that too often. Do you miss serving in the Air Force?"

"I did at first, but working for the FBI has allowed me to learn new skills and have experiences I otherwise wouldn't have had. There's never a boring day."

"I think not."

"Enough about me. I want to get to know Julianna Pakulski, the mysterious aide to the deputy prime minister."

"Trust me, I'm not all that exciting. I work in the background and prefer it that way. Sterling, are you hungry yet?"

"I'm starved. Are we eating here?"

"Not here, but downstairs in the Marconi restaurant. The executive chef has prepared a special menu just for us."

Over dinner, Gray steered the topic of conversation back to work. He still hadn't heard from Gorecki about Fadel.

"I can tell you right now a team of investigators is questioning Fadel. I assure you his rights are not being violated, and he's being treated well."

"Well, that's good to know. I'll be frank with you. I really would like an opportunity to sit down with Fadel and question him."

"As you should. I'm sure when the team is done, you'll have an opportunity to see Fadel. I'll pass it along just so that it's noted and not forgotten."

"Thanks, Julianna. I appreciate it."

Pakulski had been nothing but polite and friendly since the beginning of the night. However, Gray still couldn't help but think her entire reason for being there with him was to hold his hand and watch over him. But Gray wasn't about to bring that up. If this was how the Polish government did things, so be it. He was there to consult, not take over and lead an investigation.

After they finished dinner, the night was still young, and Pakulski had more entertainment planned.

"I wasn't sure we'd finish dinner in time, but it looks like we can catch the opera tonight."

"Now I understand the reason for a tuxedo," Gray said.

"Even if we didn't make the opera, you look dashing in it."

Pakulski and Gray sat in a private box that was front and center. They had champagne on ice and a personal attendant waiting on them. Gray had never experienced this sort of hospitality on an assignment, ever.

"You do this for all guests of the state?" Gray whispered.

"Just the handsome ones," she whispered back.

After the opera, Pakulski insisted on a nightcap, arguing Gray had nowhere he really needed to be in the morning. Who was Gray to push back? They walked arm in arm to a small bar not far from the opera house.

～

The following morning, Gray woke with a case of dry mouth. All that alcohol the night before had left him dehydrated. He glanced over at the bedside clock: it was almost ten. Gray recalled leaving the opera house, but everything after that was a blur. He couldn't even remember coming back to his room and climbing into his bed. Strewn across the floor were various pieces of Gray's tuxedo.

Surely I would remember stripping down.

Gray sat up and realized something was sticking to his rib cage. It was a black thong. He then noticed the handwritten note on the pillow next to him. It read: *I had a wonderful time last night—Julianna.*

I wish I remembered it, he thought.

22

After a shower and a few cups of coffee, Gray began to feel normal once again. He still couldn't recall much after the opera. He put another call in to Gorecki and left a message reminding Gorecki that he wished to speak to Fadel. Gray wanted assurance that they had the right guy.

He did remember Pakulski saying she'd pass along his wish to question Fadel but didn't want to leave it to chance. That request had been made before a long night of champagne-filled indulgence. He figured she might need the day to recover from the previous night's events.

While waiting for a return call, Gray flipped on the TV and found a news channel. There was a large graphic off to the side of the newscaster that read: *Breaking News.* Suddenly the graphic changed to a photo of someone familiar. It took a beat, but Gray recognized the man. It was Fadel. The crawler at the bottom of the screen read: *Serial Killer Captured.*

The graphic changed to video footage of Fadel sitting behind a table in handcuffs with guards around him. Gray turned up the volume.

The news reported Fadel, a migrant from Syria, had confessed to murdering little girls in the camp.

Confessed?

The newscaster went on to say that Fadel was experiencing significant stress in the camp, and it drove him to do despicable things. The footage cut to Fadel speaking through a translator.

"We're treated like animals by the Belarusian soldiers. They beat us daily. Rape our women and daughters. Steal whatever of value we have. All we wanted was to escape the persecution in our own countries and live a better life in the EU, but now we're trapped in Belarus. Everyone in the camp is suffering."

Gray couldn't believe what he was watching. He had so many questions about the confession from Fadel. Was Fadel coerced into giving it? What evidence did he provide that corroborated him as the actual killer? Was it just his word? Was there other evidence discovered that Gray was unaware of? It was shocking how fast the Polish government had moved to hold Fadel up as the man responsible.

Did my requests fall on deaf ears?

The footage cut to a government spokesperson addressing the media. "Poland always has and will continue to support the migrants in the camp with food, water, medical treatment, and more. If we must police the camp ourselves to keep them safe, then that is what we will do. Belarus clearly has no interest in the migrants. Nothing was done when the murder of three innocent girls was reported. When it was brought to our attention, we, the Poles, could not stand by and allow this to happen. So we did what was necessary. We handled business that should have been handled by them. Now we're asking Belarus to do what is necessary. Stop using these people in your efforts to have well-deserved sanctions placed on your country lifted. These are human beings, not pawns in your game of political chess."

Gray felt like he'd just been punched in the gut. It all made sense. The way he was handled and compartmentalized. The Polish government didn't want to solve the crime. They wanted someone they could hold up to the world and say, "See? We care." It was politics and nothing more.

As the facade crumbled, Gray felt like an idiot. He'd been played, used just like Fadel. The Polish government was doing exactly what they were accusing Belarus of doing. They'd politicized the murders of three young girls and were using them to their advantage. Fadel was a mere puppet in their plan, and Gray had hand-delivered him to the Poles. This was never about catching a killer. This showed the world that Poland and the EU were the good guys and Belarus was the bad guy.

Gray sat on the edge of his bed, dumbfounded and speechless. He still couldn't believe he'd been taken advantage of like that. *I guarantee Fadel is innocent, but it's too late for him. The Poles have their scapegoat.*

Just then, the hotel phone rang.

"Gray, it's Gorecki."

"Gorecki, you got a lot of explaining to do. I just saw the news conference."

"I know, I know. I'm on my way to your hotel now. I'll explain everything when I see you."

23

Gray was waiting for Gorecki in the lobby. As soon as he saw Gorecki walk through the entrance, Gray jumped to his feet. Before he could open his mouth, Gorecki held up a hand, stopping him.

"Not here. There's a place nearby where we can talk in private."

Gray bit his tongue and followed Gorecki out of the hotel and to a restaurant not far away.

"They have great cheeseburgers here," Gorecki said. "We both need to eat." He went ahead and placed their order with a server.

"I know you're angry," Gorecki said. "I would be too."

"You knew I wanted to interview Fadel."

"I know, but I don't have that authority. I'm not bullshitting you. I informed my superiors, and they took it under consideration. I found out about the news conference fifteen minutes before it happened."

"What do you know about Fadel's confession?"

"He admitted to killing all three girls. He said he used candy to lure them into the woods."

"One of the girls was reported to have gone missing during the night. She was there when the family went to sleep and gone when they woke. How did Fadel explain that?"

"He would target little girls who seemed adventurous, always out roaming around the camp on their own. All were told to meet him at night, and he would give them the sweets and more so they could surprise their families in the morning. These people have nothing. These girls realize that. And for them to have a chance to do something great for the family, like bring them additional food, they'll jump at the opportunity. You may find it hard to believe, but family units in the Middle East are tight. There's nothing a family wouldn't do for one another."

"He was able to pinpoint the crime scenes?"

"From what I understand. The one you visited, I'd passed that information along to investigators. Fadel corroborated it. As for the graves, Fadel wouldn't have knowledge of that. But he knew enough."

Gray shook his head and looked away. The server appeared just then with their food.

"Gray, I know you had your doubts about Fadel."

"I still do. Look, I know the real reason why your government wanted to catch the killer. It wasn't to stop the senseless murders. It was so they could show the world that they were the good guys."

"But by doing that, the murders were stopped. Do you really care about the real reason? Gray, you were brought here to do a job: deliver a profile. My job was to deliver a suspect. If the investigators decided Fadel was innocent—"

"What? They would say sorry and return him to the camp?"

"I don't know. That's not my decision. Gray, you're used to seeing an investigation through to the end. That's not the reason why your help was requested. It doesn't matter that my government politicized this. The killings were stopped. Isn't that what you wanted? Wouldn't that have been the outcome, politicized or not?"

What Gorecki said was true. Gray was just bugged that stopping the killings happened to be a pleasant outcome to the real objective: demonizing Belarus.

"What's next for Fadel?" Gray asked before stuffing a few fries into his mouth.

"He'll be sentenced and jailed."

"And his son?"

"What about him?" Gorecki took a large bite of his burger.

"He has no father now."

"That might be a good thing. His father was a rapist, and now it's been proven that he's also a killer. The boy is better off without him. For all we know, he might have been grooming the kid."

Gorecki motioned for Gray to eat his burger as he chewed. The two ate in silence for a while until Gorecki cleared his throat.

"You did a great job, Gray. We both did. I know you're not aware of this, but everyone is happy with your efforts. The deputy prime minister is very pleased. Not a lot of outsiders have an opportunity to shine like you did. Enjoy your efforts."

"It's a little hard when I feel like I was left out of the loop from the very beginning."

"Think of this every time you feel that way. This wasn't your investigation, Gray. You were a consultant. You played your role, and it all worked out. Tonight the deputy prime minister is throwing a party to celebrate. A lot of important people will be there, and you're invited. I suggest you be on your best behavior."

~

Later that evening, Gray left his hotel in a freshly pressed tuxedo to attend dinner. The affair was held at the Presidential Palace, a five-minute drive from Gray's hotel. It was the official residence of the Polish president. With invitation in hand, Gray passed through the metal detectors and underwent a quick pat-down by the security team before he was escorted into the palace.

The neoclassical building was impressive with its beautifully lit exteriors. Out front in a large courtyard was a statue of a man on horseback pointing a sword.

"That is Prince Jozef Poniatowski," the young man escorting Gray said. "He was a very famous Polish general."

"Does the president actually live here?" Gray asked.

"He does, but the building also houses government offices."

"Is the party inside the palace?"

"Cocktails are being served on the patio overlooking the gardens. It's stunning there. Dinner will take place inside in the dining hall."

The man led Gray into the front of the palace and then directly out the back onto a large patio area adjoining the gardens. A sizable crowd had already arrived before Gray, all dressed similarly.

"Hi, Sterling."

Gray turned to find Pakulski standing before him. She had her hair down this time and wore an elegant black dress with a single strand of pearls around her neck. She handed Gray a flute.

"I hope you haven't had your fill of champagne."

"Hi, Julianna. You look amazing."

"Thank you. This tuxedo suits you well. You may take it with you when you leave."

"That's very generous. I think I will. I don't own one. Oh, by the way, I have something for you."

Gray removed a small envelope from the inside of his jacket and handed it to Pakulski. She peeked inside, and upon seeing her panties, a smile appeared on her face.

"I was wondering what happened to it."

"Gray." Gorecki approached, wearing a tuxedo.

"You clean up well," Gray said.

"I'll take that as a compliment. There are a lot of people who want to meet with you tonight. You're a star. But don't worry, it's a very intimate group. No one outside of these walls will know of you."

"Good to know."

"Deputy Prime Minister Aleksy Salamon has requested you. If you'll excuse us, Julianna."

"Of course. Sterling, we'll talk later."

Gorecki led Gray to the opposite end of the patio. He recognized the deputy prime minister speaking with a group of men.

"Special Agent Gray," Salamon said as he offered his hand.

Gray shook it. "Deputy Prime Minister. Thank you for the invitation. It's beautiful here."

"I'm glad you could make it. I just wanted to personally thank you for helping us not only end those senseless killings but resolve our differences with Belarus. The prime minister couldn't be here, but he has asked me to send his thanks and appreciation for your efforts. You remember Commander Janda." Salamon motioned to a man standing next to him.

"Of course I do." Gray shook hands with the Polish Border Guard commander.

"Wonderful job, Agent Gray. The results only reinforce

your impressive background. The problem at the border is well on its way to being resolved."

"Thank you, but it wasn't just me. Officer Gorecki here was just as involved as I was."

"Both of you men did exceptional work," Salamon said. "Enjoy yourselves tonight. You both deserve it."

Gray and Gorecki thanked Salamon and Janda once more before leaving.

"We have another official stop to make. I believe you already met the head of Poland's Foreign Intelligence, Gabriel Filipek." Gorecki motioned to a man speaking to three other men.

"I have."

"Agent Gray," Filipek said as he excused himself from the group. "Excellent work. You and Gorecki here make a great team. Everyone is pleased with the work you two did."

"Thank you. I'm glad I was able to help."

"Your help will go a long way in resolving our issues at the border."

Once out of earshot of Filipek, Gray quietly said, "Why do I get the impression that they are more pleased with how successful their political interest was in masquerading as an investigation?"

"Because that's exactly what happened."

"Be honest with me. Did you know this was their intent all along?"

"I knew it was more than just an investigation, but I didn't know that they planned on using Fadel as a poster boy for Belarus's bad behavior."

"Come on, now. Do you really expect me to believe you were that naive?"

"Did you really expect me to share that information with you if I did have knowledge? We both had orders. We both delivered. That's all that matters. Don't try to wrap it all up in a neat little bow. Not everything works that way."

Just then, an announcement was made that dinner was ready to be served and everyone needed to go to the dining hall.

Gorecki and Gray met up with Pakulski and they took their seats at the same table.

"Did you enjoy your small talk with the important men?" Pakulski whispered to Gray.

"It was pleasant and diplomatic, not nearly as interesting as the conversation we had."

Dinner started with Siberian caviar served on Melba toast with a side of crème fraîche. It was followed by a cup of cauliflower consommé. The main entrée was a rack of lamb served with a side of leeks and potatoes, and the dessert was raspberry mousse.

Gray, Pakulski, and, surprisingly, Gorecki enjoyed lively banter during dinner. Gorecki was a different person. It was refreshing not having to pull a conversation out of him.

"I've been an intelligence officer for ten years," he said.

"Any aspirations to try something else?" Gray asked.

"Maybe one day, but for now, the work keeps it interesting for me. Do you see yourself staying at the FBI until you're old and tired?"

Gray laughed. "I don't know. I'm like you. For now, it's holding my interest."

"What are your plans when you leave? Are you heading back to the US?"

"Most likely not. I'm currently based in the UK."

"Do you like working with Interpol?"

"I do because the assignments I'm given definitely span the spectrum, and I have opportunities to work outside the country. That's not typical with the FBI."

Just then, the deputy prime minister called for a toast.

"Tonight, we are celebrating a win and a path forward to resolving our differences on the border with Belarus. I'd like to give a much deserved thank-you to Special Agent Gray, without whom our efforts would not have been possible."

The room toasted Gray. By the end of the night, Gray had forgotten any grievances he held for being involved in Poland's propaganda machine. He did his part of the job and delivered.

24

The cloud nine Gray had been floating on the night before had dissipated quickly when he caught the breaking news on the television the following morning. Another little girl had been murdered in the camp.

Belarus struck back fast and hard. They claimed Poland's apprehension of Fadel was nothing but a political farce, a way to distract from their legal obligation: accepting the migrants. Belarus went on to say that they were, in fact, investigating the crimes from the very start. Poland saw an opportunity to politicize the deaths of these little girls by holding up a scapegoat, all for political gain.

The media went wild over the assertions by the Belarus government. Footage of Belarusian CIS investigators in the woods was shown. A Belarusian spokesperson stated that investigations took time and manpower. "How silly that Poland's government could state that they conducted an investigation from their side of the border and caught a killer in such a short time. It's impossible."

All the goodwill and praise the Polish government and EU

had built up had quickly unraveled into a steaming pile of crap.

Gray sat on the edge of his bed, his jaw slack as he watched the mess unfold. After the shock wore off, Gray called Gorecki but got voicemail—same for Pakulski. He even called the offices of both and left messages there.

But as the morning wore on with no return calls, Gray began to wonder if he was becoming part of the narrative, a possible scapegoat. Were the wheels in motion for him to join Fadel? He wouldn't put it past the Polish government, already having seen firsthand how they worked.

If the Polish government exposed Gray as an FBI profiler, he would lose all anonymity and hope of ever working undercover again. Not only that, but since he had been in the camp, the Belarusian government could charge him with spying, or worse, send assassins after him. It would essentially end his career, not to mention the damage it would do to the safety of his personal life.

The more Gray allowed his mind to wander, the more he began to fear he was being set up. He decided he wouldn't just sit around and wait for the other shoe to drop. He quickly got dressed and headed out. A short taxi ride later, he stood outside of the Chancellery.

Gray went inside and walked down the same hallway Pakulski had escorted him down upon his first visit. There were two guards stationed outside the front entrance to the deputy prime minister's office. Gray knew the guards remembered him from his first visit, so it was worth trying to gain entry. They, of course, didn't allow that, but he continued to plead his case until one said they would pass a message along. About fifteen minutes later, a woman that he had never met before appeared.

"Agent Gray. Please come with me."

Gray followed her inside, and she led him into Salamon's office.

"Agent Gray. You've seen the news this morning?" Salamon asked as soon as the woman left.

"I did. I'm sorry to take up your time, but I couldn't get ahold of Gorecki or Pakulski."

"It's fine. I wanted to see you anyway. Do you have any idea how much trouble you've caused me and my country?"

"The trouble I caused? How is any of this my fault?"

Salamon snatched a piece of paper off his desk and held it up. "This is the profile you created. It led us to the wrong man."

"Whoa! That's not my doing. That profile is solid."

"Is it? Did you not at any time tell Gorecki that you were fifty-fifty on the profile?"

"Yes, but that was early on. I told him it was the beginning of a profile, but I still believed we were on track. Deputy Prime Minister, you have to understand that profiles change as new information is presented."

"Did you not obtain information while in the camp?"

"Well, yeah, but I needed more to be sure."

"And yet you still turned over the profile."

"I did not turn over the profile. I shared it with Gorecki, my partner. Listen, I was not included in everything. I wasn't privy to decisions being made. I wasn't included in—"

"You're complaining about inclusion? Agent Gray, you were embedded among the migrants for almost a week. How much more inclusion in the investigation did you need?"

"That's not what I'm talking about. It wasn't my decision to take Fadel. I was still gathering information and honing the profile when he was abducted and taken across the border."

"To which you participated in, willingly, I might add."

The gaslighting had begun. Gray could see the cards being

stacked against him one by one. It was only a matter of time before the Polish government had enough to paint a new narrative. One that allowed them to gracefully exit and Gray to take the blame. It was happening. Just like he'd thought it would.

"Agent Gray. You were responsible for catching the killer. Instead, you embarrassed this government and the country of Poland. You should be thanking me right now."

"For what? For being falsely accused?"

"That you are not facing charges for gross negligence."

Gray could not believe the words coming out of Salamon's mouth.

"You are officially being ordered out of the country immediately. And I would make sure it happens as soon as possible, as I cannot guarantee your safety much longer."

Those last words were very telling. It meant the Polish government intended to out Gray and make him the scapegoat. His life could be in serious jeopardy if he remained inside the country any longer. Belarusian assassins could easily cross over into Poland and seek him out.

Before Gray could say another word, the guards entered and escorted him out of the DPM's office. Gray spotted Gorecki walking away and called out to him on the way out of the Chancellery.

"Gray, what are you doing here?" Gorecki asked.

"I just finished meeting with the deputy prime minister. I'm being ordered out of the country immediately."

"We have orders to escort Mr. Gray back to his hotel," one of the guards said.

"You know me, give us a few minutes. I'm asking for a favor."

The guards looked at each other and then nodded. "You got ten minutes."

"Thanks, I'll owe you. We'll be right over here."

Gorecki led Gray off to the side so they were out of earshot. "What happened, Gray?"

"Your government is about to pin this entire mess on me. I need you to step up."

"Believe me, I already tried earlier this morning. I argued that this wasn't your fault and that you and I needed more time, but they wouldn't listen."

"Do you understand that my career is on the line all because the Polish government wanted to politicize a serial killer investigation and it went wrong? This is not my fault."

"Don't you think I know that?" Gorecki exclaimed.

Gray grabbed hold of Gorecki and locked eyes with him. "You are the only person I know who can turn this around. You've got to try again."

Gorecki drew in a breath and let it out. "The only way to turn this around is to catch the killer."

"Exactly. If the Belarusians are saying that there's another body, then the killer is still in the camp. We can catch him. We can hit the ground running."

"My government already tried that route. They won't go that way again."

"So long as there's a killer in that camp, the Belarusian government will continue to use it against Poland and the EU as they pretend to investigate. It'll only get worse. Kicking me out doesn't solve the problem. You know that. Only capturing the real killer will do it."

Gorecki shook his head. "You're not getting it, Gray. This isn't about saving little girls. It never was. The men in there don't care about the girls." Gorecki pointed at the Chancellery. "And neither do the Belarusians. Both sides are playing the same game."

"We've got to get back into that camp."

"Impossible. My superiors are fully aware of everything we're discussing right now, and they still shut it down. If you want back into that camp, we need something else that's not only going to convince my command but the deputy prime minister to put his ass back on the line. And we don't have anything."

Gray spoke in a lowered voice. "I have something else."

Gorecki frowned. "What are you talking about?"

"What would you say if I told you a migrant didn't kill those little girls?"

"I'm not following you. Who else could have done it?"

"A Belarusian soldier. Do you think that'll grab the deputy prime minister's attention?"

25

Gorecki held up a hand, stopping Gray from saying anything more; a large group of tourists on a tour of the Chancellery passed by.

"Quick. Follow me," Gorecki said as they slipped away from the two guards unnoticed.

Directly across the street from the Chancellery was Lazienki Park. Gorecki led Gray to a bench in a secluded area.

"Tell me this isn't you just reaching for anything."

"It's not. As I learned more from the migrants about the victims and what happened, my gut began to sound the alarm."

"Why didn't you say something to me sooner?"

"I did. You just weren't listening.

"You should have made me listen."

"You were too busy following your orders. And anyway, I was still trying to work things out in my head. But the more I learned, the more I started to think a soldier could be responsible for the killings."

"You really think the serial killer is a soldier?"

"I do, and I'll tell you why. Think back to the profile I delivered.

"I said our guy was a predator, likes to be in control, and isn't afraid to display his authority in front of others. That's a soldier. But what helped me focus on a soldier was when you mentioned that many of them were conscripts. Our guy definitely has anger issues. This could derive from the fact that he was forced to serve in the military. If that's true, then it's safe to say he would harbor resentment against the migrants. Those migrants only reinforce the belief that Belarus needs a more extensive military, and to satisfy that need, they have to draft men."

"So he believes they are the reason he's forced to serve?" Gorecki said.

"Yes. This problem on the border acts like a bullhorn. If this soldier thought there might be a chance he could end his term earlier, that's all but been thrown out the window. So he's killing the girls to send a message, and to punish, but mostly to send a message."

"To who? His superiors?"

"No. It's a message to migrants who are thinking of coming to Belarus with the hope of crossing into Poland. In his head, that's the way to solve this problem. It's classic mission-oriented killing. Soldiers are given missions. This is his mission."

"Gray, proving the killer is a soldier will be damn near impossible. It was hard enough when we thought it was a migrant. We can't question a soldier."

"I know. That's why the answer can be found with the bodies."

Just then, a group of men dressed in suits with angry looks on their faces was walking straight toward Gorecki and Gray.

"Who are they?"

"They're a high-level security team. I can't stop them. You'll be escorted back to your hotel and locked in your room until your flight leaves. I'll do what I can, but I can't promise anything."

"Mr. Gray!" one of the men called out. "You need to come with us."

Gray stood up, and two men grabbed him by his arms.

"Remember, the answer we're looking for can be found in the bodies of those girls," Gray said as he was pulled away.

～

Just as Gorecki had said, the angry men took him straight back to his hotel room. His phone and laptop were confiscated, and he was told they would be returned right before he boarded his flight.

The phone in the room no longer worked, and the television had snow on every channel. All Gray could do was sit or lie down on his bed. Room service brought him a meal, but other than that, he had no contact with the outside world. He felt like a prisoner.

Soon the world would hear a different story about what was happening on the borders of Poland and Belarus. Gray figured the Polish government would paint him as a rogue agent, someone who was brought in to consult but instead had taken matters into his own hands. And there would be nothing he could do about it.

For all he knew, they could have already issued a news conference. It's probably why he had armed guards outside his room. The government probably didn't want him assassinated on Polish soil. But once his plane was up in the air, they wouldn't care what happened to him. All they wanted was to minimize the damage and see if they could spin the story to their benefit.

I'm going to have a whole lot of explaining to do when I touch down in the UK. And if the Polish government has given a news conference, I'll already be presumed guilty.

The time came for Gray to head to the airport. He had his belongings packed into his carry-on luggage. He decided not to take the tuxedo. He didn't want anything associated with the assignment. The two armed guards and two other suited men escorted Gray from his room. While walking through the lobby, Gray couldn't help but feel like every person at the hotel was looking at him—the traitor of Poland.

Gray was directed to a black SUV outside the hotel. One of the men took Gray's luggage and put it in the vehicle's rear cargo area while the other opened the back passenger door and ordered Gray inside. Gray ducked his head and scooted across the seat. He didn't see the man sitting on the far side until he bumped into him.

"Sorry," Gray said.

"Don't say sorry," Gorecki said. "Say thank you."

"Gorecki, what are you doing here? Are you coming to the airport with me?" Gray asked.

"We're not going to the airport, Gray. You got your wish. We're heading back in."

26

Gray had nothing but questions during the drive, most of it regarding why the DPM changed his mind.

"It wasn't easy," Gorecki said. "I had to first get my supervisors on board. They weren't convinced we could determine which soldier was responsible. Pointing a finger at a Belarusian soldier is different from pointing a finger at a migrant. But they know me and how I operate. They felt the mission deserved a few days."

"A few days?"

"Look, Gray, this is not an investigation. You know this already. This is about the economic sanctions placed on Belarus. The migrants, they are just pawns in this game. We will have to use alternative methods."

"What does that mean?"

"Forget about how you did things in the past. Focus on the new goal and be creative about how you get there. The deputy prime minister may have agreed to let us go back in, but he's not a fan. He expects us to fail."

"Then why are you being allowed to go back into the camp?"

"My take is he's under so much pressure, he can't take the chance."

"He has other plans in the works?"

"Of course, but nothing as radical as this. It's mostly diplomatic efforts. The more there are, the harder it will be for Poland to refuse. Legally, they have to accept them, and Belarus knows that. That was my entire argument. It's like you said, Belarus will keep letting this guy kill while they pretend to investigate."

"How much time do we have?"

"It's not based on time. It's based on objectives. I'll get into that when we meet the rest of the team."

"More IOs?"

"Yes, there are two more. They're in Bialystok at a safe house, waiting for our arrival. We'll brief there and then meet up with the rest of the DWB team in Kuźnica. It'll be the same people we paired up with the first time."

"And everything else about the mission is what we discussed in the park?"

"Yes. It's crazy, but it's our only chance."

The drive to Bialystok went by quickly. The SUV came to a stop outside of a residential building.

"From now on, we'll both go by our aliases to avoid any confusion with names. Bring your luggage. You can repack in the flat. You'll need to get rid of anything with your real identity." Gorecki said.

The apartment was on the fifth floor. Waiting inside was a man and a woman. They were sitting at a table in the kitchen, food spread across it. Gray recognized the man; he had met him at the border when they abducted Fadel.

"Took you long enough," the man said. "I thought maybe you chickened out."

"And miss out on your cooking? Never. I want you two to meet Dr. Clark Sanders," Gorecki said.

"Sanders, the talkative one is Dr. David Klausen, and the woman is Dr. Eliza Pop. They both have files you should study in case you're questioned by the soldiers. They've already seen your file."

"Sanders, let's hope things go better this time around," Klausen said.

"Let's hope," Gray said.

"Come on," Gorecki motioned to the table. "We can go over the briefing while we eat."

"Listen up, I don't need to say this, but I'll say it anyway. Our mission is ten times more dangerous than the last time. The soldiers will be watching the NGOs in the camp much more closely, so we must be on our best behavior."

Klausen raised his hand. "Teacher, may I? No offense, Sanders, but what's different this time around? Are you coming up with a different profile?"

Gray looked at Gorecki. "They don't know?"

"No, why don't you fill them in?"

Gray cleared his throat. "The profile hasn't changed, but I don't believe the killer is a migrant. We're looking for a soldier."

"Are you crazy?" Klausen asked. "You think a soldier is killing those girls?"

"I do."

Gray went over the profile and his reasoning for focusing on a soldier.

"So we need to prove this, right? That a soldier is behind it all?" Pop asked.

"That's correct," Gray said.

"Hard to think it's a soldier," Klausen said. "But I believe it."

"Good," Gorecki said. "Unless there are more questions about who we're looking for, let's go over our mission objectives. The powers that be are no longer interested in whether or not a migrant is killing the girls. They only care if it's a soldier. So we must prove this."

"Great. How the hell are we doing that?" Klausen said as he ate. "Are we abducting soldiers and questioning them? That's a plan for failure right there."

"You're right," Gorecki said. "That's why we're coming at this from an unconventional way. We'll be using science."

"I'm not following," Pop said.

"Neither am I," Klausen said.

"Add me to that list," Gray said.

"I'm surprised, Dr. Sanders. The exhumation was your idea. Autopsies will be how we move forward. The body of the first girl is buried in the camp. Sanders confirmed this the first time around. Assuming that holds true for the other girls, our first objective is to locate the gravesites of all three victims. If we do that, we buy ourselves more time. Fail, and our mission will end. We pull out."

"So right now, all we need to do is find the gravesites. That's it?" Klausen asked as he wiped his mouth with a napkin.

"No bodies. No autopsy."

"But how do we know if the autopsy will lead to something?" Pop asked.

"We don't. One of the reasons why the deputy prime minister agreed to this plan was on Sander's experience." Gorecki looked directly at Gray. "It's all on you, Dr. Sanders."

"Okay, we find the bodies, then what?" Klausen asked.

"Next objective is to dig them up. Seems easy, but I expect the soldiers are extra vigilant now. Not getting caught digging holes in the ground won't be easy. If we can't find a way to get those bodies out of the ground, the mission is over. But if we succeed, we need to get them across the border."

"That's a lot of work for a gamble that the autopsy will produce something," Pop said as she took a bite.

"That's right," Gorecki said. "There must be convincing evidence."

"Convincing evidence?" Klausen asked. "What does that mean?"

"The evidence needs to prove no one but a soldier could have done it."

"Wow," Gray ran a hand over his head.

"Sanders, this is exactly what you wanted. You said an autopsy was needed, that we'd extracted all we could get out of the migrants in the camp."

"Yes, I think that's true, but when you frame it the way you did, it seems worse than it normally is." Gray turned to the other two officers. "Look, this is normal in every investigation. Autopsies can reveal new evidence, or they may not. We don't know until one is conducted. The difference here is that we have hurdles where normally we wouldn't."

"If the autopsy doesn't reveal convincing evidence. We pack up and go home." Gorecki tore a piece off a loaf of bread.

"And if we find convincing evidence, how will we narrow it down to one soldier?" Klausen asked. "There are about a thousand soldiers in that camp. We can't question them all."

"We use the migrants," Gray said. "Earn their trust and ask questions."

"How is that different from what you did the last time in the camp?" Klausen continued to question.

"We were looking for the wrong person."

27

Crossing into Belarus took longer this time around. The entire team was double-checked at two points. They were questioned about their backgrounds, organization, skills, and even where they would go next. Gray took it all in stride and answered the best he could.

The soldiers led them to a new area in a different location. The place they had previously occupied was now filled with a Belarusian aid organization. The media was there reporting on their efforts. DWB was assigned to an area far from the cameras.

"Looks like they're intent on making themselves look like angels," Gray whispered to Gorecki.

"I'd say right now they're winning," Gorecki said.

Besides the heavier presence of soldiers, the other thing that caught Gray's eye was the military vehicles. There were several armored personal carriers parked around the camp. There were even a few infantry fighting vehicles, complete with a thirty-millimeter auto cannon. But the vehicle that stood out the most was the tank.

"That's a T-72," Gorecki said. "It's a hand-me-down from

Russia. It was the Soviet's main battle tank. Still very effective, though."

"Why would they need a tank here?" Gray asked.

"Intimidation."

"Does your government know these vehicles are in the camp?"

"They know from the satellite pictures. If it were any other scenario, they would have positioned troops and vehicles on our side. Any kind of build-up can be viewed as a provocation."

Once in their designated area, the DWB team set up their tents. Gray and Gorecki were sharing a tent. Klausen and Pop were in a tent next door.

"The other two don't seem to be convinced," Gray said as he unfolded a table.

"You got to understand, they're being pulled in on this assignment at the last minute. They don't have the history with it that we do. But don't worry. I know them well. They're professionals, and you can count on them to do their jobs."

"That's good to hear, because we got a mountain to climb."

"I won't argue there," Gorecki said. "Everything is riding on the autopsies but finding those graves and getting the bodies out of the ground and across the border will be a challenge."

"I never asked, and you never said anything, so I'll ask now. I'm assuming because I'm here, there was no news conference painting me as the bad guy."

"There wasn't. You wouldn't be able to enter Belarus if they had exposed you. I'll tell you now, the news conference was ready to go. This mission is your reprieve. You're on borrowed time, but you're not alone. My job is on the line because I backed you up."

"Why did you do that? The odds are against us."

"Believe it or not, I like you, Gray. And I believe we can catch this guy. We may have different methods of achieving results, but at the end of the day, we both get the job done."

"I appreciate you saying that."

"Glad to hear it. When the time is right, I'll fill you in on the other objectives that are being kept from you."

Gray waited for Gorecki to say he was kidding, but he said nothing more and walked out of the tent.

Old habits die hard.

28

The Belarusian military camp headquarters was located directly east of the checkpoint, near the edge of the camp, where the M6 expressway began, which served as a direct line to the capital city of Minsk. The camp headquarters housed the administrative facilities, communication center, canteens, mess hall, motor pool, medical services, weapons and ammunition storage, and most soldier barracks. Additional barracks and canteens were erected in the north and south regions of the camp as the camp grew. It was also where arriving migrants were processed before being turned loose in the camp to fend for themselves.

On the same morning the DWB team arrived, Mikola Azarenka, the commander of military operations in the camp, was holding a meeting with his top officers.

"What the Poles did, not only undermined our efforts and embarrassed the leadership back in Minsk, but it showed the world how weak we are. That the Poles could send someone into our country, take a man under the watch of more than one thousand soldiers, and escape back across the border without us knowing. I will not have anything like that happen again. Am I clear?"

"Clear, sir!" the men sitting at the table sounded off.

Azarenka walked around the rectangular conference table as he stared down at his men. He was a tall man with a bushy mustache and dark penetrating eyes that could make any man look away after a few seconds. Azarenka had served in the military his entire life, following in his father's footsteps. The latter had risen to General Lieutenant, the number two in command of Belarus's ground forces.

By the time Azarenka was thirty-five, he had risen to Lieutenant Colonel in charge of the Western Operational Command headquartered in the border city of Grodno. It was composed of two mechanized brigades and one artillery brigade. Because of his location, experience, and tenacity, Azarenka was ordered to oversee the camp.

It was clear to everyone that Azarenka was on track to becoming commander of Belarus's entire military. A rank his famous father had come close to achieving. But recent events with the Poles set off a ripple that began to tarnish Azarenka's perfect soldier image. Azarenka wanted to erase any doubt staining his commanding abilities.

"Make sure your men watch those aid organizations closely," Azarenka said. "As far as Minsk is concerned, we had our one mistake. A second one will not be tolerated."

Azarenka released his men and walked outside and lit up a cigarette. His cheeks sunk as he took the first pull, holding it in for a beat longer than usual so that he could feel that tobacco rush and then letting out a cloud of white smoke.

"Lieutenant Colonel, you gave a rousing speech in that meeting," said one of his officers.

"I'd rather hang the soldier who allowed the Poles to move a man across the border in the middle of the night."

"The guards patrolling that section of the border have already been relieved of duty, and we were able to spin that serial killer investigation in our favor."

"I don't care about that. I care about how the Poles were able to infiltrate our camp and walk out with that man so easily. We found out through a news conference."

Azarenka began to walk, and the officer stayed in step.

"I understand," the officer said. "But we will be out of this mess soon. The west can't hold out much longer, not with the world knowing little girls are dying in the camp. They will give in."

Azarenka and the officer ended up within earshot of a few other men from the meeting.

"I can't believe we're stuck here watching over these pigs," one of the men complained. "All I want to do is get out of this hell. I would do anything to leave and go to my dacha. I'd spend three or four days there, relaxing with friends, bottles of vodka, and grilled shashlik. Forget about this place."

Azarenka cleared his throat, catching the attention of the men. "It's unfortunate that the west has caused this situation to drag on. But as you know, it's vital work we're doing here. Our country is being unfairly persecuted by the west. We must stand up to them, no matter what."

The man who had been complaining snapped his heels together. "Yes, sir. Anything for our mother country."

"Good. Any dissension in the ranks will not be tolerated."

"You can count on me one hundred percent, sir."

Azarenka smiled. "I understand. I miss my dacha too."

The officer and Azarenka watched the group of men walk away. "Do me a favor. Throw that man in prison."

"For how long, sir?"

"Ask me that question again in ten years."

29

Coming into the camp for a second time with everything on the line, Gray no longer viewed himself as a profiler. He saw himself as the lead investigator. He had to take control of the investigation. That meant not allowing Gorecki to compartmentalize everyone this time around. Once they were set up, Gray insisted on a meeting with the others.

"It's not smart to be meeting like this," Gorecki said.

"You're overthinking things, Dr. Rasheed," Gray said. "This is nothing more than a staff meeting among us doctors. Listen up, I'm revising the profile to tailor it to a soldier. It won't change that much from the original, but I want to make sure there's no confusion on who we're after. Secondly, since I have a rapport with the mother of the first victim, I will use that relationship to find the parents of the other victims and those gravesites."

"And what about us?" Klausen asked.

"You will start singling out soldiers. Forget what you know about Fadel. I don't want that tainting your efforts. This soldier will be a loner."

"He still a control freak?" Pop asked.

"He is. He's also angry. He feels as if he's lost control over his life or purpose and blames the people in this camp. His mission is to stop migrants from coming to Belarus."

"The dead girls are a deterrent," Pop said.

"Yes."

"We're not looking for someone weird. He prefers to remain in the background and not be in the spotlight. He most likely interacts fine with his comrades."

"Do you think we're looking at a low-ranking soldier or one of the officers?"

"Hard to tell at the moment. For now, I want you to make notes for anyone who fits the mold. Watch them. See if they have a peculiar routine. Are they active during the day or at night? Do they interact with the migrants? If so, is it abusive or respectful? Any questions?"

No one said anything. As soon as Klausen and Pop had cleared out of the tent, Gorecki turned to Gray. "I don't appreciate you giving orders to my people without consulting with me first."

"Then, if we fail at this mission, you can blame your ego." Gray grabbed a medical satchel and exited the tent.

Gray wasn't about to get into a dick-swinging contest with Gorecki. He had too much work ahead of him. Gray headed toward the area where he remembered Sada, the first victim's mother, was located. He spotted her in the distance sitting outside of her tent and tending to the campfire. A smile formed on her face when she saw him approaching.

"Dr. Sanders, I thought you'd left and would not return."

"You can't get rid of me that easily," Gray said. "How are you and Gamila?"

"You are a very kind man for asking. I'm glad you have returned. I have—"

Sada stopped midsentence and looked around. She

motioned to Gray's satchel, and he immediately took out his stethoscope and hung it around his neck.

"Please come inside," she said as she headed into her tent.

Sleeping on a cot was Gamila. She woke immediately.

"Dr. Sanders, you came back," she said as she rubbed her eyes.

"You two were the first on my list to visit."

"Dr. Sanders, do you have news for me about the police investigation?"

"I do. The authorities in Poland are willing to conduct the autopsies, but I must locate all the bodies and exhume them. It's the best way to collect as much evidence as possible."

"But what about the man they arrested, Arif Fadel?"

"I see you heard of that news."

"Of course, everyone here knows. We were so happy to hear the killer was caught, but then there was another girl."

"It's all true. Arif Fadel was the wrong man. That's why I am continuing to help. I want the real killer to be caught."

"I found out who the parents are of the second girl who was killed. I can take you to them, but that's all. It's too dangerous for anything else."

"Why is that?" Gray crinkled his brow.

"The soldiers don't want us talking to each other."

"Why would they care?"

"I don't know, but they keep us separated. Others are free to move their tents around, but we were told we couldn't move. The parents I will take you to, they were told the same thing."

"Can you take me there now?"

"Yes."

Sada led the way through the camp as Gamila walked alongside Gray. "How long will you stay this time, Dr. Sanders?"

"I'm not sure. I hope long enough to locate all the graves."

"Do you really think the police in Poland will help us?"

"I do. I believe they are trying very hard."

Sada stopped near the rear of a tent. "Over there," she motioned with her head. "You see those cluster of tents?"

"I see them."

"They are in the middle tent."

"Do you know anything about them you can tell me, even a name?"

"I don't. I've never met them. I only know they lost a daughter just like me. Good luck, Dr. Sanders. If I find more parents, I will let you know. We must leave now," she said as she grabbed hold of Gamila's hand.

"Thank you."

Gray waited until Sada and Gamila were a safe distance away before approaching the tent. He stopped, deciding to observe for a bit.

"Hello," he said to a nearby family. "My name is Dr. Sanders. Does anybody here have health problems?"

While taking an elderly woman's blood pressure, Gray kept watch on the tent. The campfire outside burned, but that didn't necessarily mean anybody was home. After he finished with the woman, Gray approached the tent.

The flap opened just as he reached it, and a man stuck his head out. In his right hand, he held a knife.

30

"What do you want!" the man said quietly through gritted teeth.

"Easy there. I'm Dr. Sanders. I'm here to help." Gray turned his medical satchel so the man could see the DWB logo.

Instant relief came over the man's face. "I'm sorry. I've been getting threats lately. I have to be careful."

"Mind if I come in and look you over?"

"Please." The man opened the flap of the tent.

Inside, Gray found a woman and a teen boy.

"This is my wife and my son."

"Nice to meet you. I'm Dr. Sanders.

"My wife has a cough," the man said.

Gray checked the woman's vitals and then listened to her breathing. "You have a cold." He took some pills out of his bag and handed them to her. "Take one twice a day. Rest and stay warm."

Gray looked over the son and then the man. They didn't have any health problems.

"I'm sorry for your loss," Gray said.

The man's eyes widened. "You know?"

"I do. It's terrible."

He motioned for Gray to step outside of the tent.

"I don't want to talk about it in front of my wife. She's still having a hard time accepting it."

"That's understandable. Do you mind talking about it?"

"What do you want to know?"

"First, your daughter's name."

"We called her Adra. I am Gadi. We are from Syria."

"Who found the body?"

"I did. When we realized she was missing, we started searching the woods."

"Who is we?"

"I had help from a few other men in the camp. We spent all day looking."

"How long had Adra been missing?"

"She went missing in the night while we were asleep. We spent the next day and night searching for her."

"When did you find her?"

"The morning after, but it was strange. Her body was in a place I swear we had searched. But maybe I was wrong."

"I understand she was the second girl to be murdered."

"Dr. Sanders, why do you want to know all of this?"

"I have contacts with the police in Poland. They're interested in helping solve this crime."

"They arrested the wrong man. How can they help?"

"It's a bit more complicated and difficult to explain, but yes, a mistake was made, but they aren't giving up. They do want to find the man responsible for Adra's death. Is it possible for you to show me where you found Adra's body?"

Gadi hesitated as he looked around.

"What's wrong? Gray asked.

"I'm worried about people watching us. Some of the migrants are working with the soldiers. They pass information for special treatment."

"I'll see patients along the way to keep suspicions at bay."

Gadi took a few moments to think over Gray's proposal before agreeing. He stuck his head back into the tent and told his wife he would return soon.

"Is it far from here?" Gray asked as the two men started off.

"About twenty minutes that way." He pointed. "The woods over there are really thick. It's very easy to get lost. The trees blend into each other. It all looks the same."

Once they made it into the woods, it seemed like every third step required Gray to move around a tree. It was also eerily quiet and sounded like each breath and step they took was hooked up to a microphone. Gray was just about to ask how much farther when Gadi stopped.

"This is where I found Adra. She was lying flat on her back between those two trees."

"You mean like the person intentionally laid her on her back?"

Gadi nodded. "It didn't look like she fell to the ground."

"Was there anything left in the area by the person responsible? Footprints, perhaps?"

"I didn't see anything." Gadi kicked at the ground, shoving leaves away with his boot. "See how I can easily move the leaves around? I know my Adra. She would have fought back."

"We're quite far from the camp. Can you think of a reason why Adra would come this far into the woods?"

Gadi shook his head. "We come into the woods to use the bathroom, but even this is too far."

Gray agreed with Gadi's words. Adra would need a reason to come this far. Either something or someone lured her here, or it was just a spot where her body was dumped. Gray looked around but saw nothing physical to suggest a crime scene. He couldn't help but think how helpful it would be to have CSI comb the place.

"I saw in the news that the Belarusian government had a crime scene crew investigating the area where the last girl was found. Do you know where that is?"

"You think they were investigating? They weren't even in the right area. It was all for the cameras, and it was just soldiers dressed to look that way." Gadi rested his hands on his hips. "Dr. Sanders, does this information help you?"

"Anything I can learn helps. There is one more thing that I'd like to ask you that I believe can provide answers not found here."

"What's that?"

"Would you allow the police in Poland to perform an autopsy on Adra's body?"

"An autopsy? You want to dig up my daughter's body?" Gadi asked in a raised voice. "Are you out of your mind? I can't allow that. It is against our beliefs."

"I realize that. The mother of the first victim has given permission. I intend to ask the parents of every victim. Please reconsider."

"No. My answer is final. I can't allow it. I just can't."

Gadi turned around and stormed off back to camp, leaving Gray alone. Gray let out a defeated breath and looked around the site one last time. He noted the location on his phone and left.

Gray had only walked a few yards when Gadi's son popped out from behind a tree.

"What are you doing here?" Gray called over to the boy in the distance. Gadi had already disappeared from view.

"My father doesn't know I'm here," he said. "You must not tell him."

"I won't, but why are you here?"

"Because I want to help you find the killer."

31

Azarenka made it a point to stroll through parts of the camp at least once a day. This time he was in the most northern area. The tents there were spread out farther apart. In the distance, he noted a few people mixed in with the trees. Officers close to Azarenka always accompanied him along with a few trusted soldiers. His reason for the walks was to check the mood of the camp. It was important to him that none of the migrants think they had rights or, more importantly, a voice in what was happening.

"Spread out," Azarenka ordered.

His men proceeded to order the migrants out of their tents. At the same time, they searched their belongings, pocketing anything of value right in front of Azarenka. Any migrants that objected were quickly given a beating. An officer nearby fondled a teen girl as her father stood by with another soldier pointing a gun against his head. The scene put a smile on Azarenka's face.

As far as Azarenka was concerned, his job was to ensure the migrants behaved yet came across as troubled souls. The face of the camp the leadership back in Minsk wanted to project to the world was one of sorrow and despair. It needed to fit their narrative of a country whose only interest was to help these people obtain a better life, to reunite them with their relatives in the EU. Minsk was nothing more than that guiding hand. This image played an important role in Belarus's negotiations with the EU.

Azarenka disagreed with that method. He believed in ruling with an iron fist like how his motherland, Russia, had ruled in the past. Oh, how Azarenka pined for days of old. When every citizen fell into line and did as they were told. He admired his father and their comrades in Moscow for their control over the Soviet empire. He always believed weak leadership was the reason for the fall of communism. He thought Minsk had softened its approach to problem-solving over the years. Yes, they were standing up to the EU's economic sanctions, but this hybrid warfare was new to Azarenka. In the end, he was a soldier and did as he was ordered.

One of the officers returned, holding up a gold chain. "For you."

Azarenka smiled. "You keep it. You earned it."

The officer put the chain inside his pants pocket. "Do you think this camp will force the EU to lift sanctions? It's been two months. Winter will be here soon. The sick and old will not make it. That could help."

"It could," Azarenka said. "But diplomacy is a long game, a dance where each partner takes a turn leading until they are both tired. That is the end result."

"This could all be for nothing."

"It could."

"How would you have handled it?"

"I would never allow the other side to lead. And that's happening too much right now."

32

Gray took a moment to consider what Gadi's son had said. The last thing he wanted was to get involved in a family squabble. But he was also here to solve a crime.

"What's your name?" Gray asked.

"My name is Dekel. I heard what you asked my father. I can show you where my sister is buried."

"Why would you disobey your father?"

"I don't want to, but my father is stuck in his old ways. He's very traditional. I'm not. I want to see the person responsible for killing my sister beaten and hung."

"Do you understand why I want to know the location of your sister's grave?"

"I do. You want to dig her body up and have an autopsy done."

"That's correct. I need to know you're absolutely sure about helping. I don't want to cause any problems."

"I'm positive, but we must hurry. If I'm gone too long, my mother will worry, and my father will be angry."

Dekel turned on his heels and led the way. After a brisk fifteen-minute walk, they arrived at the gravesite. The soil was slightly raised where Adra was buried, but there was no head-stone or a marker for her grave. Gray stayed back and noted the gravesite location while Dekel knelt and prayed.

"Is there anything you want to ask me while we're here?" he asked after he finished.

Gray nodded, seeing as Dekel was much freer with his words than his father was. "Why isn't there something to iden-tify Adra's grave?"

"My father doesn't want the soldiers to know where she's buried. He doesn't trust them."

"Have they spoken to your family about Adra and what had happened to her?"

"They told us to keep quiet and keep to ourselves. If we cause any trouble, they will put us in jail.

"They said that?"

"I heard them talking to my father. That's why he doesn't trust the soldiers and is always watching."

"Are you aware of the man who was taken from the camp? His name was Arif Fadel."

"Yes, I know of him. He's the rapist, but I heard he wasn't the one who killed my sister."

"You're right about that. Do you know where the last victim was found or who the parents are?"

"I don't. The soldiers are keeping watch on us. If a soldier sees someone out of their section, they'll punish them."

"Your father said the location where he discovered Adra's body was too far from camp. She would never come that far on her own."

"It's true. She knew about the dangers. I think someone took her."

"Who?"

Dekel looked away.

"Tell me, Dekel. It's okay."

"Everyone thought for sure it was the rapist who killed all the girls. They wanted to believe it."

"But you didn't, did you?"

"No."

Gray crouched a little so he could catch Dekel's eye. "You think it's a soldier, don't you?"

"I do," he said softly.

"I'll let you in on a little secret. So do I."

Dekel looked up at Gray. "I thought I was the only one."

"You're not. I believe others think the same as us, but they're too afraid to say anything."

This was the first confirmation Gray had received from a migrant that he was on the right track. It meant a lot coming from Dekel because he seemed to have a good take on what was happening in the camp.

"Do you have your suspicions?"

"It could be anyone. They're all bad."

"Yes, they are, but there must be some that stand out to you. Think hard, Dekel. Was there something that one of them said or did that made you start to think a soldier killed your sister?"

Dekel shook his head. "It's just a feeling I have. And I know my sister. Someone took her by force. She would never just come here on her own. It doesn't matter who was asking her. Only a soldier can take someone like that."

"Keep thinking about it. Something might come to you later."

"Dr. Sanders, when do you think you will take Adra's body?"

"I'm not sure. I need to obtain permission from the other families. It's best if autopsies are performed on as many victims as possible. Then I need to speak to my contacts back in Poland. It will not be easy taking the bodies across the border, but I hope we can very soon."

"Let me know if there is anything I can do to help you. I'm willing."

"Thank you for doing this. I'll make sure everything possible is done to capture the person who murdered your sister."

33

Gray and Dekel split up before heading back into the camp so that no one would see them together. Back at his tent, Gray was surprised to find Gorecki seeing patients. The queue of people waiting to be seen wasn't very long, so Gray jumped in and helped until the last one had been looked at.

"Did you discover anything useful on your outing?" Gorecki asked.

"I did. I have the location of two gravesites and permission from family members to exhume the bodies. Two more to go, and we'll meet our first objective. Is there a plan in place once I identify all the graves' locations? How are we removing them from the ground? What about bringing them back across the border? Will the autopsies be performed in Warsaw or in Kuźnica?"

"Not yet, but don't worry about that. I'll have something ready to go when the time comes."

"I met the teen brother of the second victim. His name is Dekel. He's been the most vocal from any of the victims' families. He also believes a soldier is responsible. There's no concrete evidence, but his gut tells him it's a soldier, and I believe him."

"Why?"

"The spot where his sister was found was the farthest from the camp. Both he and his father confirmed that it wasn't in her personality to venture out that far on her own. She knew of the dangers."

"So she was dumped in that location?"

"It's possible the girls are being abducted and taken somewhere else, killed, and then dumped back into the woods. That could be why no one has seen anything. I've mapped out the locations of the crime scenes and graves." Gray opened a map app on his phone. "The crime scenes are nowhere near each other, but it's too early to tell if the bodies are being dumped randomly or not."

"Seems like a lot of extra work."

"It might be worth it if a soldier wants to cover his tracks. But there is the chance they're killing them where the bodies are found. No evidence suggests that isn't happening. The first girl was found crumpled against a tree, while the second was described as posed. There's leeway since we're relying on testimony from the family."

"Where are the graves?"

"Here and here," Gray pointed at the screen. "The graves, I imagine, will be spread out in the woods. Both families said that the soldiers weren't keen on the families taking the bodies and burying them. The second victim's grave is unmarked for that very reason. They don't want the soldiers to find her."

Gorecki leaned back in his chair. "I've identified several soldiers who seem to be the biggest offenders of them all. I've heard from migrants themselves that they beat, rob, and rape. One has been accused of rape. I haven't spoken to the actual victim."

"Crime in a migrant camp is always problematic," Gray said. "I would say most soldiers abuse the migrants in one form or another. But rape is a leap to the next level."

"I intend to pay closer attention to him."

"Was he accused of raping a young girl?"

"No, it was a young woman."

"Serial rapists who target children tend to stay in that age range. The autopsy will either confirm or deny if we have one on our hands."

Gorecki shook his head. "Most of the crimes reported by the migrants, except for rape, are assault and robbery. In your experience, does someone who commits those crimes suddenly start killing?"

"If someone ends up dead during an assault or a robbery, it's by accident. But for a serial killer, it's different. Their intent is to kill. For a mission-oriented killer, it's necessary to achieve his goal. They aren't interested in assaulting or robbing."

"That's my point. If that's what most of the soldiers are doing, how likely is it that it's a soldier killing?"

"Whoever is killing these girls needs to move around freely and not be questioned. Dekel confirmed that the soldiers are keeping everyone in their assigned sections. You got that impression the first time we were in here. Now it's confirmed."

"Yeah, you're right about moving around freely. It'll be hard for a migrant."

"We're struggling to connect all the dots because some of the dots are missing," Gray said. "How many soldiers have you singled out?"

"Five."

"Do they patrol together?"

"Two of them patrol together."

"Have you heard back from Klausen or Pop?"

"Not yet." Gorecki stood. "What are your plans?"

"I'm going to stay here and tweak the profile. The four of us should plan on meeting later tonight."

Gorecki nodded before leaving.

34

Gray settled onto his cot and pulled up the profile on his phone. With the idea that they were looking for a soldier, he definitely felt like this person was mission focused. They were also angry. The migrants added to that anger and triggered him to act. It made complete sense if they were looking at a young soldier, a conscript forced to serve. He might have had a gratifying life before it was interrupted with military service. Now he was stuck in a dirty camp with winter coming.

Rape, robbery, sexual assault, bullying, intimidation all are common crimes in migrant camps. Gray didn't think this soldier escalated at all. He felt the soldier had always had dark thoughts growing up, and it wasn't until he was put into his current situation that he acted on them. Gray didn't think the actual kill brought the soldier joy. But the idea that every kill brought him closer to solving a problem was probably exciting to him.

Gray still thought the soldier kept to himself. He didn't believe he was involved in petty crimes and abuse throughout the camp. Surely he witnessed it, might have even covered up for others when needed, but that was probably the extent.

This soldier was a planner. He put careful thought into his actions. Everything from the selection of the girl, to the abduction, to where the body was disposed of. It played out exactly as planned. Gorecki still thought their killer could be a sexual deviant, but the more Gray thought about it, the less he believed that to be true. He was fully expecting the autopsy to show no signs of sexual assault. Sexual gratification wasn't what this killer was after.

So why focus on girls? Why not anyone? It would be easier and still paint the camp as dangerous to any Arab thinking of traveling to Belarus. Gray knew the answer to that. Killing little girls hit harder. They had their necks sliced opened the blood drained from their bodies. That's an image for a frightening tale.

A giggle caught Gray's attention. He found Salma peeking inside of his tent.

"Hello, Salma," he said as he sat up. "What a nice surprise."

"I heard you came back. I want to return the crutches."

"Well, thank you, but you didn't have to do that. Is your mother with you?"

"No." She laughed a little. "She doesn't know I'm here."

"She doesn't?" Gray smiled back at Salma. "You know what I said last time about wandering around by yourself. You have got to stop doing that."

"I know, but I wanted to visit you."

"That's very sweet of you."

Gray fetched a box of cookies from his food stash and handed it to Salma.

"Have a seat. I want to take a look at your ankle."

While Salma munched on a cookie, Gray examined her ankle.

"It looks like it's healed quite nicely. Do you feel any pain?"

Salma shook her head.

"Well, I think it's safe for you to run around again."

Salma pointed at her ear.

"Something wrong with your ear?"

"She nodded."

Gray used his otoscope to peek inside her ear. "I think there's something in your ear. Let's see if we can get it out." Gray tickled her ear for a second before magically pulling out a coin. "There we go. Did you stick this in there?"

"No."

"Are you sure?"

"Yes," she laughed loudly.

Gray gave Salma the coin. Just then, a soldier poked his head into the tent.

"What are you doing?" he growled.

Salma immediately clammed up and looked away from the soldier.

"Nothing," Gray said, standing up. "I was examining her ankle. She twisted it the last time I saw her."

The soldier slapped the cookie out of Salma's hand.

"Hey! What are you doing?"

Gray moved in between the soldier and Salma. The soldier slammed the butt of his rifle into Gray's chest, knocking him back and the air whooshed out of his lungs. Gray took a step forward, and the soldier pointed his rifle at him.

"What is wrong with you? I'm a doctor."

A smirk appeared on the soldier's face. "I heard laughing. Your job is to treat, not entertain."

The soldier took Salma's arm and yanked her off the chair. "Go back to your tent. Now!"

Salma ran out of the tent as two more soldiers entered.

"Is there a problem here?" one of them asked.

"This doctor thinks he's an entertainer."

"Look, I already explained," Gray said in a raised voice.

The soldier slammed the butt of his rifle into Gray's chest again. This time he fell back onto the ground and groaned. Gray got back up with his fists balled. All three soldiers pointed their rifles at Gray.

"You think you can do whatever you want?" the soldier said. "Take a step forward and find out what happens."

Just then, Gorecki, Klausen, and Pop appeared at the entrance to the tent.

Gorecki quickly recognized the situation. "Hey, let's calm down. I'm sure whatever happened is a misunderstanding."

"Your doctor friend here is a troublemaker."

"No, he's not. He's new. He just doesn't understand the rules. We'll talk to him and make sure he understands how things work here."

Gorecki reached under his cot, removed two vodka bottles, and handed them to the soldier. "We are very sorry for any trouble."

Klausen opened the tent flap. "We promise to make sure he understands the rules of the camp. This won't happen again."

As the soldiers walked out, Azarenka appeared.

"Commander Azarenka," the soldier said as he and the other soldiers snapped to attention.

Azarenka looked at the two bottles of vodka in the soldier's hands, then at Gorecki and the others in the tent before turning and leaving.

"That was the commander of the camp," Gorecki said once the soldiers were gone. "His name is Azarenka. It's best to stay off his radar."

"I did nothing wrong," Gray said. "I was having a bit of fun with a patient when those soldiers came into the tent."

"Your antics could have put the whole group at risk. Your job is to treat, nothing more. Remember that the next time you decide some bedside manner is in order."

35

When Gray woke the following day, Gorecki wasn't in his cot. He stuck his head out of the tent, thinking Gorecki might be tending to a patient, but there was no one around. A queue had not even formed. Gray used a portable hot-water maker to fix a cup of coffee. He had barely gotten through his second sip when he heard someone outside his tent.

"Dr. Sanders. Are you there?"

Gray pulled back the tent flap and saw Dekel, the brother of the second victim, standing outside.

"Good morning, Dekel. What can I do for you?"

Dekel looked around, and Gray quickly caught the hint and invited him inside.

"Dr. Sanders. I have the information you were asking for. The families of the last two girls to die have agreed to meet with you."

"That's great news."

"I can introduce you to them, but I don't know anything about where their daughters are buried."

"That's fine. Can we go now?"

"Yes, of course."

Gray downed the rest of his coffee quickly before grabbing his medical satchel.

"The family I'm taking you to now is at the north end of the camp, about two kilometers from here," Dekel said. "It's better if we walk through the woods instead of the camp. We won't be questioned by soldiers."

"Are you sure you can navigate through the woods?"

"Don't worry, Dr. Sanders. We won't get lost."

The hike to the far end of the camp took almost an hour since they couldn't move as fast through the woods. When they reentered the camp, Gray saw that the number of tents had thinned.

"Have you been in this area before?" Dekel asked.

"I haven't been this far north. Do the people here receive medical treatment?"

"There are no organizations to help in this area. They must hike south to where we are. The family is actually north, outside of the camp. They're a bunch of people who prefer to live farther out, where there aren't very many people."

"Why is that?"

Dekel shrugged. "Maybe they feel safer."

"What about services, like food and water, or medical attention?"

"They must hike back into the camp."

"They must think things are pretty bad if they believe that's better."

Dekel stopped. "That tent straight ahead."

"Are you coming, or are you staying here?"

"I think it's better I stay here. Come find me when you're finished, and I'll take you to the next family."

Gray nodded and headed over to the tent. He could hear voices inside, so someone was home.

"Hello," Gray called out. "I'm Dr. Sanders from Doctors Without Borders."

A man stepped out of the tent. He had a warm smile on his face, and surprisingly he offered his hand. Gray shook it.

"My name is Caleb. I've been expecting you."

"You have?"

"Yes, Dekel informed me." Caleb looked over at Dekel and nodded. "I know why you're here, and you have my permission to perform an autopsy on my daughter, Maisha."

"I am very sorry for your loss. It's a terrible thing that has happened. I want you to know that I'll do everything possible to catch the person responsible."

Caleb gave Gray a comforting squeeze on his arm. "I must head into the camp for supplies. I'll take you to her grave first. It's farther north in the woods."

Caleb led the way deeper into the woods.

"Why do you live out here?" Gray asked as he walked in step with Caleb.

"We didn't always live like this. At first, we were farther inside the camp. It was only after Maisha's death that we moved. I feared for the safety of my family. I have two other children, both boys. One is four, and the other is twelve. My wife prefers it here even though it makes it harder for us. Every other day I travel into the camp for supplies."

"Do you mind if I ask a few questions?" Gray asked. "They're a bit sensitive."

"It's not pleasant for me to discuss what happened to Maisha, but I do understand you need information."

"Who found her body, and where was the location in relation to where you are now?"

"I found her. Our tent was about half of a kilometer south from here."

"Is it possible to take me there?"

"Yes, of course."

"When you found Maisha, what position was her body in? Was she laid down neatly? Was she curled up?"

"She was lying facedown like she was sleeping on her stomach. Why do you ask?"

"The parent of another victim said his daughter was lying on her back with her arms and legs stretched out like she was positioned that way."

"You could probably say the same for Maisha. She wasn't lying on her arm. You know the way you might fall to the ground unconscious?"

"Yes, I understand. How long was Maisha missing before you found her?"

"About a day. She went missing in the night. We found her a day later."

"Did you report her disappearance to the soldiers?"

"I tried. They didn't care and offered no help. But when I found her, they prevented us from taking her body. I had to fight with them to get my little girl. Strangely, they weren't interested when she disappeared. But when I found Maisha, they changed their minds."

"Do you have any thoughts on why they didn't want you to take Maisha's body?"

Caleb shook his head. "But I heard other parents had problems with burying their daughters."

"They did. If I understand correctly, the soldiers don't want you talking to the other parents."

"Yes, that's correct. The only reason is that they think we might figure out what happened. That's a good thing, right? But for them, it's not. I don't understand." Caleb slowed his steps and searched the area. He reached out to a tree with a small cross carving in its trunk.

"I made this so I can remember where her grave is. Out

here, everything looks the same. Maisha's grave is just over there."

Caleb counted ten trees north of the tree with the marker.

"Here it is."

Gray didn't see anything indicating a grave there except a very slight mound. Caleb knelt and began to pray while Gray pinned the location on his phone.

When Caleb finished, he stood.

"Does anyone else know Maisha is buried here?"

"No. We kept it a secret. That's why there are no markings. Dr. Sanders, what will happen next?"

"I will need to turn over all this information over to my contacts back in Poland. They will then formulate a plan to retrieve the bodies. As you can probably guess, this is not something the Belarusian government must find out about."

"In the news, they want everyone to think they are looking for the person involved, but they're not doing anything. You, Dr. Sanders, are the first person I believe can actually help."

Gray and Caleb made their way back to the tent. Caleb needed to fetch a bag for the supplies. While Gray waited outside, three soldiers approached him.

"What are you doing here?" one of them asked.

"I'm providing medical attention for people." Gray showed them his satchel with the DWB logo.

"You are very far from your tent. Don't you normally provide services there?"

"Yes, that's right, but we are far from people who live in this area. So I come here instead."

Caleb emerged from his tent. "I'm ready to take you to the —" He stopped speaking when he noticed the soldiers.

"Please, continue," the soldier said. "I would like to know where you are taking the doctor. I think everyone here wants to know.."

Caleb stuttered for a bit, unsure of what to say.

"He was going to take me to others who might need my help, that's all."

"Was I speaking to you, Doctor?"

"Well, I know the answer. I just—"

The soldier slammed the butt of his rifle into Gray's chest, causing him to drop to one knee as he choked for air.

"Do not speak unless I ask you a question." The soldier returned his attention to Caleb. "Now, where were you taking the Doctor?"

"It's what he said. I was heading south for supplies, and I know people who could use his help."

The soldier smiled as he looked back at his comrades. "Do you believe him?"

They both shook their heads.

"It seems as though we don't believe you. Do you know what happens to people who lie?"

Caleb started to answer, but the soldier slammed the stock of his rifle across Caleb's face. He fell to the ground, unconscious.

"What are you doing?" Gray shouted as he leaned over to attend to Caleb.

"My job. And now you are doing your job. Treat the people. Do not become friends with them. Is that clear, Doctor?"

"You can't just go around assaulting these people."

The soldier pressed the barrel of his rifle against Gray's head. "Do not think because you are a doctor that you have any rights here. One slip of the finger and things will get messy very fast."

Gray held his arms up. "I'm sorry."

A few moments passed before the soldier lowered his rifle.

"Return to your tent, Doctor. Your services are no longer needed here."

Gray got to his feet, his arms still up in the air as he looked the soldier in his icy blue eyes.

"Do you have something to say to me, Doctor?" the soldier asked.

Gray shook his head and walked away.

"Doctor," the soldier called out. "Don't ever come to this area of the camp again. I won't be so nice the next time."

36

As Dekel had already fled from the area, Gray headed back to his tent. He didn't blame the kid for leaving. He had seen everything that had happened. Gray avoided giving medical attention to anyone, even telling those who came up to him that they needed to come to his tent.

When he finally returned to his tent, as usual, Gorecki wasn't there, and a line of migrants needing medical attention was gathered outside. Gray didn't feel like attending to people after nearly having his head blown to bits. Still, he needed to keep up appearances. Gorecki had warned him multiple times to remain invisible, not to do anything that would attract attention. Gray's encounter with the soldiers did him no favors. It would be the gossip among the migrants who witnessed it and a story to brag about for the soldiers involved.

The migrants kept Gray busy, which was a good thing because whenever he did think about what had happened, his anger would start to bubble. After about two hours, Gray had cleared the line of people needing his services. He unscrewed the cap off a bottle of water and took a long swig. When Gray finished, his eyes caught those of another soldier staring at him. Only this wasn't some regular soldier. It was Azarenka.

Gray quickly looked away as if he hadn't locked eyes with the commander. But when he casually looked back in that direction, Azarenka was still focused on him. How long had he been watching Gray? Did he know what happened up north? Has Gray already been labeled as a troublemaker? All that thinking caused Gray's eyes to settle onto Azarenka once more. Gray quickly looked away and then back. Not once did the commander's stare waver. In fact, it appeared as though Azarenka wanted Gray to know he was watching.

"Why are you staring at Azarenka?" Gorecki asked.

Gray had been so focused on Azarenka, he didn't notice Gorecki approaching.

"I wasn't. He was staring at me."

"Well, unless you're trying to get kicked out of here, stop looking over there."

Gray followed Gorecki into the tent.

"I have good news. I found the grave of the third victim."

"What's the bad news?" Gorecki asked.

"I might have heat on me."

Gray told Gorecki about his encounter with the soldiers and how they banned him from coming to that part of the camp.

"Are you serious? What part of 'stay below the radar' did you not understand?"

"Hey, I was doing my job. Nothing I did flagged them. It was rotten timing with Caleb opening his mouth, that's all."

"You think Azarenka knows what happened?"

"I don't know. Maybe. Look, I have three locations. Do you think your command will be okay with three bodies?"

"I think that'll satisfy the objective."

Gray pulled out his phone and showed Gorecki the three locations.

"Do you have a plan?" Gray asked.

"The plan is to dig up the bodies, put them in bags, and carry them over our shoulders."

"Sounds easy enough."

"The body that's up north will be easy. It's the two that are near us that I'm worried about. The soil is hard, so taking the bodies out of the ground will take time. The probability of us being seen is high. We'll have to be careful."

"After we acquire all three bodies and we're clear of the camp, then what?"

"We walk north in the woods. Farther up, there's no fence, just border markers. It'll be easy to cross."

"What about Belarusian Border Guards?"

"If we travel far enough, there shouldn't be any. They're mostly concentrated along with the camp. As soon as Klausen and Pop return, I'll brief them. We'll make our move tonight."

The shuffling of boots outside the tent prompted Gorecki to take a peek. It was Azarenka and a couple of soldiers.

"Commander Azarenka. Can we be of help to you?" Gorecki asked.

"I appreciate your offer, but it is I who wants to do something for you. For your safety, I have decided to station these two soldiers outside your tent."

"I don't think that's necessary, Commander—"

"I don't care what you think."

"But surely there must be better uses for your men."

"Are you telling me you know how to command my men better than me?"

Gorecki paused for a moment before speaking. "Thank you, Commander Azarenka. It's appreciated."

Azarenka left without saying another word, and Gorecki headed back inside the tent.

"We got a problem," he said.

"I know. I heard everything."

37

"He had to have heard about what happened up north," Gray said in a lowered voice.

"You definitely caught his attention. It won't surprise me if he orders us out of the camp tomorrow. We have to move those bodies out tonight."

"How do we do that with his men stationed outside?"

"He doesn't seem concerned with Klausen and Pop. He's focused on you. I should be able to get out by saying I need to check on a patient. You'll stay here. Three of us can get the job done."

Gorecki reached under his cot and removed a bottle of vodka and a pack of cigarettes from a bag. "Use this to keep those soldiers entertained."

Gray transferred the location of the graves to Gorecki's phone.

"I doubt those soldiers will allow us out at two in the morning. We'll have to leave earlier while the camp is still awake."

"How long do you think it'll take?"

"Hard to tell. Three hours."

"That's a long time to be away."

Gorecki retrieved another bottle of vodka and handed it to Gray. "Make sure they drink both bottles. It'll help if we return late."

Klausen and Pop appeared fifteen minutes later, and Gorecki briefed them in their tent. The soldiers didn't appear to be concerned with Klausen or Pop's comings and goings, nor did they seem to bother with Gorecki.

"It's like I'm invisible to them," Gorecki said when he came back. "They're here to keep an eye on you. You have Azarenka's attention."

"I seriously don't think I did anything out of the ordinary."

"It could just be that you're a Yankee. Klausen and Pop will head out first. I'll leave a little later and meet with them. Your job is to stay here and make sure these two soldiers continue to care only about you. I'm serious. Stay here. Don't leave the tent."

～

Around eight that night, Klausen and Pop left. Gorecki waited twenty minutes before leaving the tent to catch up.

Gray placed three plastic cups on the table, then the bottle of vodka, and fired up some music on his phone. From the corner of his eye, he could see that he'd already caught their attention. Gray threw the pack of smokes onto the table before unscrewing the cap off the bottle of vodka. He then poured a little into each cup. Gray picked up his cup, and only then did he acknowledge the soldiers with a nod before drinking the shot.

Gray placed the cup back down and refilled it. He looked at the soldiers and then at the two other cups. The soldiers looked at each other with confusion. Gray picked up his cup, smiled at the soldiers, and then drank the shot. He refilled his cup and looked at the soldiers once more, and then at the two other cups. This time the soldiers responded by picking up a cup each. Gray tapped his cup against theirs.

"Na zdorovie," he said.

All three of them drank their shots, and Gray quickly refilled the cups and pushed the pack of cigarettes over to them. One of the soldiers smiled, took a cigarette from the box, and lit up.

∾

Gorecki and his men arrived at the burial site nearest to them. It would be the most problematic dig of them all. Not only was it within eyesight of a few tents, but an APV as well. The odds of them being seen digging in the ground, or worse, with the body, were high. They carried with them two small hand shovels and three burlap bags. There was nothing high-tech about this job. They were going to be digging the bodies out of the ground, putting them into a bag, and slinging them over their shoulders. It wouldn't be pleasant, but it was the only way.

Gorecki and the others attended to a few migrants in the area while they watched the soldiers. There were three of them hanging around the APV. No digging could start with those soldiers there.

"What if they don't leave?" Klausen whispered to Gorecki. "We don't have that much time. We still need to get the other bodies and then hike north to the extraction point."

"If worse comes to worst, we'll leave this body and just take the other two."

"Will that suffice?"

"It'll have to."

After fifteen anxious minutes, the soldiers walked off, and Klausen and Pop made their move. Their job was to get the body out of the ground while Gorecki kept watching for any passersby.

The soil was hard, and it took longer than they expected to get the body out. One good thing about the cold dirt was that it slowed the decomposition. It was still in excellent shape, and they bagged it quickly.

The three then headed south to the location of the second gravesite. Once they got that body out of the ground, the plan was to head deeper into the woods and then go north, eliminating the chances of being caught by a patrol.

There were no soldiers near the second gravesite and very few tents around, as it was beyond the edge of the camp. Klausen and Pop started digging right away. Once they had the body bagged, they headed deeper into the woods, with Gorecki leading the way. Klausen and Pop each had a bag slung over their shoulders. They were about five minutes into their trek when they ran right into a soldier who had just finished zipping up his pants after urinating.

Gorecki and the others came to an abrupt stop as they stared at the soldier. He looked them up and down, noting the shovel in Gorecki's hand and the bags slung over Klausen's and Pop's shoulders. The soldier drew a deep breath and raised his rifle a beat later.

～

Gray and the soldiers had been toasting for quite some time now. The soldiers were relaxed, smiling and slapping Gray on the back. Any walls they had between them had been broken down. Gray hadn't taken a single sip of alcohol during that entire time. He had punctured a tiny hole near the bottom of his cup, which he would keep covered with his thumb when he poured vodka inside. He would hold his cup near the edge of the table and allow the vodka to drain out between his legs. It was too dark for the soldiers to notice. He would then toast with an empty cup and pretend to drink his shot.

This charade carried on until the soldiers finished the first bottle and most of the cigarettes. The only thing that stopped their merry-making were gunshots in the distance.

38

The worst scenario possible raced through Gray's mind: his team had been compromised and shot dead. Surely if Gorecki and the others had been caught, he was next. But as he contemplated the situation, the two soldiers grabbed their rifles. They took off in the direction of the gunshots.

Gray tried to think through the situation. If Gorecki and the others had been caught, his best move was to get out of the camp. Gray watched as other soldiers ran toward the sound of gunfire. Migrants had begun to stir and climb out of their tents. It was only a matter of time before the camp was a hive of busyness. Gray could easily make his way to the border checkpoint without suspicion. Now was the time to act if that's what he wanted. Or he could find out what happened.

Gorecki's words came back to Gray. "Stay here. Don't leave the tent."

A beat later, Gray grabbed his medical satchel and ran after the soldiers who had been guarding him. The way he saw it, his job was to keep the soldiers' attention focused on him. He couldn't do that if they'd left. And anyway, if there was a chance he could help Gorecki and the others, he had to try.

"Excuse me, pardon me," Gray said as he sidestepped around people. He'd already lost sight of the two soldiers, but he knew he was heading in the right direction. The migrants were either pointing or looking south.

Gray figured Gorecki had already secured the first body and worked on the second body south of his tent when things went sideways. He knew the exact location of the gravesite and headed there. As he neared, there was a lot of shouting in Belarusian. More soldiers appeared, and it looked as if even they were unsure of what had happened.

As he neared the edge of the camp, Gray slowed to walk and kept his cool.

"What happened?" he asked a man who stood with his arms folded across his chest.

"Someone was shot," he said.

The heavy feeling in Gray's stomach grew with every step. His heart thumped in his chest as his eyes searched for clues. *Come on, Gorecki. Don't let me down.*

A group of soldiers appeared from the edge of the woods. They were walking toward Gray, clearly escorting someone.

Gray recognized the person. It was Dekel. He had both arms restrained by soldiers as he limped along. As they neared, the light from a few campfires revealed his bloodied pants. He'd been shot.

Gray rushed toward Dekel to administer first aid, but a few soldiers stepped in front of Gray, blocking his path.

"He needs help," Gray said as he moved around them to get to Dekel.

A soldier slammed the butt of this rifle into Gray, knocking him back. Gray wheezed as he struggled to catch his breath. Another gun slammed into his side, and Gray dropped to the ground in pain. Soldiers quickly circled with their rifles aimed at him.

"He's injured. I can help him," Gray managed to say.

None of the soldiers responded to Gray's offer. Then all at once, they looked away. Gray looked to see what had grabbed their attention. Azarenka had arrived.

Gray watched as Azarenka had a discussion with a few soldiers. They were pointing to Dekel. Gray was too far away to hear what was said, but assumed Azarenka was being briefed.

The soldiers forced Dekel down to his knees as Azarenka approached. Words were exchanged between Azarenka and Dekel. Then, without warning, Azarenka removed his handgun from its holster and shot Dekel in the head, killing him instantly.

"No!" Gray shouted. "Why did you do that?"

Azarenka's attention turned to Gray, and he slowly walked over until he stood a few feet away. He pointed his handgun directly at Gray.

"You have a problem with the way I punish people in my camp?"

"Punish? You murdered that boy."

"Boy? He was practically a man, responsible for his own actions. He killed one of my men."

"Killed? How?"

"Dr. Sanders, if I were you, I'd focus on giving out medical treatment to those who need it and stop playing judge. It's a very dangerous role to assume." Azarenka ordered his men to take Gray back to his tent. Without another word, Azarenka left.

Two soldiers yanked Gray to his feet.

"Move," one said as he jabbed his rifle into Gray.

Gray tried to talk to the soldiers during the walk to his tent, but they refused to answer questions. The last thing Gray remembered was entering his tent and then feeling a sharp pain in the back of his head.

39

Gray's eyes fluttered briefly before he opened them. He was lying face down on his cot. He peeled his face off the pillow and looked around. Gorecki wasn't there, and it didn't appear that his cot had been slept in. Gray rolled over to his side and was immediately reminded that he'd been hit multiple times by a rifle. He touched his rib cage. He didn't think he had any broken ribs, but they were bruised. He also had a splitting headache. Gray forced himself to sit up. He grabbed an old bottle of water and drank what was left, erasing the stickiness in his mouth.

He could hear murmuring outside his tent: the migrants were already lined up, waiting for medical treatment.

Gray hurt and felt like crap, but he looked at the bright side. He was alive. He could not say the same for Dekel. He still had trouble believing Azarenka shot the boy in cold blood in front of many soldiers and migrants. And he did so without a single worry of repercussions, for that matter.

There was a tender bump on the back of Gray's head. He figured one of the soldiers had hit him once inside the tent. *I guess I got lucky and fell straight onto my cot.*

Gray stood and peeked out of the tent, squinting as his eyes had yet to adjust to the daylight. To his surprise, he saw Gorecki attending to the migrants.

Gorecki looked over his shoulder. "You're up."

"Can we talk for a minute?" Gray said.

Gorecki told the migrants he was taking a break and headed inside the tent.

"Care to clue me in on what happened?" Gray asked.

"When I came back, I found you passed out on the ground right there. I lifted you up onto your cot."

"Thanks, but that's not what I was asking about."

"It all went well. We got all three bodies out of the ground and across the border."

"There were gunshots. I heard them. I thought you—"

"We ran into a soldier right after we dug up the second body. I had no choice and cracked his head open with my shovel."

"Did he shoot at you?"

"No. After I killed him, that kid appeared."

"Dekel?"

"Yes, I guess he was following us and saw what had happened. He told us to leave and that he would deal with the situation."

"And you let him?"

"Gray, we needed to get those bodies across the border."

"Azarenka shot Dekel. I saw it with my own eyes. In fact, a lot of people watched him execute the boy. He said Dekel had killed one of his men, but it was you." Gray looked away in disbelief. "I can't believe he sacrificed himself."

"You obviously said enough to convince him of how important an autopsy is," Gorecki said. "He knew we had his sister in the bag."

"Dekel sacrificed himself."

"What about Klausen and Pop?"

"They're fine. Everything went as planned because of Dekel."

Gray took a moment to process what they had discussed before asking more questions.

"What about the bodies? What's next?"

"The handoff was seamless. We would have been back sooner, but because of the chaos in the camp last night, we opted to hang out in the woods until just before daybreak." Gorecki looked at his watch. "Pakulski should already be back in Warsaw."

"Pakulski? Why is an aide involved in this?"

Gorecki smiled, and it dawned on Gray that Pakulski wasn't an aide. She was an intelligence officer whose job was to handle Gray while in Warsaw.

"Figures. How long will the autopsies take?"

"Not long. The medical examiner was on standby. I wouldn't be surprised if we get word by the end of the day. I have my fingers crossed. If the autopsy doesn't produce anything that can point directly at a soldier, I've been ordered to pull out."

"Just like that?"

"Just like that. Especially after what happened last night. I wouldn't be surprised if Azarenka kicks the aid organizations out of the camp."

"He wouldn't do that. How would these people eat and drink?"

"He doesn't care. He might see it as a way to control the population. Every day, the camp grows. Have you made any improvements to the profile?"

"I have. I'll message a copy to everyone."

"Do we need to have a meeting, or is it self-explanatory?"

"I would suggest everyone keep singling out soldiers that

fit the profile," Gray stood. "I'll go check on Klausen and Pop and see if they have any questions or need clarification. If the autopsies produce the evidence we need, we'll have to hit the ground running. If you're right about Azarenka, we're already on borrowed time."

40

When Gray returned to the tent after speaking with Klausen and Pop, Gorecki, as usual, had disappeared. He figured he took off to watch the men he'd already pegged as guilty. Migrants needing medical attention had gathered outside the tent again, so Gray sat down and began looking over patients. A few hours must have passed before Gorecki reappeared.

"Let's talk inside," he said as he walked past Gray and into the tent.

"What's up?" Gray asked once inside the tent.

"I've been thinking. We need to escalate."

"What do you mean?"

"Between myself, Klausen, and Pop, we've already singled out people who fit the profile. Watching them in the camp will produce nothing more. In fact, I think they might even be on their best behavior."

"What are you suggesting?"

"Many soldiers leave the camp when they want time off. And when they do, they head to Grodno, the nearest city. I want to monitor the outside of the camp."

"You're joking, right?"

"I'm not. A lot of these young soldiers are from Grodno. They have family or a girlfriend there. It's about a forty-five-minute drive from here."

"Can we get permission to leave the camp?"

"We're not asking. But I believe it's worth the risk because it may allow them to lower their guard and show another side of themselves. Look, Gray, you've been asking to be more involved. I'm giving you an opportunity right now. I also feel you need to see these soldiers in a different environment. I don't want a repeat of Fadel. But I also understand there's tremendous risk here. I'll respect your decision either way."

"How will the four of us leave camp without anyone questioning us?"

"You and I will leave together for now. If we need Klausen and Pop to follow, they can do so later. We'll cut through the woods and connect with the M6 highway. A lot of farmers use that route into Grodno. We can hitch a ride with one. Money talks here. But once we're in Grodno, we shouldn't have any problems."

"When were you thinking of taking this excursion?"

"I want to leave this afternoon. We really can't afford to wait any longer. You have a couple of hours to think it over. I suggest you do that. In the meantime, I'll be in Klausen and Pop's tent if you need me."

Gray took a moment to think about Gorecki's offer. As much as he wanted to be more involved, to feel like he had a real voice in what they were doing, the fact of the matter was, they were operating behind enemy lines. This may have been par for the course for people like Gorecki. He and the other intelligence officers were used to working in the shadows. They had training and experience in that area.

While working back in America, Gray had the luxury of carrying a firearm, the full force of the Bureau, and the law of the land behind him. Here in Belarus, he had nothing. Even when he served in the Air Force as a Pararescue man, he had a backup team, an eye in the sky watching over him, and contingency plans in case things went sideways. Should they get caught, it wouldn't surprise Gray if the Polish government denied any knowledge of Gray and his actions. They were inches away from throwing him under the bus when the Fadel news blew up in their face.

The prospect worried Gray. Their organization wasn't authorized to leave the camp, let alone hang out in a nearby town. He already felt he was on Azarenka's radar. Though, Gorecki had made a good point. They didn't have the luxury of time. Even Gray knew in his gut that they could be ordered to leave at any moment.

Gray decided to let the decision sit while he attended to the people outside his tent. An hour had passed before Gorecki returned. He gave Gray a look that suggested he wanted an answer. Gray excused himself from the table out front and headed back into the tent. Gorecki was downing a bottle of water.

"I'm in," Gray said. "But I have a request."

"What's that?"

"Let's wait until the results of the autopsies are in. If they're inconclusive, heading into town becomes a moot point. You did say that we'd hear something by the end of the day."

Gorecki gave it a moment's thought. "Okay, we'll wait. But if it's positive news, I need to know I can count on you to commit to this mission one hundred percent. If something you disagree with happens, I can't have you changing your mind. You're all in now, or you're out. Do you understand?"

Gray nodded. "Don't worry. I'm all in."

41

Pakulski had been waiting at a section of the border where neither Poland nor Belarus patrolled. It was dense forest for miles and not the most accessible ground to navigate, especially at night. During their meeting, Gorecki had mentioned his plan to head into Grodno. He argued there was only so much information they could squeeze out of the camp. Pakulski informed Gorecki that the medical examiner in Warsaw was on standby and would do her best to expedite things.

The streets were wet and quiet that night in Warsaw. A little after two in the morning, Pakulski crossed the city limits. She was heading to the Central Forensic Laboratory of the Police, located next door to the Chancellery.

The SUV came to a stop behind the forensic laboratory. Waiting outside with a few assistants was Dr. Maria Broz, the top medical examiner in all of Poland.

"Maria, thank you so much for being here at this hour," Pakulski said after exiting the vehicle.

"When I heard you were involved, how could I say no? It feels like ages since we've last seen each other."

Pakulski and Broz had been friends for many years. Pakulski had first met Broz when she was a junior officer with the foreign intelligence office. Ever since then, she and the medical examiner had been friends.

"What do you have for me?" Broz asked as she shoved her hands into the pockets of her lab coat.

"Three bodies, all girls ages eight through ten, I believe. They all sustained lacerations to the neck."

Broz's assistants helped Pakulski's people transfer the bodies to the gurneys.

Broz looked at the burlap bags. "Is that how you transported the bodies?"

"Yes. Gorecki and his team delivered them this way. They dug them out of the ground. I haven't looked at them, but he said they were in good condition—minimal decomposition, but I'll let you be the judge of that."

Broz and Pakulski followed the gurneys as they were wheeled into the building.

"What is it that we're really after, besides confirming the cause of death?"

"We need something that can point to identifying the person responsible."

"Nothing out of the ordinary there."

"It needs to implicate a soldier, a Belarusian soldier."

"Asking for much, aren't we?"

"I know, but for Gorecki to continue his mission, he needs evidence to confirm a soldier is responsible."

"I should have known, with Gorecki involved, he would be asking for the impossible."

"Do you think there's a chance?" Pakulski asked as they walked down a long hallway.

"Anything is possible. It all depends on what I find. I'm

assuming because I'm here at this hour, these autopsies need to be completed as soon as possible."

"I'm sorry to ask this of you."

"I don't blame you. We're just doing our jobs. Look, you're welcome to stick around, but I'll need a couple of hours before I can make an assessment."

"You hungry?"

"I can always eat," Broz said as she smiled and adjusted her glasses.

"I'll go pick up some food. There's a place I know that's open twenty-four hours. I'll see you in a bit."

~

Pakulski returned about an hour later. Broz was in her examination room masked and gloved as she peered into the wound of one of the girls. She had all three bodies lying on metal autopsy tables.

"How goes it?" Pakulski asked.

Broz pulled away from the body. "I can tell you now the same person is responsible for all three deaths. Come over here."

Pakulski grabbed a medical mask off the counter and slipped it over her face.

"All three girls have lacerations across their neck. This is obviously the cause of death. There are no signs of blunt force trauma or foreign DNA in their nails."

"So the girls didn't struggle or fight back?"

"That's correct. This can suggest they knew their attacker or, at a minimum, had some level of comfort around them. I'm inclined to believe they did not fear for their lives, at least initially. Later, yes. There are signs of ligature marks around their wrists and ankles. So at some point from the time of abduction to death, they were tied up."

"They knew their attacker, went along willingly, probably to another location, where they were then tied up and killed."

"It is possible that they were drugged. We'll know when the toxicology reports come back. But let's focus on the neck lacerations."

Pakulski moved closer as Broz adjusted a lamp above.

"You see how on the right side of the neck the laceration is clean cut? No tears."

"Yes."

"But on the left side, it's jagged. The skin is torn here and here. This can suggest the knife slipped or the person pressed too hard toward the end and used the bottom of the blade, where it wasn't as sharp."

"So does that mean he was sloppy or in a rush?"

"Possible, or that this person wasn't as skilled. But when I compared the lacerations of all three girls, they were identical. They all started off with a clean cut and ended with torn skin."

"That's weird."

"But it's also why I'm positive it's the same person."

"Same style of cutting?"

"No, same knife. All three victims were cut deep enough for the blade to strike the vertebrae in the neck. Also, what could cause this jaggedness toward the end of the laceration is a blade that is also serrated."

Broz led Pakulski over to a computer monitor with microscopic photos on display.

"See this mark?" she said as she pointed at a photo. "That's from the blade striking the vertebrae. It's the same on every girl."

Pakulski shrugged. "So they all sustained deep cuts."

"Extremely deep. It explains the tears in the skin. The

person starts by stabbing with the front of the blade and then drags it across and, in the process, presses down hard, thus forcing the bottom of the blade to finish the job. This tells me it's the same knife, same killer."

"But it doesn't tell us if it's a soldier," Pakulski said.

"Not yet, but it is possible to either match the cut in the vertebrae or the actual laceration to a specific knife. I've already sent the photos to our weapons expert. Militaries usually issue the same equipment to their soldiers. If we can match this wound to the standard-issue knife used by Belarusian soldiers, then you'll have your proof."

42

Gorecki, as usual, had taken off without saying anything. Gray returned to the line of patients outside. He figured he and Gorecki were on the same page and didn't think much of it. It was late in the afternoon when Gorecki returned. He had a smile on his face as he motioned for Gray to follow him inside the tent.

"I'm guessing it's good news," Gray said.

"I just heard back from Pakulski. The medical examiner's report shows that the same knife was used on all three girls. Using a weapons expert, they identified the knife. It's a Karatel Punisher." Gorecki pulled up a picture of the knife on his phone. "It has a fixed blade that is partially serrated near the root. The incisions on the necks start clean and end in jagged, torn skin. A blade with a serrated edge near the root would cause that."

"That's great. So is that the knife these soldiers carry?"

"Not exactly. The standard-issue knife for a Belarusian soldier is an NR-40 combat knife, a hand-me-down from the Russian military. It does not have a serrated edge. However, the Karatel is a specialty knife not for sale to the general public and widely used by Russia's Federal Security Forces. Since Russia and Belarus are closely aligned, it would be reasonable to think that Belarusian soldiers have the punisher instead of the NR-40. Most likely, he's a higher-ranking soldier or even one who serves or has served in Special Forces. The good news is that was enough to allow us to stay in the camp."

"So we're not looking for your average enlistee."

"That's right. It definitely narrows it down."

"Do any of the men you were looking at fit that profile?"

"A couple. Klausen and Pop also have a few in mind. But now that we know what knife was used, we can just focus on identifying soldiers carrying that specific one."

"This is all good news. It updates the profile. It also answers questions I had myself. How did this person move around without being seen? If they're an officer, no one would question their actions or movements."

"That's right."

"So, what are the next steps now that we have new information?"

"I still want to go into town and observe."

"But we've narrowed it down. We can stay in camp and identify soldiers with this type of knife."

"Klausen and Pop have orders to do that. I still feel like we should get out of the camp and see how these soldiers act while off duty. Are you having a change of heart? You told me this morning you were all in, one hundred percent. And it wasn't with contingencies. What is it, Gray? I can't have you changing your mind based on new information."

"I'm in. I'm just thinking this through. That's all."

"Good. Be prepared to leave in an hour and wear clothing that doesn't have any DWB branding. Transfer everything you keep in your medical satchel to a normal backpack."

"Why?"

Gorecki shrugged. "Just in case."

"Anything else?"

"No. I'll be back in an hour."

～

Gorecki returned precisely one hour later, eager to leave right away.

"I spotted one of the soldiers I suspect getting onto a transport truck," he said as he changed his shirt. "He's heading into town. We need to move quickly."

A minute later, Gray closed up shop, telling the line of people outside that he was sorry and they had to come back in the morning. The two men then headed south a bit before walking east into the forest to avoid the barracks. Once in the woods, Gray and Gorecki kept a reasonably brisk pace. Gorecki wanted to reach the highway before sundown.

"Two questions," Gray said. "How long will it take to reach the highway? Do we have transport arranged?"

"The highway isn't far," Gorecki said as he stared straight ahead. "I just don't want to pop out of the woods too close to camp headquarters. For transport, we're hitchhiking. It shouldn't be a problem to catch a ride with a farmer heading into town."

About forty minutes later, Gray and Gorecki reached the M6 highway. They remained off to the side of the road, in the tree line, as the route was heavily trafficked by military vehicles.

"There," Gorecki pointed at a box truck heading in their direction. "Wait here."

Gorecki ran out to the side of the road, waved the truck down, and spoke to the driver. Gray couldn't tell if the truck was hauling a payload or not. There were also no company logos visible on the truck—a family farmer, perhaps. Gorecki turned around and called for Gray.

"He's willing to give us a lift, but we need to ride in the back," Gorecki said.

He rolled up the cargo door, and Gray was expecting to see a manure-infested cargo area, but surprisingly it was clean, except for a few vegetable crates and burlap bags. The two climbed inside. Gorecki shut the door and then pounded on the side of the truck to let the farmer know they were in.

The ride into town was quick and without incident. The truck came to a stop, and a couple of moments later, the door rolled up. The farmer stood there smiling, waving at them to come out. He appeared to be in his early fifties, with gray patches of hair on the sides of his head. He was dressed in blue jeans, rubber boots, and a black sweater.

Gray climbed out first. The truck had been parked on a narrow road next to a small park. Opposite them was a six-story red-brick building. In fact, the entire area around the park was filled with residential buildings.

"My home is this way," the man pointed at an apartment building.

"Why are we here?" Gray whispered to Gorecki.

"I forgot to tell you, Vasily here would only give us a ride if we looked over his family and made sure everyone was healthy."

"Is that why you told me to bring my gear?"

"No one really does favors for free. There's always some sort of an exchange."

"Vasily, this is Dr. Sanders. He'll be happy to examine you and your family."

The man stuck out his hand. "Vasily Morozov."

Gray shook it. "Nice to meet you," he responded in Russian.

"Ah, you speak Russian?"

"A little."

"You are American, no?"

"I am."

"Come," he said before leading the way.

Gray and Gorecki followed Vasily into the building and up the stairs to the fourth floor. He led the way into the flat. A smiling woman with short auburn hair appeared from the kitchen.

"My wife, Iryna. This is Dr. Sanders."

"Privet," she said. "It is nice to meet you."

"Nice to meet you too," Gray smiled back at her.

"I'm his colleague, Mr. Ajam."

The flat wasn't very big. A narrow living room led to a small balcony. There were two chairs and a small couch. A wooden hutch with glass doors took up almost one side of the room. Inside he saw crystal stemware, dishes, and a few vases. There was also a collection of Mariska dolls, carved wooden figurines, and what looked like folded stacks of handmade tablecloths. Just then, two young children, a boy and a girl, came out of a bedroom.

"My son, Denis, and my daughter, Liudmila." Vasily turned to his children. "Dr. Sanders will make sure you are okay. Please go into the bedroom."

Gray followed the two into the bedroom. There was a small single bed and a chaise lounge. Hanging on the wall was artwork done by one of the children. There were two dressers. The room wasn't that big, and Gray wondered where everyone slept.

Liudmila grabbed a wooden chopping board that had flowers painted on it. "I made this."

"That's beautiful. Did you also do the paintings on the wall?"

"Yes. I'm the artist in the family."

Gray removed his stethoscope from his bag and started listening to Liudmila's breathing.

"I'm studying English," she said as she switched to English.

"Your pronunciation is quite good."

"My teacher is very strict. She insists that I pronounce all the words the right way."

"She's right. It's important. Do you like studying English?"

"It's okay. My parents want me to learn. I've been studying for a year already."

"I'm impressed. You must be working very hard."

"I do it for my parents. They said it will be better for me when I'm older."

"They're right. What about your brother? Is he also learning English?"

"No, he's only seven. I'm thirteen. And anyway, my parents can only afford to pay for my lessons."

"Keep up the good work."

"I sleep on the bed," Liudmila said. "My brother sleeps on the sofa, in case you're wondering."

"And what about your parents?" he asked as he checked her blood pressure.

"They sleep outside. The sofa turns into a bed. It's very common for parents to give the bedroom to the children."

"I didn't know that."

"There's a lot I can teach you about our culture."

"I'm sure you could."

As Gray looked over Denis, Liudmila continued to talk as she danced around the room.

"Where do you go to school?" Gray asked.

"I go to school number eleven."

"That's the name of your school? Number eleven?"

"Yes, why?" She rested a hand on her hip.

"It's just that schools in America have different names."

"Well, I can't be number ten or number twelve because those names are already taken." Liudmila started to twirl around. "Tomorrow I have to face my enemy."

"Your enemy?" Gray was a little taken back by Liudmila's strong word choice and wondered if she was referring to the soldiers. "What enemy are you talking about?"

"Her name is Olga. She's in my class."

"Oh, you're talking about a classmate."

Liudmila stopped her spinning and crinkled her brow. "Who else would I be talking about? We don't like each other. She's very irritating."

After the examination, Gray and the children headed back to the living room and found a table had appeared, taking up most of the space. At least six different dishes of food had been spread across it. Gray also noted a large basket of black rye bread, a variety of fruit juices, and two bottles of chilled vodka. There was even crystal stemware to go along with it.

"We've been invited to dinner," Gorecki said. "Take a seat and enjoy some fine Belarusian cuisine."

Liudmila quickly pushed Denis out of the way to sit next to Gray. Gorecki and Denis sat on the other side, and Vasily and Iryna sat at the ends.

"Dr. Sanders, have you tried Belarusian food?" Liudmila asked.

"I haven't, but I'm excited to. It smells great."

"I'll tell you what everything is. That's Russian salad. It has potatoes, carrots, peas, and boiled eggs mixed in mayonnaise. That dish there is called selyodka pod shuba, but when you translate it to English, it's called 'herring under a fur coat.'" Liudmila giggled.

"A fur coat?"

"Yeah, it's a funny name. It's also kind of a salad. It has pickled herring, beets, onions, and potatoes in layers. The herring is on the bottom, the white is potatoes and eggs, and the reddish-purple top is from the beets. That's the fur coat. Get it?"

"Got it."

"This dish is stuffed cabbage."

"Now, that, I tried in Poland."

"Many Belarusian and Polish meals are similar," Gorecki said. "But I can tell this one will be delicious."

Vasily poured three shots of vodka for him, Gray, and Gorecki.

"Na zdorovie," he said.

The three drank their shots of vodka, while the others drank fruit juice. Over dinner, Liudmila was very happy to play translator. They learned that Vasily and Iryna were originally from Russia. They met while he served in the military. After they married, they'd settled in Belarus. Vasily and Iryna had recently opened their own shop selling fishing supplies and other household goods in the local market.

"My mother works there during the day," Liudmila said. "Sometimes I help out after school."

"And your father is a farmer?" Gray asked.

"Yes, but he will stop soon and work with my mother at the market. Dr. Sanders, how long will you be in Grodno?"

"Not long, I'm afraid."

"We're here for supplies," Gorecki quickly answered.

"Are you helping the people on the border?"

"We are."

After dinner, Gray examined Vasily and Iryna. The entire family appeared to be in good health. They thanked Vasily and his wife for their hospitality.

"Dr. Sanders, can I have a photo with you?" Liudmila

asked Gray. "I want to show my friends at school my new American friend."

"Sure."

Liudmila used her parents' phone to take a picture.

"Now they'll have to believe you," Gray said before waving goodbye and leaving.

43

Gorecki kept a fast pace as he and Gray walked along the sidewalk. Night had fallen, and streetlights lit the way. There was decent foot traffic as many residents were still making their way home from their workday.

"That took a lot longer than I expected," Gorecki said.

"How will we find the soldiers?"

"There are two known places where they hang out. We can start there."

Gorecki used his phone to figure out their location and led the way. A twenty-minute walk later, they stood outside of a restaurant-like pub called Mister Twister. Loud rock music could be heard coming from inside. The sign had a steampunk feel to it.

"A lot of residential buildings around here. Odd place for a bar like this," Gray said.

"Odd country."

Gorecki and Gray headed inside. They saw multiple tables with soldiers gathered around drinking beer and eating pizza. They were all armed with their rifles and holstered handguns.

Gray felt a little uneasy, realizing how bad things could go very quickly.

The décor inside was biker gang–themed. There were even a couple of tables where the base was an actual motorcycle. The walls had photographs of bikers riding Harley-Davidsons, road signs, and even a couple of chrome handlebars and exhaust pipes from motorcycles. The disinterested servers wore jeans and leather jackets. Gorecki motioned for a server and then placed an order for two beers.

"Do you recognize your guy?" Gray asked.

"That's him, there in the corner. Near the bathrooms."

Sitting at a single table was a soldier. He wore wire-framed glasses and was reading a book. He seemed utterly oblivious to the rousing gang of soldiers not far from him.

"Intellectual type," Gray said. "Have you seen him read in the camp?"

"No, but he keeps to himself. Only interacts with his comrades when necessary. Definitely a loner."

"He has a sheathed knife hanging off his belt." Gray used his phone to zoom in on it. "I can't tell if it's the Karatel or the NR-40."

"Yeah, they all keep their knives in the same spot. Handles look identical."

The server returned and placed two bottles of beer on the table.

"I'll try to get a closer look," Gorecki said.

As Gorecki neared the soldier, he dropped a euro on the floor right next to the man's boot. Gorecki stopped and picked it up slowly. The soldier kept his eyes on his book and didn't look or acknowledge Gorecki once. Gray found that interesting because most people would react to someone close to them, either by looking to see what they were doing or even just moving their foot out of the way. But this man did nothing, not even flinch a tiny bit.

Gorecki continued on and disappeared into the bathroom. A few moments later, he reappeared and returned to the table.

"So?" Gray asked.

"I can't tell."

"Should we engage? Offer to buy him a beer?" Gray asked.

"I think it's better to observe. If we engage, we'll forever be on his radar." Gorecki took a sip of his beer. "Any thoughts on him?"

"He showed no concern about you invading his personal space. That lack of emotion is in line with a functioning sociopath. He probably wears a mask most of the time to help him appear normal to others when, in fact, he really doesn't care about others and would rather be alone."

"Is he capable of killing?"

"Definitely. Sociopaths are impulsive by nature. Often this can be displayed through violent outbursts. Not all sociopaths kill, but the tendency to do so is there."

"So he could be lashing out at the migrants."

"Yes, he could be."

"The more I talk to you, the more I believe this is our guy."

"There's still no hard evidence. Talking to him would tell us more."

"You want to interview him?"

"In an ideal world, yeah. Questioning him would be good."

"Hey, it looks like he's leaving."

The soldier called a server over and paid his tab. He put on his jacket, tucked the book into one of the pockets, and grabbed his rifle. He walked past Gray and Gorecki without so much as a slight glance at them.

"We need to follow him," Gorecki said as he called a server over and quickly paid for their beers.

After exiting the bar, they looked up and down the street before spotting the soldier heading south. He walked with his head down and both hands buried in his jacket. He had his rifle slung across his chest, and he swung it back and forth near his hip with every step he took as if he hadn't a care in the world.

"I'm familiar with this road. It leads directly back to the city center," Gorecki said. "He's most likely catching a ride with a transport vehicle back to the camp. This is perfect."

"Why is this perfect?"

"I want you to hang back a bit, okay?"

Before Gray could ask why Gorecki had taken off toward the soldier, Gorecki was right on the soldier's butt in seconds. Gray couldn't figure out what Gorecki had planned, but he picked up the pace.

Suddenly, Gorecki slammed both hands down on the soldier's shoulders and threw him into the dark passageway . A split second later, Gorecki disappeared.

44

Gray sprinted down the sidewalk toward the passageway he saw Gorecki disappear into. At any second, he expected gunshots to ring out and Gorecki to stumble back onto the sidewalk with bullet holes riddling his body. But nothing happened. Gray even questioned if he'd seen it right. *Did Gorecki push that soldier into the alley, or did he go willingly?*

As he neared, Gray slowed to a jog, then a brisk walk, and stopped about ten feet from the opening. A group of women chatting among themselves passed by but paid Gray no attention. He took a few steps forward until he could peek inside the passageway. It was narrow, dark, and empty from what he could determine.

Where did they go?

The passageway appeared to cut directly between two buildings. He could see an opening at the other end, but it didn't look like it opened up onto a busy street like the one he had just come from. The sides of the buildings had a few windows, but there were no fire escapes. The passageway was relatively clean, with just a few pieces of paper debris lying about. It was quiet and smelled fine. Gray was about halfway through the passage when a creaking noise caught his attention. A door opened, and Gorecki appeared.

"In here," he whispered. "Hurry."

Gray entered the small doorway, and Gorecki closed and locked it immediately.

"What is this place? Where's the soldier?"

"Follow me," Gorecki said as he climbed a narrow wooden stairway. Gray followed him to the second-floor landing. Gorecki knocked three times on the only door there, and a beat later, it cracked open.

Gray stepped into a small flat and noticed right away the resemblance to the one they'd had dinner at earlier, minus the décor. This one was bare aside from a few chairs and a table in the living room.

"What is this place? Who is this?" Gray pointed to the man who had let them in.

"You can call me Lesun," the man answered in English with an accent.

"Lesun works with us," Gorecki said.

It dawned on Gray that this was a Polish safe house, and Lesun was a Belarusian asset recruited to work with Gorecki. Gray spied a closed door. He moved swiftly toward it and pushed it open. Inside, he found the soldier gagged and tied to a chair. Another man with a gun stood next to him.

Gray spun around. "You abducted a Belarusian soldier? Are you out of your damn mind?"

"We need to interrogate him. Even you said we needed to learn more."

"I didn't say to kidnap the guy. You plan on just letting him go after and hoping he keeps his mouth shut?"

"You always get caught up in the details."

Gorecki pulled a chair over in front of the soldier and sat.

He reached out and pulled the gag out of the soldier's mouth, causing him to suck in a deep breath.

"What is your rank and name?" Gorecki asked in Belarusian.

The soldier said nothing and only stared back at Gorecki.

"Actually, I don't need to know your rank. I can see clearly that you are nothing more than an enlisted soldier in your uniform. You have no rank. Does that bother you? Does it make you angry that you had your life uprooted, and now you spend your days watching over those dirty migrants in the camp? You would much rather be at home reading, wouldn't you?"

Still, the soldier kept his mouth shut and his face expressionless. Gorecki slapped the man hard.

"Do you not understand my Belarusian? I know it's not perfect, but that shouldn't prevent you from answering my questions." Gorecki removed his phone from his pocket and showed him pictures of the girls on an autopsy table. "Remember them? Remember when you passed your knife across their necks?"

Gray looked for the soldier's knife, but it had been removed. "What kind of knife does he have?"

"It's standard issue," Gorecki said.

"Then this isn't our guy."

"It didn't sound like you thought that back in the bar."

"Yes, the profile will help you identify suspects, but you still need hard evidence to tie them to the murders. Those lacerations were made with a Karatel knife."

"I'm not convinced everything hinges on that knife. And anyway, he could own one but not keep it on him. Maybe it's hidden in his personal belongings."

Gorecki focused back on the man. "I'm losing patience with you."

The soldier smiled and then spit in Gorecki's face, prompting him to strike the soldier multiple times with his fist. Blood ran from the soldier's nose, and the area around his left eye began to swell.

"Why did you kill the girls? Just give me an answer, and we'll be done here. I promise."

As Gorecki continued to question the soldier, Gray noticed jugs of water in the room. It was clear that Gorecki wanted this guy to be the right one so that he could complete his mission. But if they were wrong, that would lead to the same problem they had with Fadel.

After more questioning that went nowhere, Gorecki took a break and asked Gray to step out of the room.

"What do you think?" he asked once they were back in the living room.

"You mean about what's happening here? I disagree with it."

"I mean the soldier and his answers. You want to question him? We still have some time."

"I don't think you understand. This isn't something that's determined after a few questions. And there's still the issue of needing hard evidence. Do I think this guy fits the profile? He fits the initial profile. The revised one focuses on a soldier who is of a higher rank. This is just an enlistee."

"So you don't think this is our guy? If you don't, just come out and say it."

"Based on the information I have on him, I don't think he's our guy."

Gorecki walked back into the room, took the handgun away from the other man, and shot the soldier point-blank in his head, killing him instantly.

Gray couldn't believe what he'd just seen. Gorecki had just murdered a Belarusian soldier who was first kidnapped and beaten. To make things worse, they were in Belarusian, not Polish, territory. The last thing Gray wanted was to be involved in what was taking place. Gorecki's supervisors might have given him the okay to do whatever was necessary, but Gray was not an intelligence officer working for the Polish government. He was an FBI agent with no jurisdiction on a mission that probably wouldn't be sanctioned by Interpol or the Bureau. Even being in that apartment was criminal. And there he stood, staring at a dead soldier.

45

Lesun drove Gray and Gorecki to a drop-off point away from the camp headquarters. During the drive, Gray kept quiet, which wasn't easy as he had a lot to say to Gorecki. But Gray held his tongue, as he didn't know Lesun, and he had no interest in airing dirty laundry in front of him. Nor did he want Lesun to know any more about him than what he assumed Gorecki had told him. As soon as they were out of the vehicle into the woods, Gray unleashed.

"I can't believe you dragged me into that crap back there," Gray said. "And don't tell me it was spur of the moment. You knew damn well what your intentions were when we went into town. I thought you were cluing me in on everything."

"You knew the important things," Gorecki said.

"You think shooting a Belarusian soldier in the head isn't important?"

"It's not." Gorecki stopped walking. "Look, Gray. You knew what you were getting into when you agreed to help. You were allowed to get on a plane as soon as you were told what you would be doing here. You didn't. You stayed. So don't complain because things aren't playing out the way you anticipated. If you want safe and predictable, go back to your desk job in America."

"Don't insult me like that. Do you think going Rambo out here is a proud badge to wear? It makes you irresponsible. We're working as a team. Our actions have consequences for the others involved."

"We have the same objective, just different methods of obtaining it," Gorecki said. "If I were in your world, I'd have to play by your rules. But you're in my world, and you need to accept that."

"I need you to be more transparent. My life is on the line here."

"As is mine."

"The difference is you know what's coming. I don't. I get that everything is need-to-know, but if something goes sideways, you'll need me."

"You're right. I'll do better."

"Tell me more about those men back in town," Gray said.

"They're good people. Trustworthy. I recruited them a few years ago. Both have citizenship and families in Poland."

"So they were brought over just for this assignment?"

"Yes, that's part of the arrangement we have with them. They and their families get to live a better life in Poland, but they go with no questions asked when I call. They're also ex-military. We can count on them."

"And that safe house?"

"It's been in existence for about three years. We had another one, but that one got compromised."

"Let me ask you something, and be honest. Why did you ask me to come with you, and not Klausen or Pop? Are they not aware of what you're up to?"

"They're aware, but the short answer, I trust you to have my back. It's not that I don't trust them, but I need you there. I need you to evaluate those soldiers. That's something Klausen and Pop aren't able to do."

"I appreciate the vote of confidence. I really do, but I don't want to be involved in the abduction of any more soldiers."

"You surprise me, Gray. With your background, I would have assumed you were placed in some heated areas that didn't always go as planned."

"But we always had a clear mission."

"Like I said earlier, you were made aware of the deal. I'll admit not all the details were given to you, but operating in another country, one like Belarus... Does it really come as a surprise to you? Your law enforcement and Pararescue background combined with your profiling abilities give you a unique skill set that not many can boast. In fact, your name was the only name discussed. No one has ever done what we're attempting to do here. There is no plan, just an objective. The best people suited for this mission are standing right here. Our job is to locate and extract. I know you understand that."

Gray couldn't really disagree with Gorecki. Everything he said, Gray fully understood, and the nature of the mission, well, there was no playbook. It wasn't that long ago that he was in Thailand, stumbling along and figuring things out as he went, all while having to rely on people he knew little about. It made him feel like he had no sense of control over anything, and it was essential to Gray that he at least had control over his decisions. That wasn't always the case.

"I need more transparency. I'm serious."

"I'll do my best to see that—"

"No. I don't want you to try. I want to know everything you know. Anything less is unacceptable."

Gorecki took a moment to consider Gray's request. "Deal."

46

Gray woke early the following morning. He was up before Gorecki, who lay sleeping in his cot for the first time. Gray hadn't slept well the night before. The feeling that Azarenka and his men would burst into his tent and haul him and Gorecki away stuck with him. But that never happened. And Gorecki appeared to be sleeping very peacefully.

Gray fixed himself a cup of coffee and took a seat outside the tent. The sun, surprisingly, made an appearance that morning. The warmth on his face felt good. It almost made him forget what had happened the night before. Almost. Gray scanned the campgrounds for soldiers. They weren't yet patrolling, but soon they would be.

Relax, Gray, if they knew they had a soldier missing and connected it to the camp, they would be out in full force.

And yet they weren't. What did that mean? Were they even aware at that point? Or were they busy comprehending and scheming? It certainly wasn't a question of whether they found out but more a matter of when they will act. And what if any of those repercussions would be directed at the aid organizations.

"You're overthinking," Gorecki said as he sat down beside Gray, seemingly knowing right away what was running through Gray's mind. "They have no reason to connect a missing soldier to the camp. Paperwork will show that he was on leave in Grodno. They'll first suspect he went AWOL. Remaining in this camp is taking its toll on the soldiers. It's a likely reason for his disappearance."

"Surely they already know he's missing."

"They do. But this guy keeps to himself. He's under the radar and not important enough for swifter action. For now, we'll just carry on with what it is we're here to do. We aren't even aware there is a problem." Gorecki stood. "I'm going to check in with Klausen and Pop."

The migrants in the surrounding tents began to stir and poke their heads out. A few acknowledged Gray with a wave. It would be another day of seeing patients. That was one part of the job that Gray didn't mind a bit. He enjoyed helping them. If not for him, many would have their medical problems left untreated. He felt sorry for them, knowing they were only in that position because they wanted a better life. Belarus took advantage and used that weakness against them to further its own needs. Gray couldn't say for sure what would happen to them, but he wished them the best.

A woman bundled in a thick jacket walked over to Gray. "Are you open?"

"I am. Have a seat. I'll be right back."

Gray drained the last of his coffee and then headed into his tent and got ready for the day.

Since that first woman, it had been nonstop. Many of the migrants were coming to him with cold and flu symptoms. Winter was nearly upon them, and it would only worsen as the temperatures continued to drop. Gray knew his time there could end at any moment and there would most likely be no other teams from the DWB sent to the camp.

Gray unscrewed the cap from a water bottle and tilted his head back as he drank half of it.

"Good morning, Dr. Sanders."

Gray lowered the bottle and found Salma standing in front of him. "Good morning to you too. How are you doing?" Gray noticed her mother wasn't with her.

"I'm fine."

"And your ankle?" Gray pointed at it. "Let me take a look and see how strong it's gotten."

Salma sat on the chair, and Gray bent down and examined it. "Looks healthy to me. Is that how you feel?"

"Yes," she said as her brown eyes widened.

"Salma, you know it's not safe for someone like you to walk around by yourself, right?"

She nodded.

"You know about the missing girls?"

She nodded once more.

"Did you know any of them?"

She shook her head. Gray figured that was the most he would get out of Salma on the subject, until...

"I saw one," she said. "She was lying on the ground and not moving."

"Where was this?"

Salma pointed to the woods. "My mother and I were picking mushrooms when I found her. After, she said not to tell anyone what I saw."

"Why would she say that?"

"She doesn't want us to get in trouble."

"Was this the last girl that went missing?"

"No, it was the one before her, but I saw the last one too."

"Wait, you saw two girls lying on the ground?"

"No, just one. The other one was taken away."

"By who?"

Salma remained quiet.

"Did your mother tell you not to talk about this too?"

"She doesn't know because I snuck out of the tent. She would be angry at me."

"You can tell me. I won't get angry."

"I had to use the bathroom, so I went into the woods, and I saw the other girl."

"Did you know her?"

"No."

"Okay, so you went to use the bathroom, and then you saw this other girl in the woods. Was she using the bathroom too?"

"I don't know. She was walking, and then a soldier came to her."

"Did the soldier look angry?"

Salma shook her head. "He talked to her. And then she followed him."

"He didn't grab her arm and pull her?"

"No, they walked together."

"Salma!" a voice called out.

Gray looked up and saw Farida approaching. Gray waved at her.

"Looks like your mother found you. We'll keep our conversation a secret, okay?"

"Okay."

"How many times have I told you not to go anywhere without me?" Farida scolded.

"Hi, Farida. Salma wanted me to look at her ankle again. Everything's fine."

"I'm sorry, Dr. Sanders. I know you're busy."

"It's perfectly fine. I'm here to help in whatever way I can."

Farida grabbed hold of Salma's hand, and they walked away.

Gray watched them until they disappeared from his sight. While his conversation with Salma was short, he had learned something important. The last girl went willingly with her abductor. That was a game-changer.

47

No sooner had Salma and her mother left than a crowd of new patients gathered in front of Gray's tent. As he examined them, all he could think of was questioning Salma further. If the girl she saw had gone willingly with the soldier, it was a strong indication he had spent time grooming her. Was that how all the girls went missing? It made a whole lot of sense. No screaming. No fighting. Nothing to signal anything was wrong until the parent realized their daughter was missing.

The killer was calculating. He chose the girls he wanted and then spent time priming them to complete the other half of the abduction: to willingly come along.

He's intelligent. Charming. Has a friendly demeanor. Ted Bundy, the American serial killer, comes to mind. I need to question Salma again.

Gray continued to look for a break between patients, but the line of people never seemed to disappear. After a few hours passed, Gray told the migrants he had to take a break, and they should come back in an hour. He made his way to Farida's tent, but it was empty. He asked some of the people in the surrounding area if they knew where Farida or Salma was, but no one did. Gray looked around a bit longer before calling it quits. He'd have to try another time.

When Gray returned to his tent, the line of people had already resumed. He peeked inside the tent to see if Gorecki had returned. He hadn't. In fact, Gorecki remained gone for the rest of the day and into the night. Gray had gotten used to him disappearing for the day, but it was unusual for it to extend into the night. He'd even checked Klausen and Pop's tent, and it was empty. *Did they go someplace together?*

Gray sent Gorecki a couple of text messages asking when he planned to return and that he had vital information to relay. But the day turned into night, and still, there was no response from Gorecki or the others.

I can't believe this guy isn't answering me, especially after today's conversation.

Gray had also made two more trips back to Farida's tent, and both times the tent was empty. It felt like everyone had gone incognito.

~

Gray woke to Gorecki shaking him. "Get up, Gray," he whispered. "We need to go."

"Go where? What time is it?"

"It's two in the morning. I need you to come with me back to Grodno."

"Is that where you were all this time? Wait, tell me you don't have—"

Gorecki held a hand up. "Not now. I'll answer your questions on the way, but you must come with me."

Gray got ready quickly and followed Gorecki out of the tent. They made their way into the woods and continued until they were far enough from the camp to approach the highway.

Lesun was waiting for them in the car. Once they were inside the car and on their way, Gray asked for answers.

"You told me not to involve you in any further abductions," Gorecki said. "I did as you asked. But I need you to talk to them."

"How many did you take?"

"There are two."

"Two? And if I don't think they're the killers, you take out two more soldiers? That's three. Surely if one missing soldier doesn't cause concern, three will."

"It will. That's why we need to move quickly. There is no other way forward, Gray. We don't have the luxury of time. It has to be this way, or there is no point in us being here."

Gray drew a deep breath as he contemplated what Gorecki said. "I'm assuming you already questioned them. What are your thoughts so far?"

"They've denied everything, but I don't feel like I've broken them. There's the possibility they are lying about what they know. I'm not entirely convinced."

"So you don't think one of them is the killer?"

Gorecki paused. "I don't, but I think they know something."

"Well, let me tell you what I learned today. Salma, the little girl who hurt her ankle, remember?"

Gorecki nodded.

"She saw the last girl get abducted."

"You're kidding."

"I'm not. She said the girl went willingly with the soldier. There was no dragging or pulling. Salma said they had a short conversation, and then the girl left with the soldier. He selected her and earned her trust."

"That's why no one saw anything? What else did she say?"

"She and her mother were also the ones who found the third victim."

"This girl is a gold mine of information."

"Yes. I need to continue questioning Salma."

"What else did she say about the girl who left with the soldier?"

"Unfortunately, we were interrupted by her mother. Salma never said anything before because not even her mother knew what she'd witnessed with the soldiers. I had intended to question Salma later, but they weren't in their tent when I visited. I'm sure I can get more out of her. Does hearing this change your mind about the men you have?"

"It does. I'm not sure they are smart enough to do what you said, but I'll let you decide that."

Thirty minutes later, Lesun brought the car to a stop outside of the building where the safe house was located. Gray and Gorecki climbed out.

"I'll see you in a few minutes," Lesun said before driving off.

"Where's he going?" Gray asked.

"To park the car. Are you hungry? There's food upstairs."

Inside the apartment, Klausen and Pop were sitting at a table covered with takeaway containers.

"Dr. Sanders. Glad you could join us," Klausen said.

Gray ignored Klausen and turned to Gorecki. "Are they in the bedroom?"

Gorecki nodded and opened the bedroom door. Inside the bedroom were two soldiers tied to chairs. Both of them were stripped down to their underwear. Their faces were bloody and swollen. One seemed to be half-conscious. The other was definitely unconscious. The same Belarusian asset from the last time was watching over them with a gun.

"I need you to talk to both of them and then pick one," Gorecki said.

"What do you mean pick one? You already told me you think neither one is the killer. And you already mentioned you didn't think they were smart enough."

Gorecki slapped the face of the man with his eyes half-open. He mumbled something as his head flopped from one side to the other. He did the same to the other soldier, but he was completely unresponsive.

"What happened to him?" Gorecki called out to Klausen and Pop.

"I asked him a few more questions while you went to get Gray," Klausen said.

Gorecki felt for a pulse on the unresponsive soldier. "He's dead."

"Is he?" Klausen asked surprisingly. "Are you sure?"

"Yes, you asshole."

Klausen shrugged it off like it was no big deal.

"We all have different problems," Gorecki said quietly to Gray. "Mine is sitting over there."

Gray bent down so he could look the other soldier in his eyes. "What's his name?"

"Does it matter?"

Gray shook the soldier to try to get him to focus, but he appeared really out of it, barely conscious of his surroundings. Gray tried to talk to the soldier, but he couldn't respond or even say anything comprehensible.

"Looks like your colleagues took it too far. He's in no condition to answer any questions. This is messed up, Gorecki. You got one dead soldier and another who is teetering on the brink. You can't just keep kidnapping every soldier you think is suspicious."

"We needed to question the soldiers," Gorecki said.

"You're not thinking things through. Just based on the information I learned today, I guess you wouldn't have taken these two."

"How was I supposed to know you would come into that information? Look, I need to deliver a soldier. I can't sit around with a wait-and-see approach."

"And that's exactly your problem. You keep operating this way. You'll deliver another Fadel to your superiors. I'm not about to put myself in a position once again to take the fall for your ineptness. I want to go back to the camp now. I don't want to be around here when you do what is necessary with this one."

Just then, Lesun returned to the apartment.

"Perfect timing," Gray said. "Lesun. I need you to drive me back to the camp right now."

48

When Gray woke the following morning, Gorecki wasn't in his cot, and it didn't look like it had been slept in. Gray didn't give it more than a second of thought. As far as he was concerned, Gorecki had his methods, and he could continue with them. Gray was going to stick to what he knew. And to do that, he needed to find Salma and question her further.

Gray downed a cup of coffee before grabbing his medical satchel and setting off for Salma's tent. When he arrived, he noticed the campfire outside was extinguished and hadn't been burning for a while.

"Farida?" he called out. "It's Dr. Sanders. Are you up?"

Gray really needed to talk to Salma and keeping it from her mother no longer made any sense.

"They're gone."

Gray turned and found a woman looking at him from her tent.

"They moved to another location."

Gray lifted the flap to Farida's tent, and to his surprise, all of their belongings were gone.

"Do you know where they went?"

"She said they were moving to an area further south from here."

"Why? Did something happen?"

The woman shrugged. "People move all the time."

"Do you know exactly where they might be?"

The woman shook her head.

"Okay, I appreciate your help. Thank you."

"Wait," the woman said, stopping Gray. "I have a cough."

Gray went over to her tent and spent a few minutes looking her over. She had nothing more than a cold.

"Take one pill every six hours. Drink plenty of water. It'll help with your congestion. And try to stay warm."

Gray took no more than a few steps before another person stopped him. Within seconds, a crowd had gathered, all wanting medical attention. All Gray could think of was heading south and looking for Salma. Just then, a couple of soldiers appeared and looked in his direction. To keep his cover, Gray had no choice but to start helping the people.

It took about an hour for Gray to get through the initial group. There were no soldiers around, so Gray stopped more people from gathering, promising to come back, or, if they couldn't wait, that they should make their way to the DWB tent and the doctors there could help.

Gray avoided eye contact while searching for Salma and Farida. But as Gray scanned the hundreds of tents, he realized they could be in any one of those tents, and he wouldn't know. Gray wished he'd taken a picture of Salma to show around. His only plan at that point was to walk to the south end of the camp and back, hoping he'd come across them.

As he approached the most southern end of the camp, the number of tents began to thin. They could be near the edge of the camp, or he could have already passed their tent. A group of soldiers approached Gray.

"What are you doing here?" one asked.

Gray pointed to the logo on his medical satchel. "Helping people. Our tent is far from here, and some of these people aren't able to walk that far."

"You don't have permission to walk around the camp. Return to your tent."

"I'm already here. Let me help a few people, and then I'll go back."

"No. Leave now."

As Gray worked on formulating a response that could change the soldier's mind, he spotted Farida in the distance.

"Please, just fifteen minutes more, and then I promise I'll leave."

The soldier kicked Gray in his chest, sending him flying back to land on his butt. The air had been knocked out of his lungs, forcing him to gasp. Gray looked up at them, and they all had their rifles trained on him.

Gray raised his hands as he got back up to his feet. "I'm leaving," he said as he coughed.

He saw that Farida had witnessed the entire exchange, but there was nothing they could do at that moment. Gray walked away, looking over his shoulder occasionally. The group of soldiers kept watching him.

The upside was he knew where Farida's tent was. He could come back later, perhaps at night, when he could move in the shadows. When Gray felt he was far enough to be out of the soldier's direct line of sight, he slipped behind a tree for cover. Slowly, he made his way back, using the occasional tree or tents to shield him. Some people approached him for medical attention, but Gray simply told them he would return. Eventually, Gray was close enough to see the area where he'd encountered the soldiers. They weren't there.

Gray stood behind a tree and searched the camp for the

soldiers, but they had moved on. Also, he didn't see Farida outside her tent. Perhaps she went back inside. He knew where she was, so he could always come back as necessary. Gray took one more sweeping look at the camp before heading to Farida's tent.

"Dr. Sanders," a voice called out behind him.

Gray turned around. Azarenka and a group of soldiers were standing behind him.

"Something of interest over there?" Azarenka asked.

"I felt a little dizzy," Gray said. "I was just taking a moment."

Azarenka's eyes burrowed into Gray as if he knew everything he had just said was a blatant lie. After what seemed like an eternity of silence, Azarenka ordered two men to escort Gray back to his tent.

"Make sure he gets there safely," Azarenka said as a smile formed on his face.

"I don't think that will be necessary. I'm fine now."

"I wasn't asking you if you needed an escort."

Two soldiers grabbed Gray by his arms.

"The camp is dangerous, Dr. Sanders. You are advised to stay in your tent. Are we clear?"

Gray nodded, and the soldiers ushered him forward.

49

When Gray returned to his tent, he found Gorecki sitting outside. The soldiers waited around for a bit before leaving. Once they were out of earshot, Gorecki spoke.

"What was that about?"

"I ran into Azarenka in the southern part of the camp. He had me escorted back to my tent."

"Why?"

"He said it was dangerous for me to be roaming around."

"I don't know what you did, but that guy does not like you. Why did you go south?"

"Salma and her mother moved to that part of the camp. I wanted to question Salma further. I found them, but Azarenka showed up and had me escorted back here before I could get to them. I'll go back at night. I might have better luck. Where were you?"

"I stayed the night in Grodno."

Gray didn't bother to inquire why. He didn't want to know about anything that happened after he left.

"Klausen and Pop?"

"Same, but they're here now. Do you want me to interview the girl? It might be easier for me to move around than you."

"I have a relationship with her. It's better if I talk with her alone. I might need you to run interference with the soldiers if they start hanging around."

Gorecki nodded.

"Are you here for the rest of the day?"

"I am."

A few awkward moments of silence passed before Gorecki opened his mouth. "I'm sorry about last night. I'm not trying to screw with you. I thought leaving you out of the actual abduction would suffice."

"We have different ideas of how to get things done."

"I agree."

"Do we even have the same goal? Do you have different orders from me?"

"I'll put it this way. You want to stop the murders. I want to stop a war from brewing on my border. We can achieve both if we find the right guy."

Their conversation ended there as a group of people came for medical help. Surprisingly, Gorecki stuck around and assisted Gray.

∿

As soon as nightfall came, Gray wanted to leave. No soldiers appeared or seemed to be keeping watch on him.

"You sure you don't want me to come?" Gorecki asked.

"It'll be faster if I go alone. I'll be back later."

Gray grabbed his medical satchel and made his way to the far side of the camp that bordered the woods. He figured staying in the tree line as he headed south would keep him out of sight of any passing soldiers. When he was within forty yards of Farida's tent, Gray stopped behind a tree and took a moment to observe. He spotted a patrol of soldiers walking away from him. He waited until they were far enough away before coming out of the woods.

As he closed in on Farida's tent, he noticed the campfire outside was burning. That was a good sign. She was home.

"Farida," Gray said in a lower voice as he stopped outside her tent. "It's Dr. Sanders."

The tent flap was drawn back and Farida appeared. "Dr. Sanders. What are you doing here?" She looked around as if she was worried about being seen with him.

"Can I come inside? I need to speak with you and your daughter. It's very important."

Farida hesitated.

"What do you want with us?"

"Can we please talk inside?"

Farida looked around once more before motioning for Gray to come into the tent quickly. Gray ducked inside. Salma was sitting on her cot with a smile on her face.

"Hello, Salma."

"Hello."

"Dr. Sanders, why are you here?" Farida asked.

"I'll be frank. Earlier today, when I spoke with Salma, she mentioned that she saw the girl, the last victim, leave with a soldier."

Farida shot her daughter a look. "Salma! Is this true?"

"I'm sorry I didn't tell you, Mama."

"Why did you keep this from me? Why did you talk to Dr. Sanders?"

"It's not her fault, Farida. I urged her to talk about it with me."

"Why?"

"Farida, are you in trouble? Have the soldiers said something to you? I ask because you moved tents."

Farida drew a deep breath and released it. "A soldier approached me and told me to stay quiet. All he said was not to talk to anyone—he said I was being watched. I thought he was referring to when Salma found that dead girl. But now I'm thinking it's about this other girl. I swear, Dr. Sanders. I had no idea."

"I believe you. It's fine. But that's the reason why you moved?"

Farida nodded.

"Farida, Salma knows information that can really help the people I know in Poland with the investigation."

"Help? Haven't I done enough already? You've already taken my daughter from her grave. What has come of that? Tell me so that I know I made the right decision."

"It has helped." Gray looked at Salma, then back at Farida.

"It's fine. Salma should know what was done to her sister."

"The weapon used is one that's issued to Russian soldiers. A lot of the equipment the Belarusian military has are hand-me-downs from Russia."

"You think a soldier is the one doing this?"

"That's our theory. And given what Salma told me this morning. I think we're right."

Farida closed her eyes and shook her head. "This can't be happening. Now I know why that soldier told me to keep quiet. It has to be because of that."

"May I ask Salma a few more questions? It's very important."

"Salma. Tell Dr. Sanders everything you saw."

Gray took a seat on the cot next to Salma.

"Let's start from the beginning, okay? You went out at night to use the bathroom?"

"No. It wasn't night. It was daytime."

"The girl left during the day?"

"Yes, she was playing with us, and then she needed to use the bathroom. I followed her."

"That's when you saw her meet with the soldier, correct?"

Salma nodded.

And you're sure she wasn't forced to leave with him? She wasn't pulled by her arm or have a bag placed over her head or anything that wasn't normal?"

"No. She walked with them."

"Wait, 'them'? What do you mean by 'them'?"

"The soldiers."

"There was more than one soldier?"

"Yes, there were a bunch of them."

"And they all walked away with the girl?"

Salma nodded.

Gray sat up straight and ran a hand over his head. He couldn't believe it. There was more than one soldier. *How could I have missed this?* Gray circled through everything he knew, through all the revised profiles, and not once did he suspect more than one person was involved. None of the information he'd obtained suggested it was more than one. Even the autopsies concluded that one person using the same knife killed those girls.

"Salma, this is very important. Are you sure there was more than one soldier, and they all left together?"

"Yes, I'm very sure."

"Did they split off or keep walking together?"

"They stayed together, but I didn't follow them because I was scared. So maybe they didn't stay together."

"Did they all talk to the girl or just the one soldier?"

"Just one soldier, but the other soldiers were standing there, listening. Did I do something wrong?"

"No, not at all, Salma. In fact, you did a very good job. Your memory is excellent. Do you think you could point these soldiers out if you saw them again?"

Salma nodded.

"No," Farida said. "I won't allow you to take her around to look for this person. It's too dangerous."

"You're right. How about I bring photographs of soldiers, and Salma can tell me yes or no?"

"That's fine. But promise you won't tell anyone you heard this information from us. It's simply too dangerous."

"I promise. No one will find out." Gray stood up.

"Dr. Sanders, I couldn't help but notice you are surprised it's a soldier."

"I'm not surprised it's a soldier. I am surprised that more than one is involved."

"I see."

"I must go now," Gray said. "I'll be in touch."

Gray left the tent still shocked by what he had learned. If what Salma said was true, they weren't chasing a serial killer. They were chasing something devious, a false flag planted by Belarus.

50

As Gray hurried back to his tent, he recalculated his approach to the investigation, starting with whom they were really chasing. Serial killers don't typically work in groups. They're loners. But one could deem these soldiers a gang that set off on a killing spree. It's possible, but spree killing is focused on multiple murders in a short period. The victims may be random or not. Based on what Salma said, these girls went along willingly. They trusted the soldier. That told Gray they were selected.

Could the group leader be compared to cult leaders like Charles Manson or Jim Jones? Did he earn the trust of the other soldiers and, over time, convince them to have the same viewpoint that he did? It was possible. Gray still felt that the person responsible had anger issues, and the migrants amplified it. He could have brainwashed the other soldiers into accepting his viewpoint. Gray wasn't dismissing the cult theory, but he also wasn't accepting it as the answer. There was still the thought that the killings were mission-oriented and meant to solve a problem. Nothing about that changed in his mind.

Gray wrestled with the idea that a serial killer in the camp could have been invented. And if that was true, was it the brainchild of the soldiers or from a higher power? Say, the Belarusian government?

It was evident that the government was active in hybrid warfare. They'd successfully manufactured the problem of migrants seeking refuge in the EU. Why would it not be conceivable for them to invent a serial killer to heighten the crisis?

Gorecki was standing outside the tent with Klausen and Pop when Gray returned.

"How did it go?" Gorecki asked.

"Could you all step inside the tent?" Gray requested as he walked past them.

As soon as everyone was inside, Gray relayed the additional information he had learned and his thinking.

"Are you serious?" Gorecki asked.

"Very."

"So we're looking for someone who's the leader of a cult? Why would they want to kill little girls? What does that achieve? I thought this was an angry loner we were looking for? Someone who wanted to exterminate the migrants because he believed they were the problem."

"All of that could still hold true, but I don't want you guys to get caught up in the reasoning. What's important now is that we're not looking for one soldier. We're looking for a group. Forget about a serial killer. I don't think there ever was one. It was fabricated just like the migrant problem, most likely to amplify the crisis."

"And you think the government is behind it?" Pop asked.

"What I believe is that I think this isn't the brainchild of the soldiers. I think they're acting on orders."

"So to clarify, these soldiers are not serial killers. They

never were and are simply loyally following orders?" Klausen asked.

"Correct. It's not a serial killer problem. It never was. It is just a way to amplify the situation. The bigger the crisis, the harder it is to ignore. The end goal of this migrant problem is to make the EU fold to Belarus's demands."

"It's more hybrid warfare," Gorecki said. "This changes our approach. I'll need to notify the command about this. We all thought we were chasing one person. We can't bring in the Belarusian government," Gorecki said.

"No, we can't, but we can try to identify who is leading this group of soldiers. We can take it from there, but I'm sure that alone will paint a strong enough picture of what is really happening here."

Gorecki looked Gray in the eyes. "You're positive about this?"

"As much as I can be."

"But this is all based on the testimony of a little girl," Klausen said. "How reliable is her word?"

"I believe her. We need to start putting photographs in front of her. She is the only person right now who can ID these soldiers. We have to see this through. Also, you're all aware that I've got the attention of Azarenka. I can't shake the feeling that, any day, he might kick me, or even the entire organization, out of the camp. We need to move fast."

"Gray's right about that," Gorecki said. "Azarenka probably never wanted aid organizations in the camp. It won't take much to either expel us or hamper our efforts."

"So should we discount anyone we currently have under suspicion?" Klausen asked.

"It won't hurt to show their pictures to Salma," Gray said.

"Is this girl's word really enough to go on?" Pop asked. "I'm just saying."

"We'll see how command wants to handle this," Gorecki said. "But being that we've come this far, I can't see them pulling us out early. This could be the smoking gun they're looking for. If we can prove this, it'll be easy to prove that the migrant problem was created by them."

"How do we prove that, though?" Klausen asked. "It's one thing to identify the culprits, but proving the Belarusian government made up the idea of a serial killer to conduct more hybrid warfare seems damn near impossible."

"Yeah, what really are our options here?" Pop asked.

"We could just assassinate the soldiers," Klausen said. "That would at least stop the murders."

"It would," Gray said. "But it wouldn't solve the bigger issue. Those soldiers could be replaced. We need to expose them to have the biggest effect. Plus, if she can't identify them all, killing one or two won't do much to affect them, but it'll put the camp on high alert and speed up our departure."

"He's right," Gorecki said. "If we can get our hands on one of the soldiers involved, we might be able to flip him and find out who is really directing this. That's juicy enough for command to want to continue this operation. There's no longer anything to gain from capturing a serial killer or assassinating the soldiers responsible for the killings. We need more."

"I agree," Gray said. "Based on what we know now, I'm afraid capturing the person who is actually killing the girls won't suffice. It's too easy for the Belarusians to say those men were bad apples. We need to catch the guy in charge and prove he's doing what we suspect he is."

"Sounds easy in theory," Klausen said.

"It always does," Gray said. "Like Gorecki said, if we can identify one, we can start around-the-clock surveillance. Watch them like a hawk. And I can't believe I'm saying this, but if that proves positive, we need to do whatever is necessary to flip him and see how far up the food chain this goes."

"If this girl singles out one of them, why watch?" Pop asked. "We should take him and work him over."

"How well did the last two abductions go?" Gray asked.

Pop remained quiet.

"We have a small window here," Gorecki said. "If we make too much noise, we'll spook them. We need to blindside the person in charge. It's too easy for them to stop and wait it out. They have the time. We don't."

51

The following morning, Gorecki and the others left early to collect photos of their suspects. Gray remained at the tent, tending to patients just in case Azarenka stopped by to check on his safety. By the time noon rolled around, Gray had been sent seven photos. He messaged Gorecki to come back or send Klausen or Pop to cover him so he could visit Salma. Pop came back to cover Gray.

"Good luck with that," she said. "I have my fingers crossed."

"I'll relay word once I have something."

Gray took the same route, moving south just within the tree line of the woods until he was facing Farida's tent.

The area was busy with soldiers patrolling or standing around in small groups. He moved until he had an angle on the front of Farida's tent. Her campfire was burning, so they were home. He didn't think the soldiers would clear out of the area. All he could hope for was that the group closest to Farida's tent took a walk. And they did, ten minutes later.

Gray moved in, using the tents as cover. He didn't bother to announce himself and headed straight into the tent, hoping he wouldn't catch Farida or Salma at the wrong time. But as he was approaching, Farida had started to exit her tent.

"Farida," Gray said as he hooked an arm around hers and ushered her right back inside.

"Dr. Sanders. Is there trouble?"

"I don't think it's a good idea for the soldiers to see us talking."

"Do they know about our conversation? Tell me the truth."

"No, they don't. I promise. It's just added safety precautions. That's all." Gray looked over at Salma, who was lying on her cot. "Hello, Salma."

"Hello," she said with a wave.

"Farida, I have some photos to show Salma. You should look at them as well."

Gray sat next to Salma and pulled up the photos on his phone. "Salma, please look at these men and let me know if any of them were with the girl who went missing."

Salma kept quiet as she slowly swiped from picture to picture.

"Take your time. There's no hurry," Gray said.

She continued until she reached the last one and then looked at them in reverse until she stopped on one.

"Is that one of the soldiers you saw that day?" Gray asked.

She shook her head. "I'm sorry, Dr. Sanders, but I don't know any of these men."

"It's fine. Take another look just to be sure."

Salma did as Gray asked, but her answer was the same. Farida also didn't recognize any of the soldiers in the photos.

"I'm sorry we wasted your time," Farida said.

"You didn't waste my time. This is a process. We'll do it again when I have more photos."

Gray quickly sent off a message to the team informing

them that Salma didn't recognize any of the soldiers and to continue collecting photos.

"When will you come back?" Farida asked.

"I'm not sure. Soon, I hope. Thank you both."

Farida peeked outside of the tent. "It's safe. You can go now."

Gray slipped out of the tent and quickly went back into the woods. As he headed back north, a commotion in the camp caught his attention. He watched from behind a tree. One of the relief organizations was packing up while soldiers watched over them. Not that much further along, he spotted another organization packing up. This time he moved out from the forest and over to one of the workers.

"What's happening?"

"We've been ordered out of the camp," the woman said.

"Why?"

She shrugged. "They didn't say. They just want us out right away."

"Are they ordering all aid organizations out?"

"I'm not sure. Have they said anything to you?"

"I don't know. I was out making rounds."

"You might want to hurry back to your tent and find out."

"Thanks," Gray said.

Gray walked briskly through the camp back to his area. He paid attention to the migrants and the soldiers he passed that would signal something was seriously wrong, but they all seemed to continue their day like they usually would. But as soon as Gray got within sight of his organization's area, he saw that they were packing up. Gray picked up the pace and made a beeline to his tent.

"I'm glad you're back," Gorecki said as Gray approached. "DWB has been ordered out of the camp. They're making all the organizations leave."

"Did they give a reason why?"

Gorecki shook his head. "None. Just said to get out as soon as possible."

"Will we be able to come back? I mean, what does it mean for us?"

"For now, we have no choice but to leave."

Gray leaned in closer. "What about our mission? We're so close to figuring things out."

"I know. I have a plan, you won't like it, but I'll need an answer right away."

"What is it?"

"You and I stay behind and camp out in the woods."

"Wait, you mean hide out literally in the woods?"

"I do. Also, nothing I'm suggesting to you has been sanctioned. There's no time to reach out to command and explain. We need to make a move now."

"Are you seriously talking about going rogue?"

"I am. We don't have any other options right now. I can square things away with my superiors later. But we have to act now. I'll send Klausen and Pop back to help coordinate support, but until they do that, we'll be completely on our own."

"But if we get caught, that's it. Game over."

"That's one way to put it."

"But there's no way you can do this alone. You need me."

"That's right, I do. So, Dr. Sanders, are you in?"

52

Because of the size of the DWB organization and the number of supplies they had, it would take two trips across the border to move everything out. The border checkpoint was always a busy hive. It would be extra chaotic since all the organizations will be trying to cross at once. Gorecki suggested that during that time, they slip away.

"You don't need to ask me again," Gray said as he and Gorecki packed up their tent. "I'm in."

Gorecki nodded.

"When do you think we should make our move? After we get our stuff across?"

"If we go through the border once, one of the border guards might notice us not coming across again or something. We shouldn't cross right now. Klausen and Pop can deal with our things. We just need to wait for the right opportunity to break away."

Gorecki looked around the camp as he stuffed some items into a bag.

"Should we take any supplies with us?"

"Your medical satchel for now. Lesun will bring us

supplies later. I think it might even be better to head back into Grodno with him and stay at the safe house for a few days."

"We won't be effective from there," Gray said. "We still need to collect photos and get them in front of Salma. We need to camp in the woods."

"You're right. I'll have Lesun bring clothing that will help us blend with the migrants when we walk around. Listen, I think it might be better if we left separately. Those soldiers over there are walking away. Go now. I'll meet up with you later in the woods."

Gray grabbed his satchel and walked straight toward the woods. With each step he took, he kept expecting to hear a solider call out to him. Sweat poured down the sides of his face, and his heart thumped. Another confrontation was the last thing he wanted.

No one is paying attention. Just keep walking.

A few migrants up ahead spotted him and walked toward him, blocking his path.

"I have to go to the toilet," Gray said quietly to them as he walked by. "I'll find you later."

Gray headed toward the woods feeling as if his back were a large target that any soldier could be pointing their rifle at.

Relax. Walking into the woods is perfectly normal. People come in here all the time to use the bathroom. You've done it daily since you arrived. This is no different. Just keep walking. You'll be out of sight soon.

Gray entered the woods and continued walking until he felt he was deep enough. He even pretended to use the bathroom just in case someone was watching. After a few minutes, Gray began to breathe easier. He looked around at his surroundings. Satisfied he was alone, he disappeared farther into the woods, where he would wait for Gorecki.

~

Gray went farther than one would typically go to use the bathroom, though some migrants did appear in the distance. But none of them were Gorecki. He had it in his head that Gorecki would follow within minutes of leaving the camp, but he was a no-show so far. It was just another reminder that he and Gorecki thought differently. But as thirty minutes turned into an hour, and that into two hours, Gray wondered if he had heard Gorecki wrong.

I swear he said we'd camp in the woods. And he definitely said he'd meet up with me later. "Later" could cover a wide range of timing. Gray glanced at his watch: two and a half hours had passed.

The sun was beginning to set. Gray figured either it was taking longer to get across the border and Gorecki was helping or he was still waiting for an opportunity to disappear. Unless problems erupted at the border checkpoint, the DWB organization should have already finished moving out of the camp. *Maybe he's waiting for night to come.*

Gray began to wonder if there was a problem at the third-hour mark, but he told himself to remain calm. Gorecki would be coming soon, and Gray would need to watch for him.

But what if Gorecki didn't come straight into the woods like Gray had? What if he was forced to take a different route?

Wait, did he assume we'd meet at the same spot along the highway? Maybe he's already waiting for me there. But if he's not and I leave, I could end up missing him here. And it could send him to the highway in search of me.

Gray decided to wait it out a little longer before making a decision. But at the fourth-hour mark, the sun had already set, and darkness had fallen over the woods. Even though Gray had a heavy jacket on, he only wore jeans, and the cold was beginning to penetrate his legs. He blew into his hands and rubbed them for warmth as he shifted his weight from foot to foot.

A noise in the distance caught his attention, and he froze. Someone had coughed. Gorecki, perhaps? Gray stood behind a tree, keeping his eyes peeled. In the distance, he spotted movement. Gray waited just in case it was someone else and not Gorecki. It was definitely a person, but the shape didn't quite match Gorecki as the figure came closer. This person was shorter. Gray figured a migrant had come to use the bathroom. But there was something different about the person, the way they stood. And then Gray spotted it: an ushanka. It was a soldier. Gray remained motionless until the soldier finished his business and left.

Where the hell are you, Gorecki?

Again the thought of whether to head to the highway entered his head. He even considered making his way to the safe house. If he decided to do that, he'd have to leave right away. The later it got, the less civilian traffic was on the highway.

As Gray tossed the idea around in his head, another person approached. Gray moved back behind the tree and watched. This person was not wearing an ushanka. Migrant? They were definitely moving cautiously. Someone needing to use the bathroom wouldn't necessarily move that way. That's got to be Gorecki.

Gray was about to take a step toward the person when they began to urinate. Gray shook his head. It was just another migrant.

A beat later, a hand clamped down over his mouth. And an arm hooked around his chest, pulling him back into its owner.

"Shhhh, it's me, Gorecki. To the left," he said as he calmly removed his hand.

In the distance, Gray spotted three men: more soldiers. They called out to the migrant using the bathroom and told him to get back to the camp. The person hurried away. Gray and Gorecki watched as the patrol passed before them until they were out of their eyesight.

"What took you so long?" Gray asked.

"Problems at the checkpoint. Come on. We need to meet Lesun at the highway."

53

Lesun had supplied Gray and Gorecki with suitable clothing for the outdoors since they would be sleeping in the open. He also had backpacks filled with food and water and other necessities needed for camping. Gorecki didn't anticipate more than two nights. That would give them two days to see if Salma could identify a soldier.

Because it was already late at night, Gray and Gorecki found a spot to camp that wasn't far from the highway. There was no need to sleep near the camp and risk a patrol stumbling across them.

"You think it's safe to build a fire?" Gray asked.

"I think we'll be fine with a small one."

Gorecki gathered a few branches and got a fire started. A small kettle was included with their gear, and Gray used it to boil water for some coffee. They then settled in with a cup.

"Honest talk, Gorecki. Say Salma can identify a soldier. We watch him for a day, but nothing comes out of that. Really, I think we need a few days at a minimum, but that's an entirely different discussion. What will you do? Take the guy anyway, or keep watching?"

"Take him."

"You're not interested in observing, are you?"

"I'm not. If the girl identifies someone, I want to get as much information out of him as quickly as possible. If we're lucky, he's in charge of this whole thing. If that's the case, I'll move him across the border."

"I appreciate the candor."

"It's just you and I now, Gray. We're on our own."

"Did you talk to your command?"

"I didn't. At least not yet."

"Why?"

"Because I know they'll order me out. Klausen will convey what's happened during his debriefing. It's a way to buy us time. We have one or two days at the most. We need something to happen, or else we return on their orders."

"But what about telling them everything we've learned in the last twenty-four hours? We've made progress."

Gorecki took a sip of his coffee. "They don't care about making progress. They want someone they can blame. Unless we have that, we have nothing as far as they're concerned. This isn't like your typical investigations, where you have time and resources. If the Belarusian government ever found out what we were doing and caught us, not only would it be a major embarrassment for my country, but it would also probably force the EU to lift the sanctions against Belarus. Also, we'd be tried in a Belarusian court and sentenced to death. They use firing squads in this country."

"I get it." Gray adjusted the scarf he had wrapped around his neck and face. "Support is minimal when you're working in the field, and you are always off the record. By the way, I didn't have any weapons in my bag. Did you have any in yours?"

Gorecki dug into his bag and removed a small handgun.

"This is a PB. It's a nine-millimeter based on the Makarov and was created for the KGB. It's still in use by the Russian FSB. Magazine only holds eight rounds, but it's small, covert." Gorecki handed Gray the weapon and a suppressor. "Don't lose it. I don't have another one for you." Gorecki watched Gray look over the handgun. "You have a problem handling a gun you're not authorized to have?"

"No. None at all." Gray tucked the weapon into his bag.

"These guns are for worst-case scenario only. Don't bring it into the camp. If you get searched, it's over. You're dead."

"Remind me to never ask you to make a goodwill toast."

"Grab some sleep. I'll keep first watch."

～

Gorecki woke Gray at dawn with a shake of his shoulder. Gray's eyes fluttered briefly before he sat up.

"You didn't wake me for my shift."

"Seemed like you could use the sleep. Plus, I wasn't very tired. Get your stuff together. We have a busy day ahead of us."

By the time Gray and Gorecki reached the camp, the sun had risen, and migrants were stirring outside their tents. The two waited within the tree line, watching.

"There are three soldiers I know I want photos of," Gorecki said as he pulled the beanie on his head lower. "While I search them out, what are you planning on doing?"

"I'm not sure. I might go check on Farida and Salma to make sure they haven't moved locations again. Farida might have already heard that our organization was kicked out of the camp and freaked out. She's on edge."

"I wonder if it makes sense to keep her and her daughter at the safe house so that they don't go missing again. We can always return them to the camp later."

"Is there a downside to that scenario?" Gray asked.

"If they're caught outside of the camp, there will be nothing you or I can do for them."

"I'm not opposed to that, but let me meet with them first, see what the situation is like. We can make a decision later in the day."

"Be careful, Gray. If Azarenka catches you in the camp…"

"I know, I know."

Gray and Gorecki parted ways, with Gorecki heading north and Gray heading south.

Gray took his time walking to Farida's tent. He didn't want to move too fast and happen upon a soldier using the bathroom in the woods. Once he had Farida's tent in sight, Gray headed deeper into the woods and stashed his backpack, which had his weapon. He didn't like the feeling of leaving it behind, but he knew if for some reason he was caught and searched, having the weapon on him would be an endgame.

With his belongings hidden, Gray made his way to Farida's tent. He didn't bother to announce himself and quickly stepped inside. To his surprise, the tent was empty.

Gray's initial thought was that he'd lost them again. But he quickly noted that their belongings were still there. He figured they might have gone for a walk or most likely went into the woods to use the bathroom. That made the most sense. They wouldn't have left without their stuff.

Maybe I should head into the woods and look for them.

Gray ruled out that option. He could miss them if he left and they came back. It was better to wait in the tent. It had been no more than fifteen minutes, but it felt like he'd already been waiting for an eternity.

As the minutes passed, Gray began to get antsy. His and Gorecki's whole reason for remaining in the camp hinged on regrouping with Salma and having her identify one of the soldiers. Without her, their mission was over.

Gray peeked out through the tent flaps. Most of the camp was awake by that point. He noted soldiers patrolling the area. In fact, there was a higher number than what he had recalled the last time he'd visited Farida and Salma. Even if he wanted to leave and look for them, he couldn't at the moment.

He sat back down on the cot, running through possible

next steps should it come to pass that Farida and Salma had abandoned the tent.

Interview migrants in the surrounding tents: that would be tricky with the soldiers patrolling, but it would have to be done.

Check their previous tent: they could have returned to it. But why leave their belongings? Did they need two trips to make a move? There wasn't much. They could have carried it all at once.

Lastly, he had to consider that they went to the north end of the camp. If they were spooked or received more trouble from the soldiers, it was reasonable that Farida would want to move again.

Gray rested his head in his hands as he wrestled with the situation and what he could do about it. The shuffling of footsteps just outside the tent grabbed Gray's attention. A moment later, Farida entered the tent. She gasped upon seeing Gray.

"Dr. Sanders, you scared me."

"Farida, thank God you are here. I was worried. Where's Salma?"

"I dropped her off at a friend's tent. She likes to play with their children. Is something wrong?"

"No, no. Everything is okay. I just came to check on you two. But when I saw that your tent was empty, my imagination got the best of me."

Farida took a seat on the cot opposite Gray. "Dr. Sanders, I heard your organization had left the camp. Why are you still here?"

"I stayed behind but unofficially. No one must find out that I'm here."

"I don't understand. Are you in trouble? Did something happen?"

"No, it's nothing like that. It's... Well, it's very complicated."

"Then you should take your time when you explain it to me because I think that is what is needed right now. An explanation. You don't act like a normal doctor. Where's your medical bag? Why are you dressed like everyone here in the camp? Why did you stay behind when your organization was ordered to leave?"

Gray took a quick moment to think about the next steps and whether or not to give Farida just enough of the truth to satisfy her curiosity or simply deny.

"You're right. You deserve an explanation. But I need your word that you won't relay what I tell you. Not only will doing so endanger my life, but yours as well."

"I promise. Not a single word."

"I am a trained medic. There is no worry there, but I did not come to this camp to treat people. I was hired to investigate the killings of the three girls, now four. That's why I have an interest in information relating to this."

"You work for the police?"

"No, but I am working with them. I can help. I want to help. I believe Salma is the only person to have seen the killer."

Farida's mouth hung open for a minute before she drew a quick breath and spoke. "You're talking about that day she saw the girl go off with the soldiers. If one of them really is the killer, and if they saw her, that could put Salma in danger."

"Yes, but according to Salma, she says they didn't see her. That's why it's important we not lose touch with each other. I have a partner gathering more photos for Salma to look at. If we can identify the person, I'll be able to bring him to justice."

Farida sat quietly, taking in everything Gray had said.

"I want you to know I do care about the people in this camp. It's why I'm risking my own safety by staying after my organization was ordered to leave."

"I believe everything you're saying. I do, but what will happen to Salma and me?"

"What do you mean?"

"After you leave, if you catch this man? Will we stay here? If people find out we helped, maybe there could be trouble, maybe not."

"Why do you think there would be trouble?"

"I don't trust anyone here."

"I understand what you're talking about. I will find out what the Polish government can do about bringing you into Poland."

"Yes, that would make me feel much better and safer. Dr. Sanders, have you eaten?"

"I haven't."

"I have leftover mushroom soup. I'll heat some up for you. Wait here."

Farida left the tent to tend to the campfire. A little while later, Gray was spooning hot soup into his mouth.

"This is delicious. You're an excellent cook."

Gray and Farida spent the next hour or so talking about things that had nothing to do about the camp or the Polish and Belarusian governments. Gray told her a little about his life back in America, and Farida talked about her life back in Syria. Gray enjoyed the conversation so much, he'd lost track of time. It wasn't until he received a text message from Gorecki that he realized it was nearing noon.

"It's my partner. He sent more photos for Salma to look at. You should take a look as well."

Farida looked at the pictures closely before shaking her head. "I don't recognize any of them."

"We should get these photos in front of Salma as soon as possible."

"There are a lot of soldiers outside. It's better if you wait here and I'll go get her."

While he waited, he answered Gorecki's text, letting him know he was with Farida. Salma was playing with some other children. As soon as Farida brought her back, he'd let Gorecki know if she identified any of the soldiers.

About thirty minutes passed before Farida popped back into the tent. She was out of breath and frazzled.

"Farida, are you okay?" Gray helped her over to the cot. "Did something happen?"

"It's Salma. She's missing."

55

It took a beat for Gray to comprehend what Farida had just told him. And then it hit him hard, like a punch in the gut. Gray did his best to calm Farida.

"Tell me exactly what happened," he said.

"The other children said she was playing with them, and then she was gone."

"She just left without telling anyone?"

"I think so. I don't know." Farida's voice cracked.

"Okay, and when they noticed she was gone, what did they do?"

"Nothing. You know, they're children. They just kept playing, thinking she got bored and left. Only when I came did anybody start to think something was wrong." Farida grabbed Gray's arm. "I told her not to leave that area. I would come back and get her. I told her that!"

"I believe you."

Gray already knew what Farida was thinking—Salma had been abducted.

"I fear the worst, Dr. Sanders. I know you do too."

"We have to consider that. I need you to take me to this place."

Gray sent a text message to Gorecki telling him what happened, and as soon as he had a location, he would send it. Gray peeked outside the tent, there were a few soldiers nearby, but time was an issue. He couldn't wait and he hoped they would walk away.

"Farida, I need to avoid the soldiers as much as possible. If we walk through the woods, can you still get to this location?"

"Yes, I think so."

"I want you to walk to the woods like you need to use the bathroom and wait for me."

After Farida left, Gray watched the soldiers from inside the tent. As soon as they looked away, he slipped out and walked straight to the woods.

Just walk normally. You look like another migrant from behind. There is no reason for them to single you out.

Gray entered the woods and, a few seconds later, found Farida. Gray retrieved the belongings he'd hidden earlier before following her. Every once in a while, she'd have to pop out of the woods to confirm her bearings. It was only a twenty-minute walk from her tent. Along the way, Gray continued to pick Farida's mind.

"Did Salma say anything to you about the soldiers in the woods that she might have forgotten to tell me? Anything. Don't worry if it's trivial or not."

"I think everything she told you, she told me," Farida said.

"Do you think Salma might have gone back to the place where she saw the soldiers?"

"I told her not to, but you know, children. Sometimes they don't listen."

"Farida, do you know this area where Salma saw the soldiers?"

"Yes. It's not far from where my old tent was. We can go there first, if you want."

When they arrived at the spot, Gray didn't see any obvious signs that this area might have been a meeting point for more than one of the girls. He didn't notice any boot prints or heavily trodden trails. However, it was near the camp head-quarters. Gray knew the girls were held for at least a day before being killed. They might have been kept somewhere at camp headquarters or driven to another location.

"Salma said she was hiding here. The soldiers were over there." Farida pointed.

Gray walked over to the area she pointed at and examined the ground for fresh tracks. There were none, but he did find an old cigarette butt. It was made out of cardboard. Gray picked it up and put it in his pocket. Before leaving, he noted the location on his phone, just in case he needed to return.

As they neared the location where Salma had been play-ing, Gray and Farida approached the edge of the tree line cautiously.

"This is it," Farida said. "You see that tent over there? The woman I'm friendly with lives there with her family. The chil-dren were playing over there."

Gray sent the location to Gorecki. He wasn't that far away and arrived shortly after. Gray and Gorecki searched the woods while Farida stuck to the camp. They agreed to meet back in one hour.

"What are your thoughts?" Gorecki asked as they walked through the woods.

"She's been abducted. They might have taken her by force if they knew she'd seen them that day in the forest. Before we came here, Farida took me to where Salma saw the last victim leave with the soldiers. I found this."

Gorecki took the cigarette butt from Gray. "I know this

brand. It's Belomorkanal. It's one of the oldest Russian cigarettes brands and the reason for the cardboard butt."

"So most likely a solider was smoking it."

"Yes, but it's not a young soldier. It was popular in the Soviet Bloc countries. Mostly the older generation still familiar with that era smokes this brand."

"Older would suggest a higher rank. This could be the cigarette of the person in charge of the abductions."

Gorecki nodded in agreement as he glanced at his watch. "So it's been about three hours since the mother last saw Salma?"

"That sounds about right. They're not killed right away. We have about a day to try to find her. Two places come to mind: the camp headquarters and Grodno. I was kept in a small room when the soldiers were interrogating me. Salma could be in that room or one similar."

"I don't know how we would even infiltrate the headquarters without being seen or recognized. It's too dangerous. Grodno is a big city. It's like looking for a needle in a haystack."

Gray raised an eyebrow. "Don't tell me you've given up already."

"I wonder if we're better off waiting in the woods when they dump the body."

"Are you serious?"

"I'm presenting options. You're emotionally attached to this girl, and that's fine. But we also have a job to do. The odds of rescuing Salma are slim. But we still have a shot at catching the person responsible. If we don't, our mission is over. Salma was the only reason for us to stay."

"I can't just wait it out. I have to try to find her."

Gray and Gorecki reached the spot where Salma saw the girl leave with the soldiers.

"This is it. I found the cigarette butt right there." Gray pointed. "Salma said the girl went willingly with the soldiers. That means they gave her some incentive to come with them. Most everyone, even the children, is afraid of the soldiers. So what is it they could tell them that would make them overlook that danger?"

"The promise of food?"

"It's possible, but they have access to food from the relief organizations. I think it would have to be something that's not easily attainable."

"Shopping? The promise to take them into Grodno and buy necessary goods for her family."

"Better."

Gorecki looked at the cigarette butt again. "There's a large cigarette factory in Grodno. In fact, if I'm correct, these cigarettes are made in Grodno."

"So the person who smokes this brand is from Grodno?"

Gorecki nodded. "If they are holding the girls for a day, they're probably doing it in the city. They still need to keep what they're doing under wraps from the rest of the soldiers. They convince the girl to go with them, take her to a civilian car, not a military one, and drive into the city. It's strange, though, why they feel the need to keep them alive."

"We can't deny that the person involved could still have characteristics of a serial killer, specifically the need to control or have power over others. These are all traits of a leader, more so in the military. The answer could be as simple as wanting to explain to them why they're being killed. A need to make sure the girls understand that it's their fault."

"An officer is a perfect person to head this up," Gorecki said. "A damn wolf in sheep's clothing."

"He would also know exactly which hot buttons to press."

Gray stopped walking and scanned the woods around them. He snapped his fingers a second later. "Freedom."

"What do you mean?" Gorecki asked.

"The promise of being escorted across the border or even something as far-fetched as being flown to Germany. He promised the girls freedom."

A smile formed on Gorecki's face. "Securing her family's safety and future... You're good."

Gray glanced at his watch. "It's been about an hour. Let's head back."

Gorecki tugged on Gray's arm. "Up ahead."

A soldier was walking through the woods while talking on his cell phone.

"He's coming toward us," Gorecki said.

Gray and Gorecki moved farther back and knelt down behind a couple of trees. As the soldier got closer, Gorecki could make out parts of the conversation.

"He's looking for something," Gorecki whispered. "Whoever he's talking with is giving him instructions."

"Maybe one of the soldiers that took Salma dropped something."

"Seems like it. Can you act drunk?"

"Why?"

"Don't question, just do it and follow my lead."

Gorecki stood up and started swaying back and forth as he walked forward, slurring his words. Gray immediately fell into step and did the same.

"My friend," Gorecki called out to the soldier.

The soldier got off his phone and pointed his rifle at them.

"We come in peace. Come and drink with us."

"What are you doing out here?" the soldier asked. "Get back to the camp."

"We finished a bottle of vodka. We have two more."

The soldier lowered his rifle. "Where did you get the vodka from?"

"We have a connection. We can get you a couple of bottles, free, of course, if you keep this secret between us."

Gorecki had managed to get right up next to the soldier without raising suspicion. He slammed his fist into the soldier's face a second later, knocking him out. Gorecki took the rifle from him.

"Let me guess. We're going to interrogate him?"

"We need to know who he was talking to. You object?"

Gray shook his head. "This time, I think your actions were spot on."

Gorecki began to pat the soldier down. "We can use his shoelaces to tie his hands behind his back." He found the man's wallet and identification. "His name is Fedor Skok. Secure his hands and gag him while I call Lesun. We need to move him to the safe house quickly."

56

Gorecki and Gray moved the soldier to the highway and waited for Lesun. Gray held Skok by an arm while Gorecki kept the rifle pointed at him. Skok had been cooperative from the moment he regained consciousness. Not once did he try to fight back or question what they were doing.

When Lesun arrived, Skok willingly climbed into the back seat without question. Gorecki had already mentioned to Gray not to make any conversation until the soldier was secured inside the safe house.

More men were waiting at the safe house when they arrived.

"More assets?" Gray asked.

Gorecki nodded.

The men quickly secured Skok to a chair in the bedroom. Gorecki pulled another chair over and sat in front of Skok. He eyed Skok for a moment or so and watched him repeatedly swallow as he looked back and forth between Gorecki and Gray. Perspiration had bubbled across his forehead and upper lip.

"Do you know why we took you?"

Skok shook his head.

"How long have you been serving in the military?"

"Eleven months."

"How long have you been assigned to the camp?"

"Since it was first created."

Gorecki held up a wallet. Skok's eyes locked on it.

"You recognize this?"

"Yes, it's mine."

Gorecki removed a piece of paper from the wallet. "This is your home address. You live in Grodno."

Skok nodded.

Gorecki removed a photograph of a woman and a newborn.

"This is your wife and child?"

"Yes."

"I know where you live. I know what your wife and child look like. If you lie to me or withhold any information, I will retrieve them and bring them here and force you to watch me do things to them that are unimaginable. Am I clear?"

He nodded. "I'll answer all your questions. Just don't hurt them."

"Back in the woods, you were talking to someone on the phone."

"Yes, another soldier. My friend."

"Does this friend have a name?"

"Vadzim Polonsky."

"And what was Vadzim asking you to do in the woods?"

"He lost his lighter. He wanted me to look for it."

"Were you with Vadzim when he lost it?"

Skok shook his head.

"Why was Vadzim in the woods?"

"I don't know. Maybe to take a piss."

"I don't believe you." Gorecki waved the wallet in front of Skok.

"I swear. I wasn't with him. He called and asked me to look."

"Why didn't Vadzim just look for the lighter himself? Why bother you with this task?"

Skok shrugged.

"You're lying, and my patience is running out," Gorecki said in a raised voice.

"He wasn't in the camp. He had to come into Grodno. I don't know why. I swear. That's all I know. He just asked me for a favor."

"Do you have a photo of Vadzim on your phone?"

Skok nodded and told Gorecki how to find it.

Gray snapped a photo of Vadzim with his phone. "We know what he looks like. That's good news."

Gorecki turned his attention back to Skok. "My friend here has a few questions for you," he said as he motioned with his head to Lesun.

Gorecki and Gray left the bedroom so they could talk in private. No sooner had they closed the door than they heard loud smacking coming from the bedroom that could only be caused by a fist hitting someone.

"Don't worry. Lesun knows not to kill him. We'll talk to him again when he's had some sense knocked into him."

"You don't believe what he said?" Gray asked.

"I'm not sure yet. And you?"

"I don't feel like he's lying. He's been cooperative with us from the very start. I think he hates being in the military and hates being away from his family. To lose his life over something he hates, there's no advantage to lie to us."

"If Vadzim is part of this abduction team, he must trust

Skok enough to send him to the crime scene. We need to find out where he is."

"I agree," Gray said. "We could make Skok call Vadzim and tell him he found the lighter and ask where he is. But I think we sweeten the pot right now. We don't have time for games."

"What are you thinking?"

"He's already screwed. There's no way he's walking out of here alive. You and I both know that. So does he. We need to convince him that's not true, that if he cooperates, he will live."

"Why would he believe that? I can't let him live."

"You can if you promise him and his family amnesty...a new life in Poland. It's the only real way for him and his family to remain alive. Do you think that's possible? It needs to be real. I think he'll sniff it out if we're lying to him."

"I'm not sure. I'd have to have a conversation with command and bring them up to speed on everything that's happened. Amnesty just to get him to talk, that's a hard sell. But amnesty based on the type of information we get in return, that's more likely, but it all hinges on what Skok knows."

"This is the same psychology that was used on the girls. Skok has to think the promise of a new life is real. We don't have time to go back and forth."

Gorecki nodded and then headed back into the bedroom. Skok had a bloodied face, and Lesun was breathing hard.

"That's enough," Gorecki said as he patted Lesun on the back.

"Skok, I'm going to be very honest with you. There is no way you'll walk out of this room alive. I'll say the same to your family. All three of you are dead. But I'm going to give you a chance to change that. You hold up your end of the deal, and I will do the same. All three of you will live."

"Who are you?"

"Never mind who we are. Do you want to save yourself and your family?"

"How do I know you're telling the truth?"

"You don't. Your choice is to believe me or die."

Gorecki handed the photograph of Skok's wife and child to Lesun, along with the address. "Bring them here."

"Hey, what are you doing? You said I had a choice."

"You do. But if you screw with me, I'll give them a painful death right in front of your eyes."

~

It didn't take Lesun very long to grab Skok's wife and child and return to the safe house. He showed his wife a picture of her beaten husband, and she willingly came along. In the meantime, Gorecki spoke to command about amnesty. As he had thought, there were no guarantees, as it hinged on whether they could locate Vadzim and what information he could provide. The best that Gorecki could offer was a consideration.

"That won't work," Gray said.

"What's your gut say? You think he knows anything?"

"Hard to say. He might know something without knowing what he knows. There's also the possibility that Vadzim may not be connected to any of this. But if he is, any information Skok can reveal about him will be helpful. I can't believe I'm about to say this, but to truly know what we have, we need Vadzim in that chair."

"I agree."

Gorecki headed back into the bedroom. "Skok, your wife and child are here. They're in the bedroom next door."

"What do you want? I'll do anything. Just don't hurt them."

Gorecki fetched Skok's cell phone. "I want you to call

Vadzim. Tell him you found his lighter and that you had to come to Grodno for some other business. Ask him to meet you." Gorecki leaned in and whispered in Skok's ear. "But if you go off-script just a tiny bit, the deal is off."

"I understand."

Skok gave Gorecki Vadzim's phone number, and he called it. He held the phone up to Skok's ear but also had his own ear close by so he could hear.

"Vadzim, it's Fedor. I have good news. I found your lighter."

"Spasibo, spasibo. I'll get it when I see you."

Gorecki nudged Skok.

"I'm already on the way to Grodno for supplies. Where are you? I can bring it to you. It's no problem."

Vadzim didn't answer right away, but there was a ruffling noise as if he covered his phone with his hand.

"Just hold on to it," Vadzim answered. "I'll get it later."

"What? Are you busy with your mistress or something?" Skok asked jokingly. "Don't worry, I won't tell your wife."

There was more silence.

"Okay, can you meet me in thirty minutes?"

"Yeah, sure. Where?"

"Mister Twister."

57

With only thirty minutes, Gray and Gorecki had to work fast to devise a plan. The good news was that Mister Twister wasn't very far from the safe house, both men were familiar with the place, and they knew what Vadzim looked like.

"I think you should stay here and continue questioning Skok," Gorecki said. "I'll leave Lesun with you, but I'll take the others to help me grab Vadzim."

"How exactly do you plan on abducting a soldier and bringing him back here? Also, what if he's not alone when he arrives or is someplace with other soldiers? They'll start to wonder why he hasn't come back."

"We'll assess the situation and react accordingly. Hopefully, he comes alone."

"I can't help but think we're digging ourselves deeper into a hole."

"We are. But we can still escape from it if need be. No one knows we're here. We'll pull out and head back across the border if it comes to it. Mission over."

The plan was simple: Gorecki and two other assets would go to Mister Twister. Once they had eyes on Vadzim, Gray would send a text message from Skok's phone letting Vadzim know he was five minutes away. Gorecki planned on playing it by ear from that point on.

"If you hear gunshots or we aren't back in thirty minutes, have Lesun get you out of here. He'll know exactly where to drop you off, and you'll have to make your way through the woods and cross the border."

"What about Skok and his family?"

"Don't worry about them. Worry about saving your life."

~

After Gorecki left, Gray headed into the bedroom to talk to Skok. Up until that point, Gorecki had done all the talking. Gray sat down in front of Skok.

"My family, are they safe?" Skok asked.

Gray looked at Lesun and nodded. Lesun disappeared, then reappeared at the doorway with Skok's wife and child a few moments later but only for a few seconds before he ushered them away and closed the bedroom door.

"Do you feel better?" Gray asked in Russian.

"Your accent. You're American?"

"Where I'm from isn't important. What is important is your cooperation. It's important to keep you and your family safe. I can't stress that enough. I know you're scared. But I want you to understand, there is a way out of this."

"A way out? There is a way out only if my information is useful to you. And I have no idea what it is you still want from me except to meet with Vadzim."

"Yes, you're right. You might have better information without realizing it. You're aware of the girls who were killed in the camp, right?"

"Yes, of course, but I had nothing to do with it. You think Vadzim is responsible?"

"You tell me. People talk. You hear things. You see things. You know Vadzim well enough to go look for his lighter in the woods."

"I don't know anything about him killing those girls."

"Yes, but you know something."

Skok looked away.

"Remember, your life and your family's lives are in your hands. Now is not the time to be loyal to a friend. You must choose your family. Tell me what you know."

Skok licked his lips and let out a heavy breath. "I don't know anything about him killing girls. He and some others are always going into the woods and coming to Grodno together."

"Did this happen around the time the girls went missing?"

Skok nodded.

"Do you know where they go when they're in town?"

"No, but I know they're staying longer than they're supposed to. We aren't allowed to stay more than three hours, and I know he spends the night in Grodno."

"Is he with family or a girlfriend?"

"His family is from Brest, it's a large city in the south, near the border of Ukraine. I don't know if he has a girlfriend here. He might."

"So he and the other soldiers all spend the night here in Grodno?"

"They don't return until the morning, so I'm guessing. You think they're responsible for those girls?"

"I don't know yet."

"Why do you care? Who are they to you?"

"I'll remind you that this is not about me. It's about you and your family. So focus on them. Think about a new life in

Poland or anywhere in the EU. Do you have family outside of Belarus?"

"Yes. My wife has a sister who lives in Germany."

"Think about that. Think about all the good that will come if you move your family there and have a fresh start, away from the mess happening here. I'm sure your wife would want that. That's why it's important to tell me everything you know. No one is looking out for you. Vadzim can't help you."

"Vadzim is dangerous."

"How so?"

"He's crazy. I don't trust him."

"Why are you friends with him?"

"To keep the peace. Better to be on his good side than his bad side. It doesn't end well for other soldiers who cross him."

"Does he attack them?"

"Sometimes, yes. Sometimes they are demoted."

"What is Vadzim's rank?"

"He's a senior sergeant."

"So he has a lot of power in the camp."

"Yes."

"Why is he in the camp? Did he volunteer? Do you know where he was posted before he came to the camp?"

"I don't know much about his background, but I heard he was stationed in Minsk. He was Spetsnaz."

"Special Forces?"

"He had a nickname there: the Butcher."

"Why do people call him that?"

"He likes fighting with a knife."

58

It was late in the afternoon when Gorecki and his men hurried over to Mister Twister. His plan was to intercept Vadzim outside the biker pub and move him into a nearby alleyway where they had a car waiting to spirit him back to the safe house. It would be a textbook abduction. Gorecki had done it more times than he could count.

Gorecki stood directly across the street. Asset one was positioned just outside the pub. Asset two was standing at the entrance to the small alleyway. The plan was for asset one to intercept and guide Vadzim away from the pub and across the street, where Gorecki would then get involved in ushering the soldier to the alley.

Gorecki was the first to recognize the soldier walking toward the pub. He couldn't determine if the soldier drove, was dropped off, or came out of one of the nearby buildings. But he was happy to see he wasn't carrying his rifle, nor did he have a holstered weapon on his hip. He signaled to the asset across the street.

As Vadzim neared the entrance to the pub, asset one walked past and bumped Vadzim in the arm, dropping a bunch of money in the process. He began to apologize as he bent down to pick up the money. Gorecki wanted to see if Vadzim would try to take advantage and steal the money. He didn't.

The asset popped to his feet and slammed his fist into the back of Vadzim's head as hard as he could. He swore at the soldier and then took off running. That got Vadzim's attention.

Both men were running right toward Gorecki. Gorecki followed in pursuit as soon as they passed, staying just far enough behind Vadzim that he wouldn't notice. Asset one headed straight toward the alley, all while looking over his shoulder and mocking Vadzim.

Asset one cut into the alleyway, disappearing from Gorecki's sight. Vadzim followed, and Gorecki was right behind him. He slammed into Vadzim from behind, knocking the man to the ground. Surprisingly, Vadzim handled the hit well and rolled up to his feet, producing a knife in the process. A second later, he had passed it across the neck of asset one, sending him down to one knee as he tried to stem the flow of blood with both hands. Vadzim slammed his knee into the face of asset one, rendering him unconscious.

Gorecki wasted no time moving in with his shoulder tucked to drill Vadzim from the side. The hit was brutal and sent Vadzim flying into the building. Still, he recovered quickly and slashed out at Gorecki, catching him on the forearm just as he jumped back.

Asset two charged with a broomstick he found in the alley, slamming it down across Vadzim's wrist and disarming him. Vadzim countered with a series of fist strikes while using his forearms to block the broomstick. Vadzim was highly trained in hand-to-hand combat.

Vadzim raised his forearm, and the broomstick snapped in

half when it struck. Vadzim moved in with fist strikes, backing the asset away.

Gorecki moved in from behind, hooking an arm around Vadzim's neck. At the same time, he applied pressure with his other arm, executing a chokehold. The asset struck him repeatedly in the abdomen with the remaining half of the broomstick. But the chokehold and the strikes didn't seem to be affecting Vadzim very much.

"Hit him harder," Gorecki yelled. "I'm losing my grip."

The asset did one better and kicked Vadzim in his crotch. He stopped struggling, and Gorecki was able to tighten the chokehold. After a few seconds, Vadzim went limp and dropped to the asphalt. They quickly moved Vadzim and their downed asset into the car and drove off. On the drive back to the safe house, Gorecki called Gray.

"We got him. We're five minutes away. Have Lesun meet us downstairs."

~

Gray was keeping an eye on Skok and his family when Gorecki and the others showed up. He peeked out from the bedroom.

"Where's Vadzim?" he asked as they entered the apartment.

Gorecki motioned for Lesun to take Gray's place in the bedroom.

"We have a problem," Gorecki said once the bedroom door was closed. "Vadzim's dead."

"What the hell happened?"

Gorecki shrugged. "This guy wasn't a simple conscript. He was well trained—I lost a guy. He almost had all of us."

"Skok mentioned he was Special Forces while stationed in Minsk."

"That bastard. Information like that would have been worth knowing before we left. I had to use more force than I anticipated. I thought I had only choked him out."

Gray shook his head in disappointment. "Vadzim was key to learning more. What are we supposed to do now? Every time we take a step forward, we get knocked back two steps."

"Look, I'm not happy about the situation. It's my fault. I screwed up. But I do have good news. Vadzim attacked us with a knife." Gorecki opened up a plastic bag he'd been holding and removed a knife. "This is a Karatel. It's got the serrated edge."

Gray took the knife from Gorecki. "This was the type of knife used to kill the girls. Skok mentioned Vadzim had a nickname when he was in Minsk. He was called the Butcher because he liked to fight with knives."

"This is the guy responsible. It's got to be."

"Where are the bodies?"

"My other guy is disposing of them, but I have photographs of Vadzim's body. I also have all of his belongings." Gorecki shook the plastic bag. "Between this stuff, the knife, and Skok's testimony, I think we can make the case that Vadzim was behind this."

Gray didn't say anything.

"What's wrong? Are you pissed that you didn't get to question Vadzim? I am too, but it looks like we have our guy."

"Salma said there was a group of them. Vadzim is only one."

"But he owns the Karatel knife. So I think we can assume he was the one who slit the necks of those girls."

"He probably did, but he's not the one in charge."

"How can you be so sure of that?"

"Skok overheard Vadzim talking on the phone right around the time the fourth girl went missing. Skok said his exact words were, 'We have the girl.' Vadzim was reporting back to someone. Vadzim isn't running this operation. He's taking orders."

"Do you know who Vadzim was talking to?"

"Yes, because Skok said Vadzim addressed the person on the phone. It was Azarenka."

59

Gray and Gorecki stood in the kitchen staring at each other. The hole they'd been digging themselves into had just gotten a lot deeper.

"Does Skok know for sure that Vadzim was talking to Azarenka?" Gorecki asked.

"He was positive. So if the dots we connected to Vadzim are true, the girl he mentioned on the phone was one of the victims. He was talking to Azarenka, so everything we theorized is true. The Belarusian government is behind this, and Azarenka is their hatchet man. Who better to pull off this scheme than the commander of the camp?"

"I can't believe it's him, but if what you said is right, we have a serious problem. What we have won't be enough to connect Azarenka, at least not in the way my government would want to use the information. We'll need more. I'm not sure as of yet what that is. Still, if he really was in charge of orchestrating the killings, my country would be able to end this mess on the border right now. My government can salvage its reputation."

"It is highly likely Vadzim was with Azarenka before he

was called to meet with Skok. Did you see where he came from?"

"I didn't, but it's gotta be in walking distance of that pub." Gorecki ran his wound under the faucet to clean it. "There's a first aid kit in that cupboard. Grab it for me."

Gray got the kit and placed it on the table. Gorecki dug around inside of it until he found a suture kit.

"If Vadzim was with Azarenka, he'd be expecting him back soon. About an hour has passed."

Gray looked at Vadzim's cell phone. "I don't see any recent calls, but they'll come soon."

"We have hard decisions to make and not a whole lot of time to think them through. I completely understand if you want to reconsider. Because now would be the time to get out of here. We're fifty kilometers away from a safe crossing point along the border. That may not seem that far, but when you're moving on foot with soldiers hunting you, it can seem like an eternity."

"You thinking of cutting out?" Gray asked as he watched Gorecki stitch up his wound.

"I'm considering it, as should you. Proving Azarenka is responsible won't be easy. We don't even have access to him. Vadzim is dead. I was hoping we could have made a case with his body and what we know, but you're right. We need the man in charge. Not the one following orders."

"Plus, it would be too easy for the Belarusian government to separate themselves from this. They can easily say Vadzim was a bad apple. Pinning Azarenka to the killings will put a stain on the entire camp."

"I have no idea how we do that, but if we're going to leave it needs to happen now. Vadzim was part of Azarenka's inner circle. He can lock down the city and the surrounding area. If that happens, we're screwed. Also, I feel like I need to relay this newest information to my command. We might need back up, at the very least an extraction team to assist us."

"Let's take a look at our situation." Gray began typing notes on his phone. When he finished, he showed the list to Gorecki.

- One dead high-ranking officer—Vadzim
- One soldier being held hostage—Skok
- One dead asset
- Three previous soldiers were abducted and killed
- The commander of the camp is responsible and involved in the murders—Azarenka
- Currently no backup or support
- Short on time

"This doesn't even include Skok's family, who we would still need to get across the border. He delivered. We owe him."

"When I look at it listed like this, the odds are heavily stacked against us," Gorecki said.

"Plus, those soldiers you killed early on are bound to catch up to us," Gray said. "But if we stop now, everything the Belarusian government is doing will continue. What we have won't be enough to condemn them. Everything that happens will be for naught."

"You're right. But this situation, even I couldn't have predicted it would get this ugly. I'm responsible here. I have you, Lesun, Skok, and his family to consider. I think you should get out while you can. This, what we're doing here, it's not part of your job description."

"If I leave, what will you do?"

"I don't know yet. I'll have to call this in and see what my command says."

"Make that call right now. I want to know what they say."

Gorecki grabbed his phone and made the call. When he finished, he sat back down at the table.

"Because of the situation, the amnesty for Skok and his family is a go. They'll have an hour to collect their belongings. I can have one of my assets escort them to the border where an extraction team will be waiting."

"That's good. Now, what's the bad news?"

"They've ordered me to stay. They want me to obtain some type of photographic or video evidence that will implicate Azarenka."

"You're kidding."

"It's an impossible task, but it doesn't apply to you. They left the decision to stay or leave up to you. You can travel back to Poland with Skok and his family."

"What they're asking you is damn near impossible without support. We don't even have supplies or proper equipment."

Gorecki walked over to a wall in the kitchen, pushed it, and popped it open, revealing a secret storage space. Inside was a stockpile of weapons.

"I have this. But this isn't an operation that will go on for days. We have today to make something happen."

"What exactly do they expect you to deliver? A confession?"

"They didn't say. You have an hour to make a decision."

"I've already made my decision. I'm not leaving you here alone. I've come this far with you. We'll see it through together."

60

Knowing there would be no support for them so long as they were inside Belarusian territory, Gorecki pressed Gray once more about his decision.

"If we are caught, my government will deny everything, even go so far as to develop a story that we'd gone rogue. We'll both be the scapegoat for a failed mission. Do you understand that?"

"I do. And it doesn't change my mind. There's a strong possibility that Salma is still alive. We have to try to save her. If we can't, we make a run for the border. She was abducted. She'll be key to filling in large holes in the story. Also, there's Farida. She can help round out the story. We need to get her out of that camp as well."

"You're right. I'll have Klausen and Pop figure out a way to get her through the checkpoint."

"What are your initial thoughts from here on out?" Gray asked.

"Someone will be calling for Vadzim real soon. I answer, pretend to be him, and we take it from there. Any objections?"

"Nope."

"I'll tell Skok what's happening," Gorecki said as he stood. "Go talk to his family."

Gray went to check on the wife and kid in the other bedroom.

"Hi. How are you doing?"

"Who are you? What's happening?" the wife asked.

"My name is Dr. Sanders. Everything will be fine. We've made arrangements with the Polish government. They will be giving you, your husband, and child amnesty. It's too dangerous to remain here any longer."

"Amnesty? Why?"

"I can't get into the details of why, but once you're in Poland, you can stay there for as long as you want, legally. Your husband mentioned you had a sister in Germany."

"I do. Can we go there?"

"Yes, you'll be able to move around inside the EU."

"Why are you doing this for us? I don't understand. You beat my husband, and now you are giving us a new life in the EU. This makes no sense?"

"Your husband was helpful to us. We promised him this in return, and now we are delivering. You will have one hour to collect a few belongings from your home, and then you will be taken to a crossing point along the border where an extraction team will be waiting for you."

Just then, Skok appeared in the doorway with Gorecki and immediately ran over and gave his wife and child a hug. Gray joined Gorecki outside the room.

"They okay?" Gorecki asked.

"They're fine. What about him?"

"He's still a little skeptical... He probably won't fully believe me until he's across the border."

Just then, Gorecki's other asset returned from disposing of the bodies. "It's done."

Gorecki had a short conversation with his guy, explaining that he needed to get them to an extraction point.

"You understand?"

"Yeah, we should leave now before it gets too late."

The asset ushered Skok and his family out of the apartment, leaving Gray, Gorecki, and Lesun behind. Ten minutes later, Vadzim's cell phone rang.

"Allo," Gorecki said with a cough to disguise his voice. "Da, da."

Gorecki continued to cough while saying as little as possible. The call lasted only a minute.

"So?" Gray asked after Gorecki ended the call.

"They thought I was Vadzim. Whoever was on the phone wants me to bring pizza back from Mister Twister. His exact words were 'Azarenka wants a sausage pizza.'"

A smile formed on Gray's face. "I can't believe it. We nailed it. And that son of a bitch is nearby."

Gorecki nodded. "Finally, something is going our way. I have the number. I'll call back later, telling them I need help carrying the pizza. That will be our chance to see what building a soldier comes out of."

"And then what?"

"Lesun, I'll need you to deal with the soldier when he comes to the pub. Keep him there or immobilize him. Do whatever is necessary to buy Gray and me some time."

"No problem."

Gorecki looked at Gray. "You and I will go to the building and try to locate the apartment."

"And if we find it?" Gray asked.

"We assess the situation and react accordingly. I know that sounds screwed up, but we're running blind here. Ideally, the girl is there and still alive. We grab her, and we make our way back to the border."

"Lesun, after you deal with the soldier, come to the building. But if things go sideways, don't worry about us. Save yourself. Understood?"

Lesun nodded.

"I want to be clear with everyone," Gorecki said. "Once we put this plan in motion, there is no turning back. We could have the Belarusian military hunting us within an hour." Gorecki glanced outside the window. "It's almost sunset. We'll head out as soon as night falls."

61

Gray and Gorecki opted to keep the handguns they originally had. Concealment was more important than firepower. They did take knives, extra ammo, and a balaclava. As soon as the sun dipped below the horizon, they left the apartment. Gorecki positioned himself to the south of the pub and Gray to the north while Lesun went inside to order the pizzas.

Gorecki had already received a text message asking what was taking so long. He replied that the place was busy. As soon as Lesun messaged Gorecki that the food was ready, he texted the number asking for help carrying the food. He said the owner had given them extra pizzas and a case of beer for free. The response took longer than expected, but they got the answer they wanted. Someone was coming to help. He sent a text to Gray to keep an eye out. They were on.

Gray stood against a building with his hands buried in his pockets for warmth and a scarf covering half his face so just his eyes showed. A second later, a door across the street opened, and out walked a soldier. He was heading toward the pub. Gray quickly messaged Gorecki to come to his location.

"It's this building right here," Gray said as Gorecki approached.

The building was small, two stories, with a shop on the ground floor. It was closed.

"This works in our favor," Gorecki said. "At most, there will be two apartments on the top floor."

They crossed the street and entered the building. Gray and Gorecki put on their balaclavas and equipped their handguns with suppressors before heading up the narrow stairs.

Gorecki led the way. When they reached the landing, he listened carefully. Voices could clearly be heard behind one door.

"I hear at least three different voices," Gorecki whispered. "If Azarenka is in there, let's try to keep him alive. Execute everyone else."

"Are you serious?"

"I am."

Gorecki stomped on the stairs to indicate he was coming up and then knocked on the door. "Open up," he said. "Pizza is here."

Footsteps approached the door, and it cracked open, revealing the face of a soldier peeking out. Gorecki fired, striking the man in the middle of his forehead and then pushing the door open.

He pushed inside the apartment, firing multiple times, immediately killing two more soldiers. Gray followed behind and spied Salma sitting in the corner of the apartment. A soldier standing next to her reached for a rifle leaning against the wall. Gray shot him in the arm, wounding him. Gorecki fired, striking that soldier in the head.

"Don't move," Gorecki said as he pointed his gun at Azarenka.

He moved in and took the handgun from Azarenka's hip

holster. He also grabbed the knife he had hanging from his belt.

"Look here, a Karatel knife."

Gray knelt down next to Salma. "Are you hurt?" he asked as he looked her over.

"No, I'm fine, but I'm scared."

"Don't worry, you're safe now." Gray looked up at Gorecki. "We need to move, now!"

Gorecki used his phone to film Azarenka, the dead soldiers, and Salma. At the same time, he commented on what had just happened.

"Commander Azarenka, what do you have to say for yourself? This girl that you kidnapped from the camp, was she to be your fifth victim in your serial killer scheme?"

Azarenka said nothing and only stared at Gorecki.

"This is a Karatel knife. It is the same type of knife used to kill the other four girls, a knife that's popular for Russian Special Forces but rare in the Belarusian military. Tell me, Commander. Are you the brainchild of this plan? What would you call it? A new form of hybrid warfare?"

"Polish intelligence," Azarenka finally said. "I should have known. He looked over at Gray. "You must be CIA. You might have figured out what is happening here, but our secret is safe in this room."

"That's where you're wrong, Commander," Gorecki said. "The world will know what kind of inhumane leader you are, using these people for your own ill gains. Did you like killing the girls? Did it excite you?"

Azarenka smiled. "You have no idea. And gutting you will give me great pleasure."

"Bold words for a man who's all alone with a gun aimed at his head."

Azarenka began to chuckle. "I am not alone." He shifted

his eyes to the ceiling. There was a tiny security camera in the corner. "You are not the only one with a spotlight on them. You can't escape now. It's over." Azarenka's chuckle turned into all-out laughter.

Gorecki fired, and Azarenka dropped to the floor dead. He then fired once at the camera, destroying it.

"Do you think that was a live feed?" Gray asked.

"We'll have to assume—"

A gunshot rang out, and Gorecki keeled over. The soldier they had seen previously was standing in the doorway aiming a small handgun at Gorecki. A beat later, another shot, and the soldier fell to the floor. Lesun appeared and fired once more into the soldier's head.

Gray hurried over to Gorecki to assess the wound. "You took it in the gut," he said.

"Yeah, I didn't need you to tell me that."

Gray grabbed a jacket off a chair and did his best to stem the bleeding. "Lesun, we need to get him medical help quickly. Is there a place we can go?"

"Yes. I can bring the car here."

"No, no, no," Gorecki said. "There isn't any time. If that camera was a live feed, you've only got a few minutes to get out of here before an army of men convenes on this place."

"You need medical help now. You won't last if you try to cross the border in this condition."

Gorecki gave Gray a few comforting slaps to his arm. "My friend, we all have a role to play. Now your role is to get this phone and that girl back to Poland. Don't let this"—Gorecki pointed at his stomach—"be for nothing." He coughed.

"I'm not leaving you. No way."

"You have to. You have no choice. Give me that rifle. I'll do my best to hold them here as long as possible. You still have to get across the border. That'll be no easy feat, I assure you. Lesun, you know where to take Gray."

Lesun tugged on Gray's arm. "We must go, or else everyone in this room will end up dead."

"Tell the story, Gray. Let the world know what happened here. This is your chance to redeem yourself."

Lesun yanked Gray to his feet. "We must leave."

Lesun took Salma's hand and led her to the door and down the stairs. Gray looked back at Gorecki as he stood in the doorway.

"Did anyone ever tell you that you're a pain in the ass to work with?" Gorecki asked. "Always ignoring orders. Go. I'll be fine."

62

Lesun and Salma were waiting for Gray outside the building.

"We must hurry back to the safe house," Lesun said. "The car is parked there."

"Where to after that?"

"I will drive you north to the woods. It'll be the safest place to cross, with very little chance of running into border guards in that area. Once Azarenka's death is discovered, it'll be too difficult to cross anyplace else. Also, reception in that part of the woods isn't strong. You can't call for support until you cross into Poland. Just keep walking west. You'll know you've reached the border when you see a clearing, probably no wider than eight meters. You'll also see wooden border markers."

"How long do you think it'll take for us to cross?"

Lesun took a moment to think. "A full day. Moving at night will be difficult. The woods are thick. My advice is to get deep into the woods and then find a place to camp. At sunrise, it'll be easier to navigate, and you'll be able to move faster. I have some food and water in the car you can take. It should last you two if you ration it."

"What about you?"

"Don't worry about me. I'll find a way across."

Just then, a large transport truck drove by. Gray looked back over his shoulder and watched it stop outside of the building they had been in. About a dozen armed men climbed out and made their way into the building. Gunfire erupted a few seconds later.

"Hurry," Lesun said. "Our window is closing quickly."

～

"Dr. Sanders, is everything okay?" Salma asked as she climbed into the back seat of the car.

"Everything will be fine, Salma," Gray said as he joined her. "You're safe with me."

"What about my mom? Where is she?"

"I'll get her across," Lesun said as he started the engine. "It won't be a problem."

"Right now, we have to focus on getting to Poland, okay?"

Salma nodded.

As much as Gray wanted to ask Salma to tell him everything that happened from when she disappeared to when they found her, he knew this wasn't the time or the place to have that conversation. When they were alone, in the woods and relatively safe, perhaps he would broach the subject with her.

Lesun took backstreets to get out of the city and onto the highway, but even then, he did his best to stick to small rural roads.

"Do you know how the military will mobilize?" Gray asked.

"They'll start by sealing off Grodno and searching for you. That'll buy time. They'll probably set up checkpoints along the major highways."

"Will they lock down the camp?"

"I don't know, but I'll enter from the north by foot. Do you know where in the camp her mother is?"

"I do. Her name is Farida. I'll send you a location and photo of her."

Gray also snapped a photo of him, and Salma and sent that to Lesun.

"She doesn't trust anyone, so that photo should help if convincing her to go with you is a problem."

It took nearly two hours for Lesun to reach a drop-off spot. He parked the car.

"That's west," he said. "Keep walking until you cross the border. Good luck."

"Thanks, Lesun. Good luck to you too. We'll see you on the other side."

Gray and Salma got out of the car and headed into the woods.

63

Gray and Salma did their best to keep up a fast pace, but it was nearly impossible, as Lesun was right about the woods. At times he found himself twisting his body around the tightly packed trees. It helped a little that their eyes had adjusted and the bark of the birch trees was white. But Gray still felt like a zombie walking with his arms out in front as he bounced off and around the trees. He was keen on putting as much distance between them and the edge of the woods as they could. The deeper they got, the safer they'd be.

"How are you doing, Salma? Do you need to rest?"

"No, I'm okay. But I'm thirsty."

Gray removed a water bottle from his backpack and handed it to her.

"Take small sips," he said. "If you drink too much, you might overhydrate."

"What does that mean?"

"It means the sodium levels in your body can become too diluted, and you can get leg cramps."

"Huh?"

"Just drink slowly and enough to wet your throat."

She took another sip before handing the bottle back to Gray.

"Salma, do you feel like talking about what happened?"

"I guess," she said as she grabbed hold of Gray's hand while they walked.

"Can you tell me why you left the kids you were playing with?"

"I had to go."

"Go where?"

"I had to meet one of those soldiers, one from the apartment, who was killed."

"Was this one of the soldiers you saw in the forest when the other girl went missing?"

"No, but I had seen him before."

"Why did he want to meet you? What did he tell you?"

"He said he was in charge of finding people who were ready to go to Poland. He said my mom had recommended us, so he had to interview me."

"Did he tell you this beforehand?"

"Yes, the day before. But he said not to tell anyone because people would get jealous about us going to Poland. He said not to tell my mom and to wait to surprise her."

"I see. Is that why you asked your mom if you could play with the other children, so you could meet this soldier?"

"Yes."

"Were you scared to go with him?"

"No, because he was very nice, and he gave me sweets to eat along the way."

"So it was just him? There wasn't a group of them like there was with the other girl?"

"At first, it was just him, but when we got to a car, there were other soldiers there. I recognized them from the forest."

"Did that worry you?"

"No, because they were all being nice. And they were smiling and laughing with each other."

"You know who Commander Azarenka is, right?"

"Yes."

"Was he there?"

"No, he came to the apartment later."

"When you got to the apartment, did you think anything was wrong?"

"No, because everyone was nice."

"You were at that apartment for a long time. What happened there?"

"It was very boring. I just sat there. They told me they had to wait for the person who was going to ask me questions."

"Did they feed you or anything?"

"They gave me a sandwich and chips."

"Did any of the men touch you?"

"No, they were busy on their phones until the commander came."

"When did he show up? Less than an hour before I came or more?"

"I think less."

"Did he say anything to you?"

"No, he only talked to the other men. I didn't understand what he was saying. Then he made a phone call and talked to the camera."

"The one in the ceiling?"

She nodded. "And he pointed at me when he was talking."

"And you still didn't think anything was wrong?"

"I started to think a little because we had been there for so long, and I was worried about my mother. They told me we would only be gone for an hour. They lied."

"They did."

Gray wasn't sure if Salma realized she was almost the fifth victim.

"My legs are tired, and my feet hurt," Salma said.

Gray checked the time. They'd been on the move for about an hour and a half. They were far enough into the woods that he felt comfortable taking a break.

"We'll rest for a bit, but then we have to keep trying to move. The sooner we get to Poland, the sooner you can see your mother."

"Dr. Sanders, do you have a daughter like me?"

"No, I don't. But if I did, I'd want her to be like you."

"Really?"

"Sure, you're a wonderful little girl."

"Do you have a son?"

"No, I don't have any kids. I'm not married."

"Why? Don't you want children?"

"I guess someday I do, but I need a wife first."

Salma laughed. "Yes, that's true."

Just then, Gray heard some voices in the distance and then noticed light beams coming their way.

"Shhhh," he said. "There are soldiers."

He and Salma crouched down. By Gray's count, the patrol was made up of five soldiers, and they were spread out in a line, walking slowly west. Most of them were south of Gray and Salma, but the man closest to them would come within fifteen feet of their position should he stay on his intended course.

Gray removed his handgun from his bag just in case. The men didn't really pay attention to anything other than their lively discussion. With each step the patrol took forward, the man on the far left of the line came closer and closer to them. He wasn't actively involved in the discussion. If Gray or Salma made a noise when he was closest to them, he'd hear it.

The soldier stopped about twenty feet from them and lit a cigarette. The end of it burned a bright red as he took a long pull. He then continued walking, but that little stop had changed the trajectory of his course. He was now walking at an angle toward Gray and Salma.

"He's coming to us," Salma said quietly.

"Shhhh."

Gray screwed the suppressor onto the barrel of the handgun and then pointed it at the soldier. He didn't seem to realize that every step he took was taking him farther from his patrol. The soldier stopped at about ten feet away, his gaze settling on their location. He took another long drag on his cigarette before flicking it away. Like a tiny projectile with a red burner, it flew through the air, landing just a couple of feet away from Gray. A second later, he turned and began walking back toward his patrol, who had veered south, away from Gray's location.

"Come on, we should keep moving," Gray said.

Gray decided to head even farther north before going west. It would add more time to their trek, but better safe than sorry.

The two kept moving for another hour and a half before Salma complained that she was tired. Gray wasn't excited about sleeping out in the open. When he researched Belarus, he knew the woods were populated with wild boar. They tended to be most active at night when they searched for food. It wouldn't be pleasant to come across a mother with her young.

Gray checked his reception on his phone. He had none. He'd been using a compass he'd taken from the safe house to navigate so there wasn't any real danger of walking in circles.

"Are you sure you can't keep moving, even if we walk slower?" Gray asked, even though he already knew he was pushing her far more than he should.

"I'm tired," Salma complained.

"Okay, we'll rest. Let's just look for a place where the trees aren't as close together."

Gray walked a bit farther until he happened on what looked like a trail. Either that or just how the trees were growing made it look like a narrow pathway. Gray decided to follow it in hopes it led to a small clearing. It didn't. It led to a small hut: a dacha.

"Does someone live there?" Salma asked.

"I'm not sure. It might just be something that hunters use. Stay here while I go check it out."

Gray gripped his handgun tighter as he moved in closer. If someone were inside, they would be sleeping, because there weren't any lights showing. As he got closer, he noticed a tiny window. He leaned up against the side of the hut and listened. He didn't hear any snoring. He then peeked through the window. It was dark inside, and he could barely make anything out. Gray removed his cell phone and turned on the flashlight app to see inside better. The place was empty. He checked the doorknob; it was locked, but the door wasn't that sturdy. He put his shoulder into it twice, and it cracked open.

"Salma," he whisper-shouted.

Salma came running over and straight into the hut. Gray shut the door behind them and barricaded it with a chair he found. There was a small bed. It seemed clean enough and sturdy.

"Go ahead and lie down and sleep," he told Salma.

She didn't argue and did as he said. Within seconds she was sound asleep. Gray poked around the hut. It was definitely something used by hunters to rest. There was a lantern, but it was out of kerosene. He didn't see any food or water, which was fine because they had a supply in his backpack. Aside from the bed and two wooden chairs, there was a small table and some shelving on the walls held a few random tools. Gray assumed whatever gear hunters would need, they brought with them. The hut might be public and not owned by anyone in particular, hence the reason for no personal belongings.

Gray sat against the door and rested his feet on the other chair. A few seconds later, he too had fallen asleep.

64

Gray woke the following morning with a sore neck and a numb behind. As he sat forward, he felt the other aches in his body. Salma was still asleep on the bed. He stood and stretched his arms above his head. When Gray looked back at Salma, she was staring at him.

"Good morning," she said.

"Good morning, Salma. Did you sleep well?"

"Yes. I feel much better. I'm hungry."

Gray handed Salma a box of crackers and a water bottle. He then checked the time. It was a little after six thirty. "We can't stay here too long. We should keep moving."

Gray peeked outside the window. Everything seemed fine, but he knew a patrol could be nearby. Surely by then, the military would be searching for them. He urged her to finish eating so they could go.

Once outside, Gray checked the compass to get his bearings. He wanted to head north for a bit farther before turning west toward Poland.

"Do you know if my mother is still in the camp?" Salma asked as they walked.

"I'm sure by now Lesun has taken her out. She's probably already in Poland waiting for you."

"I hope so. I miss her a lot."

Gray gave Salma a comforting squeeze of her shoulder. Gray and Salma did their best to move quickly around the trees for the next hour or so. They had developed a system where Gray led the way and Salma followed in his exact footsteps right behind him.

Gray stopped to check the compass. They were still heading north. "I think we can start going west now."

"How far is Poland from us?" Salma asked.

Gray still didn't have reception on his phone, but he could open up a map app and see their location. The map didn't have any landmarks or markers until the Polish side of the border. It was probably because the surrounding area was just woods, or Belarus blocked it.

"I'm not exactly sure, but we'll reach it today. I'm positive of that."

As they walked, the last of the water and crackers were depleted.

"I keep thinking about food," Salma said. "Maybe we can make mushrooms soup if we find mushrooms."

"That sounds delicious, but we don't have equipment."

"When we get to Poland, I'm going to eat a lot."

"You might not need to wait that long," Gray said as he veered to the right. "We just got lucky."

Up ahead were a bunch of bushes scattered across the ground. He knelt down next to one of them and plucked a blueberry.

"I know this," Salma said with excitement. "I tried some back in the camp."

She picked a few and popped them into her mouth. Gray did the same. For the next fifteen minutes or so, they ate their fill.

"Look at my hands." The tips of Salma's fingers were stained blue. "You have the same too."

"Yup. We're twins."

They ate for a bit longer and then picked enough to fill the empty cracker box Gray had kept in his backpack.

"That was wonderful," Salma said as she rubbed her belly. "I wonder what else we'll find to eat."

"Keep your eyes open."

After more walking, Gray noticed that the spacing between the trees was opening up. He wondered if they were nearing the border. He got his answer a few minutes later. Through the trees, he spied what appeared to be water in the distance. As they approached the tree line, a large lake revealed itself. The map on his phone didn't indicate a body of water in the area.

"Maybe there are fish we can catch," Salma said as she hurried her steps.

Gray knelt at the edge of the woods. From there, he could see the entire lake. It was huge, too large to see the opposite shoreline. The calm blue waters stretched at least half a mile across to the other side. Impossible to cross without a boat, and he didn't see one nearby. If they wanted to continue west, they'd have to go around the lake.

"What are we waiting for?" Salma asked. "I want to go to the water."

"We need to be sure it's safe. There could be soldiers around."

Gray scanned the shore of the lake for a few minutes before they walked out. It was then that Gray was able to grasp the lake's size. It was oblong-shaped, and if he had to guess, it stretched about three miles in length, maybe more. The water was crystal clear, giving them a view of the smooth pebbles at the bottom.

"Look, fish." Salma pointed.

A school of large silver fish swam past them.

"Looks like perch," Gray said.

Gray looked north, and the distance to that end of the lake looked farther than the distance to the southern shore.

"Let's keep moving. I don't want to stay out in the open for very long."

Gray and Salma walked south along the banks close to the tree line. Gray couldn't help but think they were targets out in the open. He made sure to keep watch in all directions. They kept up a brisk pace until they reached the south shore. It narrowed to a point, so getting around to the other side didn't take very long.

"The water looks so cool. Can we please just go inside for a little bit?" she asked.

Gray scanned the shores on the east side once more. "Okay, but just for a little bit."

Salma quickly took off her shoes and walked to the water's edge. "This feels so good."

She bent down and splashed water on her face. A few seconds later, Gray removed his shoes and joined her. It was cold but refreshing and immediately boosted his energy.

"Do you think it's safe to drink?" Salma asked.

Silt from the lake's bottom had clouded the water where they were standing.

"I think so, but we should move over there. Just be careful not to disturb the bottom of the lake too much and only drink the water if it's clear, okay?"

Salma did as Gray said, and they both drank their fill. Gray was still eager to get back into the cover of the woods. It was too dangerous to be out in the open for very long. They took a seat on a fallen tree trunk and slipped their shoes back on.

Just then, a familiar whizzing sound zipped right past Gray's left ear. Someone had just shot at them.

65

Sniper!

Gray dove over to Salma and forced her down behind the tree trunk.

"Crawl to the woods!" he shouted.

More whizzing noises could be heard flying overhead. From what Gray could tell from the sounds of the bullets flying past them, the sniper was on the east side of the lake. He might have even been tracking them all along.

Gray was right behind Salma, crawling on his belly while urging her to move faster.

"When you reach the woods, don't stand up; keep crawling until I say stop."

Salma kicked her legs and pulled her arms as she shimmied across the ground. Gray made sure they were deep enough into the woods before getting to their feet and running. The trees would provide cover.

"The soldiers found us," Salma said as she ran alongside Gray.

"They did, but they're on the other side of the lake. They still have to go around it."

Gray decided to move at an angle, heading north instead of straight west, thinking whoever was shooting at them would continue straight toward the border. Plus, Gray worried reinforcements could be directed to the border ahead.

"What if they have a boat?" Salma asked.

"Don't worry too much about what they are doing. We're not that far from the border. We just need to keep moving as fast as possible."

But Gray knew what he had told Salma wasn't a fail-safe. If the Polish side of the border was also woodlands, whoever chased them could simply cross and continue hunting them. Gray wouldn't be safe until either Polish border guards, military, or police met up with them. It would be too easy for the sniper to shoot them dead and then cross back over the border. Having wild boar scavenge his dead body wasn't a thought that thrilled him.

There was a silver lining. If they continued on their current trajectory, they should throw the sniper off their trail. Lesun said the border north wasn't patrolled, nor was there a fence. Crossing into Poland wouldn't be a problem. As soon as he had cell service, he would call Pakulski for an extraction.

Gray hung on to Salma's hand to keep her moving and from tripping and falling.

"You doing okay, Salma?" Gray asked.

"I'm scared," she said, clearly out of breath.

Gray stopped and bent down so he could look her straight in the eyes. "I'm not going to let anything happen to you, understand?"

She nodded as she sucked in air.

Gray removed his backpack and slipped it on so that it rested against his chest. He then motioned for Salma to climb onto his back. He would piggyback her until she caught her breath.

"Better?"

"Yes."

Gray kept up a decent pace even with Salma on his back. She was tiny, so carrying her wasn't taxing. After an hour of moving, Gray stopped to catch his breath. He also checked their location on his phone. If the GPS was correct, they were right up against the border.

"We're near the border. Be very quiet."

They moved slowly, cautiously, until Gray spotted the clearing in the distance. It was the border, exactly how Lesun had described it: a grassy clearing about twenty-five yards across. No fencing, but he saw the markers. As they moved forward, Gray also kept an eye out for any electronic devices that could detect movement.

When they were near the clearing, Gray and Salma crouched. Running across the clearing would take no more than five seconds max.

"I don't see anyone," Salma whispered.

"Me neither. On the count of three, we run across, okay?"

"Okay."

"One. Two. Three."

They stood and took a step, but Gray quickly pulled Salma back down and held a finger in front of his lips. He then pointed.

Two heavily armed Belarusian Border Guards with a German shepherd had appeared in the clearing, walking directly down the middle. They weren't on their radios or peering into the woods. Instead, they walked casually while having a chat. Even their dog seemed distracted as it sniffed at the ground occasionally. Maybe word about what happened hadn't reached them yet. Gray even wondered if the Polish border guards walked the same path and whether or not both sides passed each other with a wave.

Gray grew anxious. With every step, the guards seem to move slower and slower. That feeling that the sniper could come up behind them at any second gnawed at him. It was a real possibility, as they didn't have that much lead. Also, there might be more than one hunting them. Gray looked back over his shoulder. His gaze searched for the slightest of movement.

The guards stopped directly in front of Gray and Salma. One patted his pockets until he found a pack of cigarettes. He popped one into his mouth and gave one to the other guard. He then patted himself down again, searching for a lighter.

Gray couldn't believe their rotten luck. Now both guards were searching themselves, looking for the damn lighter. It was clear they wouldn't take another step until they had their cigarettes lit.

Gray looked over his shoulder again. They'd already been in that spot for ten minutes. Every minute they weren't moving brought the sniper closer.

Salma tugged on Gray's arm, and he focused his attention back on the soldiers. They'd found a lighter and lit up. They both took long pulls before falling back into their conversation, only they weren't moving. They continued to stay put. While Gray was sure they couldn't see him and Salma, there was a chance the dog might pick up their scent.

The dog was busy sniffing the ground, and then it got into position to use the bathroom. The guard holding on to the leash yanked back, but the dog was determined. The guard shouted out something that Gray didn't understand before pulling the dog over to the Polish side of the border, where it eventually used the bathroom.

Okay, you got your cigarettes lit, and your dog took a crap on Poland. Time to leave.

The border guards eventually continued their patrol

south. Once they were far enough away, Gray and Salma ran across the clearing into Polish territory. As they moved deeper into the woods, Gray checked his phone—still no cell service.

66

"Are we safe now?" Salma asked.

"Not quite. We still need to get out of the woods."

Gray rechecked his phone. There was one bar, but it came and went.

"As soon as I have service, I'll call for help. Until then, we need to keep moving. How do you feel?"

"I'm fine. I don't want to stop again."

They both kept quiet and moving quickly, focused on getting out of the woods. Gray occasionally looked back over his shoulder, expecting to see someone. He never did.

"Look," Salma said.

In the distance, the woods appeared to be opening up. They picked up the pace. As they neared the tree line, they slowed and then stopped behind several trees.

The woods opened up to a large field that had been freshly plowed. It stretched across about a mile and a half. Gray could see two structures in the distance. One was definitely a barn. He wasn't sure what the other one was, perhaps a home. The woods continued around the edges of the field for a bit before thinning out and stopping. From there on, it was all farmland.

"Do you think there's anyone around?" Salma asked.

"I'm not sure, but the land looks like it was recently plowed. If there is someone, they might be in that barn."

Clearly, they were inside Poland, and while Gray should be breathing a sigh of relief, he wasn't. His gut continued to warn him that they were still being tracked.

"Let's get to that barn," Gray said.

The moment they left the security of the woods, Gray felt like an easy target. It didn't help that the soil was uneven and soft, making it challenging to run. Salma kept tripping and falling down.

"Salma, climb on my back."

Gray continued as he piggybacked Salma. It was even difficult for him to keep his balance. Parked up ahead was a tractor. The barn wasn't that far beyond it, but as Gray neared the vehicle, the voice inside his head screamed for him to take cover.

Gray continued to gauge the distance to the barn. It wasn't that far. Maybe a few more minutes of running, and they'd reach it. But the alarms continued to sound, telling him to take cover behind that tractor. A heavy feeling grew in Gray's stomach. He couldn't explain it, but it felt as if the sniper was standing at the tree line and was targeting them.

The barn isn't far, just another minute. You can make it.

As he was about to pass the tractor, Gray stopped and ducked down behind it. A whizzing noise flew right by. The sniper had caught up with them.

Gray scrambled behind the tractor's large rear wheel, pulling Salma with him. *Ping!* A bullet struck the vehicle.

Gray removed his handgun from his backpack and peeked

through an opening between the wheel and the tractor's frame. *Ping!* Gray pulled his head back behind the wheel.

Just then, the barn door opened, and out walked an elderly man dressed in overalls. He started yelling at Gray and Salma in Polish. Gray couldn't understand him, but it was clear that he wasn't too happy about them being on his property. A second later, a bullet ripped right through the man's head, and he dropped to the ground. Salma gasped and gripped Gray's arm tightly.

"He killed him," she said.

Gray checked his phone; he had three bars. He only knew of one person to call, and that was Pakulski. He hoped to hell she answered.

"Gray, is that you?" Pakulski asked.

"Yes, it's me."

"Where are you?"

"Listen, I'm in deep trouble and need an extraction. I'm in Poland, near the border on a farm. I'm pinned down by a Belarusian sniper who also crossed over."

Ping!

"He's firing at us. I need help now!"

"Gray, send me your location. I'll orchestrate a team from Kuźnica to come and get you. Are you alone?"

"No, I have a little girl with me. Gorecki and I rescued her from the camp commander, Azarenka. He's responsible for all of this."

"I know. I've already spoken to Lesun. He made it safely across the border. So did the soldier and his family. We've been debriefing them since their arrival. You were the only missing piece"

Ping!

"Hurry, Pakulski. I have a handgun and limited ammo. I won't be able to hold him off for long."

Gray sent Pakulski his location and then focused back on the tree line. He still couldn't see the sniper.

Are you just going to sit there and watch us? See if we make a move?

Gray knew they'd be better off in the barn than behind the tractor, but the sniper had already picked off the farmer. It wouldn't be hard to do the same to them.

"Are we going to die?" Salma asked.

"No, we're not. I promise you that."

67

The clouds in the sky had opened up, and the noon sun was beaming down on Gray and Salma. They were both perspiring heavily, and Salma complained about being thirsty. It was dead quiet in the field, and Gray could clearly hear the flies buzzing around the dead farmer. If there were anyone else on the property, they'd be in the house. But it was far enough away that they wouldn't have heard the gunshots.

Gray checked the time on his watch. Around thirty minutes had passed without any more shots fired. Gray wasn't sure what the sniper was up to, but he continued to watch the tree line through the tractor framework. Gray had considered the sniper might be waiting for backup, but then that would mean more Belarusian soldiers on Polish territory illegally. Gray didn't think that would happen.

If the sniper tried crossing the field, Gray would easily spot him unless he crawled on his belly. But even then, Gray felt like he would pick up on movement unless he was moving an inch at a time. Or worse, attempting to flank them.

Off to the left side of the tractor was an open field leading to thinning woods. The sniper could approach from there, as there were still enough trees for coverage. Gray's phone buzzed. It was Pakulski.

"Gray, I have a team from Kuźnica heading to your location by air. They are thirty minutes out. Any markers I can relay so they know exactly where to go?"

"We're in a field taking cover behind a tractor. There's a barn about thirty-five feet from us. A dead farmer lies on the ground between the tractor and the barn. I believe the sniper is still somewhere in the tree line to the east of us."

"Okay, got it. Hang tight. Help will be there soon."

Ping!

"Crap, he's flanking us."

Gray popped up to his feet, yanking Salma up with him, and they scurried around to the front of the tractor just as another bullet pinged the vehicle. Straight ahead was the barn. With the sniper on the move, they couldn't remain where they were. They had to get into that barn. Gray grabbed hold of Salma and turned her so she was facing him.

"Listen, I need you to run to that barn as fast as you can in a zigzag. Do you understand?"

She shook her head. "What's a zigzag?"

"Like this." Gray made a motion with his hand. "Can you do it?

She nodded. "I think so."

"Whatever you do, don't stop no matter what. Just keep running until you're in that barn."

"Okay."

"On the count of three, we go. One. Two. Three. Run!"

The two took off running. Gray shot right and then left. He looked to his side and caught a glimpse of Salma running a few steps behind him. Just then, a bullet kicked up dirt in front of him. Gray pivoted right so that the sniper couldn't lock onto him. After a few strides, he cut left. He looked over to his side, expecting to see Salma, but she wasn't there. Gray looked back over his shoulder and found her stopped dead in her tracks.

"Salma! Keep running!"

But the girl remained stationary with her eyes wide and her jaw clamped tight.

A bullet whizzed by Gray's head. He was a much bigger target than Salma and couldn't afford to stay still. He spun on his heels and ran back to Salma while zigzagging. Another bullet screamed past him.

"Salma! Run toward me!"

But no matter how much Gray urged the girl to move, she remained frozen like a statue.

At any moment, Gray knew the sniper could target Salma. He gritted his teeth and ran as fast as he could. As he neared, he reached out with both arms and scooped Salma up just as another bullet zipped by them. That one grazed Gray's arm.

With Salma safely in his grasp, Gray pumped his legs as fast as possible, running past the farmer's body. They were six feet from the entrance to the barn.

Come on, Gray. You're almost there.

Four feet away. Another bullet whizzed past his left ear.

Crap, that was close.

Three feet away.

Gray cut right, dodging another bullet. The barn door was still cracked open. There were about two feet of wiggle room to slip through. Gray reached out. A bullet slammed into the barn door. Splintered wood burst everywhere.

Two feet away.

Gray dove into the opening, holding Salma tightly against his chest as he twisted his body to the side to take the brunt of the impact on the ground. They landed hard, and she bounced out of his grip, tumbling forward end over end. Gray rolled up to his feet and spun around, focused on closing the door. He pulled the door shut and locked it just as the sniper fired. A bullet punctured right through the door, narrowly missing Gray's face.

He dropped to the ground and crawled over to Salma. "Are you okay?"

"Yes, I'm fine."

They kept low as they moved to the rear of the barn, where bales of hay were stacked high.

"Stay here behind the hay. Don't come out, okay?"

She nodded.

Gray ran to the front of the barn and climbed up the rafters to the landing. From there, he peered out a small hole in the wood. He couldn't see the sniper, but he knew he was hiding somewhere in the trees.

Gray wiped away the sweat that dripped into his eyes and concentrated on the tree line, looking for movement. And then the sniper appeared.

He walked out of the woods dressed in military fatigues and a balaclava covering his head and face. His sniper rifle was slung across his back, and he carried an AK-47 in one of his hands. That rifle would definitely cut through the sides of the barn. The wood panels were old and weak. He could easily walk around the barn while shooting, hoping to hit them.

Gray took the handgun out of his backpack. The sniper was too far away at the moment to take a shot at. The PB pistol Gray had was perfect for concealment but not for magazine capacity. The magazine only held eight rounds. Gray had two extra magazines in his bag for a total of sixteen rounds. He had fired it once in the apartment, leaving the gun with seven rounds. He had twenty-three shots to hold off the shooter until help arrived.

The sniper made his way to the tractor's rear and took

cover. He was in range, but Gray didn't have a shot, even with him popping his head up every now and then.

You'll never have a perfect shot. What are you waiting for?

Gray took aim and waited for the sniper to stick his head above the tractor's rear. When he did, Gray fired. The top of the tractor chair deflected the bullet. His shot was too low. The sniper ducked back down.

Show your head again. I won't miss this time.

The sniper's arm briefly appeared. For a second, Gray thought he had waved, possibly a ceasefire. But the truth couldn't be any farther from that. Gray caught sight of the grenade flying through the air. He followed its arc until it landed on the ground in front of the barn door.

The boom reverberated throughout the structure as an explosion ripped through the barn entrance, blowing the door off its hinges. Debris rained down on Gray as he covered his head with his arms. He looked back outside, and the sniper was standing off to the side of the tractor in full view. Gray fired, forcing the sniper to retake cover. A few seconds later, the sniper unleashed a hail of bullets onto Gray's location, turning the wooden panels into Swiss cheese.

Gray backed away and quickly climbed down from the rafters. He ran back toward the bales of hay and found Salma crouching behind them, her legs pulled up tightly against her chest and her face buried into the top of her knees.

"Are you okay?"

"Yes, I'm fine," she said as she looked up with tearful eyes.

Gray gave her a quick hug. "You're doing well, Salma. You're being very brave and strong."

"What was that loud noise?"

Gray peeked over the top of a bale and spotted the sniper standing in the destroyed door of the barn. But that wasn't the worst of it. The explosion had ignited the dry wood. Fire began licking its way up the sides of the barn near the entrance. Thick black smoke billowed upward, gathering near the roof. Not only did they have to make it past an armed sniper, but they were also at risk of being trapped inside the barn by the fire.

The sniper must have been thinking the same thing because his stance looked relaxed. Was he content to watch them burn alive? Gray squeezed off a few shots and the sniper returned fire, sending a hail of bullets into the bale, and forcing Gray down.

"Lie flat! Don't move!" Gray shouted at Salma.

Gray popped back up when the gunfire stopped, but the sniper had disappeared. A second later, he stepped back into view and fired. The firepower of the AK-47 was overwhelming. It also didn't help that the barn was filling with smoke. The crackling and popping of burning wood also grew louder. The fire was spreading.

Gray crawled around to the other side of the bales, hoping to gain a better angle. But the sniper had read Gray's movements and fired as he stuck his head out from behind the bale. He peeked again and spotted the sniper reloading and took advantage, coming out from behind the stack of bales and firing.

The sniper moved out of the entranceway and took cover behind the side of the barn. Gray quickly reloaded and continued his assault with precise shots. He began shooting through the burning wall of the barn, where he thought the sniper stood. Within a few seconds, he had emptied the magazine. He fell back behind the cover of a wooden column. The heat from the fire was intense and stung against his face.

The sniper stepped back into the opening and fired, chipping away at the column. It wouldn't hold up for much longer. But Gray didn't have many options at that point, and help hadn't arrived yet. He and Salma were dead if he couldn't take out the sniper with his last remaining bullets.

He loaded his last magazine and fired, backing the sniper away before stepping out from behind the column. He moved toward the entrance, firing through the wooden side of the barn, while using a forearm to shield his face from the heat. The sniper returned fire through the wall. Gray ducked and continued to fire until the slide locked back. He had fired his last round.

"Arrrrgh," the sniper yelled.

Gray couldn't believe it. He'd actually hit the sniper. He quickly released the magazine and shoved the slide back into place so it wouldn't look like his gun was empty.

With his gun still trained on the area where he thought the sniper was, he sidestepped for a better view through the door until he spotted the sniper propping himself up on one knee.

"Drop your gun!" Gray shouted. "Now or I'll shoot you dead."

The sniper straightened up. "Your gun is empty. I count shots and I don't think there was a magazine exchange." He threw the AK-47 to the ground. "But so is mine."

But Gray could easily see the sniper rifle still slung across his back as well as the handgun tucked into the drop leg holster. The sniper chuckled as he hobbled into the entranceway and unslung the rifle.

"I win," he said.

"Are you sure?" Gray asked.

The familiar *chuff*, *chuff* and whirling helicopter blades caught the sniper's attention. He turned around, and off in the distance was a low-flying attack helicopter converging on the barn. The sniper quickly took aim and fired multiple rounds.

A moment later the twenty-three-millimeter cannon on the front of the aircraft unleashed a barrage of bullets, striking the sniper. Gray dove to the side, hitting the ground and rolling out of the line of fire. Curled up into a ball, he shielded his head with his forearms as he watched the large caliber bullets rip through the sniper, kicking up a dust cloud behind him. His body jerked, and his arms flopped around before falling to the ground in an unrecognizable heap of smoking flesh.

The attack helicopter set down outside the barn, and a team of armed men climbed out. They had their rifles aimed at Gray as they closed in.

Gray held his hands up. "Don't shoot. Don't shoot," he said, coughing from the smoke.

"Are you Sterling Gray?" the soldier asked as he neared.

Gray nodded.

"Where's the girl?"

"Behind the bales. Hurry, the fire's spreading fast."

68

It didn't take very long for the extraction team to load Gray and Salma onto the helicopter. They flew to the 23rd Air Base, where they were met on the airfield by Pakulski. She and two other intelligence officers quickly escorted them into an SUV, and minutes later, they were on the road.

"Sterling, thank God you made it out of there in one piece."

"Your guys showed up just in time," Gray said.

Pakulski focused on the little girl clutching Gray's arm with both hands.

"Hello, my name is Julianna. What's your name?"

"I'm Salma," she said softly.

"It's nice to meet you, Salma."

"Julianna, I need to—"

Pakulski held up a hand, stopping Gray in midsentence. "I know you have a lot of questions, but I'm under strict orders to keep all conversation to a minimum. We're on our way back to the agency's offices, where you'll both be debriefed. Once you're through that process, I'll come to find you, and we can talk."

An hour later, the SUV came to a stop outside the offices of the Foreign Intelligence Agency, where Gray and Salma were immediately separated. Gray was taken to an empty room with a single table and two chairs. A mirrored window hung on the wall, which Gray assumed masked a viewing room. A few minutes later, two men entered the room and took a seat. One of them had a black bag.

"Welcome back, Agent Gray. Everyone here is pleased to see that you are safe and well. My name is Birger Wozniak, and this is Dr. Nowak. He'll look you over while we chat. Feel free to tell him if you're experiencing any pain or have nonvisible injuries."

Gray spent the next three hours telling Wozniak everything since he and Gorecki decided to remain in Belarus after their organization had been ordered out. During that entire time, Wozniak mostly listened and asked questions for clarification. He didn't even ask why he or Gorecki made any one decision. They fed Gray and provided him with anything he wanted to drink.

"I'm sorry," Gray said. "You have yet to acknowledge Lucjan Gorecki since I've started talking. I'm curious, why is that?"

"I have no idea who this Lucjan Gorecki is. I assumed he was a migrant or some other person that you recruited for help."

"You're kidding, right?"

Wozniak said nothing.

"Lesun? Where's Lesun? Tell me he made it back here."

"Ah, now that's a name I know. Yes, Lesun is back. He brought a woman with him. I believe she's the mother of the girl you came back with."

"Yes, she's the mother, and her name is Farida."

Wozniak smiled.

"What about the Belarusian soldier, Skok? Did he and his family make it across the border?"

"Fedor Skok is also here, but I'm not aware that he was a Belarusian soldier."

It was evident to Gray that the foundation of a cover-up had already started. And Gray understood why. If it ever got out that Poland not only had active spies working deep inside Belarus but that they were responsible for the murder of a high-ranking military officer, it could be seen as a grievous act of aggression.

Gray finished telling his side of the story, filling in whatever gaps the Polish government had about what had happened. Wozniak thanked him and then left the room. A few minutes later, the deputy prime minister came in.

"Agent Gray, I want to be one of the first to congratulate you on a job well done."

"Thank you, Deputy Prime Minister Salamon. It's refreshing to speak to someone willing to acknowledge the truth about what really happened."

"Agent Gray, I'll be candid with you because, quite frankly, the truth is something that can come back and cause a lot of unnecessary trouble for you and for us. I don't need to tell you what will happen if the Belarusian government discovers your real identity. I want you to know we will do everything in our power to prevent that from happening, but..."

"You need me to return the favor, right?"

"It only works if both parties are in agreement."

"Will you also pretend you don't know who Gorecki is?"

"No, I won't. You and Lesun were the last two people to be with him while he was alive. Hearing you both tell your version of events was extremely helpful and cathartic. Knowing that Gorecki did his job all the way up until his last breath, well, I don't think anyone could have asked for more.

He was an upstanding and loyal patriot. And he will be deeply missed. But once we leave this room, neither of us can ever mention his name again."

"What about Salma and her mother? Where are they?" Gray asked.

"They are both fine. They will be given new identities, but you will never be allowed to see or speak to them again. It's better this way. Skok and his family will also be given new identities and transported to Germany. The same rules apply for them as well."

Gray allowed his gaze to fall to the floor as he took in everything Salamon had just said.

"Are you okay?" Salamon asked.

"I'm fine. What happens to me now?"

"We've already arranged for you to take a flight back to the UK tonight. You must be out of the country before the morning."

"Is that when breaking news will take place?"

Salamon smiled. "Agent Gray, is there anything I can do for you, or any other questions I might answer for you?"

"No, you've been helpful enough."

Salamon looked at the mirrored window and nodded. He offered his hand across the table. "On behalf of the Polish government, I thank you for your invaluable service. You are a true ally."

Gray shook his hand. "You're welcome."

Salamon stood, and as he left the room, Pakulski came inside and took a seat across the table from Gray.

"Let me guess, it's your turn to ask the questions?"

"I only have one. Would you like to have a drink with me?"

"I thought you'd never ask."

69

Gray spent the remainder of his time in Warsaw with Pakulski, discussing as much as she was allowed to with him. This time she didn't take him to a fancy rooftop bar. She took him to a small dive bar where they could talk freely. A lot of it centered around Gorecki.

"I'll be honest with you. My initial thoughts on the guy were that—"

"Wait, let me guess," Pakulski said. "You were going to say he's an asshole, right?"

"Yes." Gray laughed. "But let me finish. In the end, he had changed my mind completely."

"Gorecki had that effect on everyone he met. He was very standoffish at first, but if you earned his respect, you got his trust. If he had your back, you were in good company. I'll miss him very much."

"Did he have any family?"

"No, he didn't. I hate to say it, but the agency was his family. He lived for it."

"He was a good guy," Gray said. "I'm glad to have met him. Everything that the deputy prime minister said about the others, Salma and Farida, Skok and his family... Was that true? Are they really being taken care of?"

"I'm pleased to say they are. You have nothing to worry about with them."

"That's good."

Gray raised his beer bottle. "To Gorecki."

"To Gorecki," Pakulski said as she tapped his bottle.

"You know, not to change the subject, but I am. I have to ask you something, and I want an honest answer."

"Okay," Pakulski said.

"That night, we went for drinks, dinner, and the opera. What happened back at my hotel... Was that real, or were you handling me?"

"Everything that happened in your room was one hundred percent real. Everything before that, well, I handled you like a pro." She smiled.

Gray wagged a finger at her. "You're good."

~

It was nearing eleven thirty p.m. when Gray's flight touched down at Heathrow International Airport. By the time he got back to his flat in London, it was almost one in the morning. Gray took a quick shower and hit the sack.

When he woke the following day, the events of the last two and half weeks seemed like a dream, but Gray knew it wasn't. He still had some bruising across his body. There was also the brand-new tuxedo hanging in his closet, courtesy of the Polish government.

With a hot mug of coffee, he took a seat on the couch and flipped on the television. There was breaking news. Playing right before Gray was the footage that Gorecki had captured of Azarenka. The bodies were blurred out, but one could clearly tell what they were. Gray was also pleased to see that his face had been pixelated. The newscaster said the Polish government did not know who the people in the video were. An unnamed source in the Belarusian government handed over the footage. This person was disenchanted by what his country had done and could no longer stand by. He admitted that his government was secretly recruiting these migrants and forcing them into the camp to manufacture a crisis to lift the sanctions the EU had placed on Belarus.

Gray smiled as he watched the newscast. He remembered what his friend Gorecki had said. If he and Gray pulled off the impossible, Poland and the EU would get what they wanted: a huge political win. And Gray would get what he wanted: an end to the murders.

Gray lifted up his mug. "You were right, Gorecki. Boy, were you right."

It was a little after ten on a Saturday morning, and the last thing Gray wanted was to sit alone in his flat. He put a call in to Gaston and Pratt and told them he was back in town and asked if they were up for brunch.

Gray couldn't be any happier to see those two familiar faces at the pub.

Pratt gave Gray a hug. "Sterling, welcome back."

"Good to see you again, mate." Gaston slapped Gray's back.

"When did you get back?" Pratt asked as she took a seat at the table.

"Late last night. It's great to be back home and here with you two."

"Aww, well, we love having you here," Pratt said.

"Yeah, mate. The pub ain't the same without you," Gaston said.

"So, seems like everything worked out well with your investigation," Pratt said.

For a second, Gray wondered if Pratt was talking about the fake murder investigation or the news that broke earlier that morning. Before he left Poland, Pakulski had mentioned to him that Interpol and everyone involved would have no knowledge of what Gray had actually been up to. She said they had been sent status updates created by her agency.

"Yeah, it all worked out okay," Gray said. "They have some sharp investigators over there. It was a real pleasure working with them." Gray grabbed Gaston's shoulder. "But I'll tell you, none of them can hold a candle to the Metropolitan Police's very own DI Gaston."

"Cheers to that," Pratt said, holding up her pint.

"Cheers," Gray and Gaston said.

"Hey, I'm not sure if you saw the news, but what a shit show on the Polish border with the migrants," Gaston said.

"I hadn't watched the telly this morning," Pratt said. "What happened?"

"Turns out the Belarusian government created that entire migrant problem. Not only that, to make it worse, they made it look like there was a serial killer in the camp to make the problem bigger. What did they call it?" Gaston snapped his fingers as he thought. "Hybrid warfare. That's it. Can you believe that? What kind of sicko thinks up that crap?"

"That's just evil," Pratt added.

Gaston bumped his arm into Gray's. "Can you imagine trying to solve those murders? What a bloody mess that would have been."

Gray smiled. "I couldn't have said it better myself."

THE GREEN SAMURAI
A STERLING GRAY FBI PROFILER NOVEL

When a violent turf war between rival Yakuza clans exposes a burgeoning black market gun trade in Tokyo, FBI profiler Sterling Gray must hunt a shadowy criminal mastermind.

After a brutal battle for supremacy between opposing Yakuza syndicates goes south, gun violence explodes in the Tokyo underground and quickly spreads throughout the city. Desperate to curb the influx of firearms, the Tokyo Metropolitan Police Department is forced to seek help from Interpol.

Special Agent Sterling Gray is adept at taking down international fugitives...but in the world of the Yakuza, being a foreigner paints a target on his back. Teaming up with TMPD investigator Mariko Tamura, the pair are tasked with profiling the invisible ringleader behind the complex arms trafficking network.

But as a clearer picture of their quarry begins to take shape, the details just don't seem to add up. The culprit is poised to slip through their fingers, and Gray can't escape the feeling that he's missing something critical. If he wants to uncover the truth, he'll have to seek help from the unlikeliest of allies— and put his mind and combat skills to the ultimate test.

Get your copy today at
severnriverbooks.com/series/sterling-gray-fbi-profiler

ABOUT THE AUTHORS

Brian Shea has spent most of his adult life in service to his country and local community. He honorably served as an officer in the U.S. Navy. In his civilian life, he reached the rank of Detective and accrued over eleven years of law enforcement experience between Texas and Connecticut. Somewhere in the mix he spent five years as a fifth-grade school teacher. Brian's myriad of life experience is woven into the tapestry of each character's design. He resides in New England and is blessed with an amazing wife and three beautiful daughters.

Ty Hutchinson is a USA Today best seller. Since 2013, Ty has been traveling nonstop worldwide, all while banging away on his laptop and cranking out international crime and action thrillers. Immersing himself in different cultures, especially the food, is a passion that often finds its way into his stories.

Sign up for the reader list at
severnriverbooks.com/series/sterling-gray-fbi-profiler

Made in the USA
Las Vegas, NV
23 January 2023

66109415R00194